Praise for Christ

"A story that not only touches but plays at every string of your
—Chandrani Shome

"Two people so very broken in different ways, and their journey to becoming whole again. This is Christi Caldwell at her absolute best!"
—Kathryn Bullivant

"One of [Christi] Caldwell's strengths is creating deep, sympathetic characters, and this book is no exception . . ."
—Courtney Tonokawa

"Christi Caldwell shows us that there's more to a person than meets the eye and that redemption through love is possible in a story that feels real, heart-wrenching at times, soul inspiring, and overall beautiful to read."
—Marcela Macias De Hadzimehmedi

"Christi Caldwell has a way to redeem dark, broken characters and make you forget their past sins and fall in love with them."
—Sharon Coffey

"Wounded dark heroes, defiantly strong heroines, love at its finest equals a Christi Caldwell classic."
—Kari Maass

"Christi Caldwell continues to amaze me with the depth of emotions she puts into each character, slowly peeling back each layer to reveal the person behind the mask he/she portrays to the world."
—Dee Foster

"Only Christi Caldwell can take a rake/rogue/scoundrel (all rolled into one) with the blackest of hearts and show that there is more to him than meets the eye."

—Dee Foster

"As always, Ms. Caldwell has written a tale that will pull at every emotion and leave you with a smile."

—Dee Deacon

THE
WOLF
of Mayfair

OTHER TITLES BY CHRISTI CALDWELL

The McQuoids of Mayfair

The Duke Alone

The Heiress at Sea

A Sure Duke

Wantons of Waverton

Someone Wanton His Way Comes

The Importance of Being Wanton

A Wanton for All Seasons

Lost Lords of London

In Bed with the Earl

In the Dark with the Duke

Undressed with the Marquess

Heart of a Duke

In Need of a Duke (prequel novella)

For Love of the Duke

The Heart of a Scandal

In Need of a Knight (prequel novella)

Schooling the Duke

A Lady's Guide to a Gentleman's Heart

A Matchmaker for a Marquess

His Duchess for a Day

Five Days With a Duke

Lords of Honor

Seduced by a Lady's Heart

Captivated by a Lady's Charm

Rescued by a Lady's Love

Tempted by a Lady's Smile

Courting Poppy Tidemore

Scandalous Seasons

Forever Betrothed, Never the Bride

Never Courted, Suddenly Wed

Always Proper, Suddenly Scandalous

Always a Rogue, Forever Her Love

A Marquess for Christmas

Once a Wallflower, at Last His Love

Endlessly Courted, Finally Loved

Once a Rake, Suddenly a Suitor

Once Upon a Betrothal

Sinful Brides

The Rogue's Wager

The Scoundrel's Honor

The Lady's Guard

The Heiress's Deception

The Wicked Wallflowers

The Hellion

The Vixen

The Governess

The Bluestocking

The Spitfire

The Theodosia Sword

Only For His Lady

Only For Her Honor

Only For Their Love

All the Duke's Sins Prequel Series

It Had to Be the Duke

One for My Baron

Scandalous Affairs

A Groom of Her Own

Taming of the Beast

My Fair Marchioness

It Happened One Winter

Loved and Found

A Regency Duet

Rogues Rush In

Nonfiction Works

Uninterrupted Joy: A Memoir

THE
WOLF
of Mayfair

CHRISTI
CALDWELL

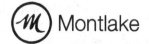 Montlake

Text copyright © 2024 by Christi Caldwell
All rights reserved.

No part of this book may be reproduced, or stored in a retrieval system, or transmitted in any form or by any means, electronic, mechanical, photocopying, recording, or otherwise, without express written permission of the publisher.

Published by Montlake, Seattle

www.apub.com

Amazon, the Amazon logo, and Montlake are trademarks of Amazon.com, Inc., or its affiliates.

ISBN-13: 9781662518164 (paperback)
ISBN-13: 9781662518171 (digital)

Cover design by Hang Le
Cover image: © KathySG, © Anterovium, © VladaKela / Shutterstock

Printed in the United States of America

THE
WOLF
of Mayfair

Chapter 1

I wish that all those, who on this night are not merry enough to speak before they think, may ever after be grave enough to think before they speak!

—*Ann Radcliffe,* The Italian

"A visitor has arrived, my lord."

While the rest of Polite Society departed for the winter months, ensconcing themselves in their cozy country estates, the Marquess of Wingrave took refuge in London. It spared him the tediousness of being shut away with his family, the annoyance of putting up with the domineering influence of his father, the Duke of Talbert.

When the duke left and took his subservient wife with him, Wingrave remained in this coveted residence and envisaged a time when it would belong to him—when *all of it* would.

Few things fired his lust more, though much did.

Conveniently, in remaining in London, Wingrave found there was no end to the debauched pleasures awaiting him.

Leaning over the billiards table, he assessed the green velvet surface for his next shot.

"A visitor has arrived, my lord."

"I heard you the first time." He drew back his cue and propelled it effortlessly forward.

Out of the corner of his eye, he caught the mottled color splotching the stout fellow's big cheeks. "I thought you might care—"

"I don't." Wingrave didn't care about anything or anyone. The world knew that. Apparently, however, his family's recently hired butler had not received the memorandum.

"This particular visitor claims to have business here—"

"I'm not expecting anyone."

"No, she indicated as much."

She.

His curiosity picked up. Over the years, there'd been any number of bold widows, married ladies, and lusty mamas who'd sought him out. Always in his bachelor's residence, though—never the ducal townhouse.

Now, *that* was a titillating prospect. An image slipped forth: of him and some wanton fucking in every room, in every bed, on every table, until Wingrave had succeeded in marking this place thoroughly and completely his.

He went hard.

The other man finally had his attention.

"A lady of the night?"

The servant dissolved into a choking fit. "N-no, my lord. I'd never dare let such a person in the ducal household."

Wingrave's erection wilted in an instant. "As long as I'm here, I am in charge. I do not care if the most notorious trollop on God's green earth arrives naked on my doorstep, you'll let me decide whether she remains or goes. You'd do well to remember that. For someday," he whispered icily, "this residence will belong to me. And your employment? Will depend on me. Is that clear?"

His butler gave a juddering nod. "Y-yes, my lord," he croaked. "It i-is understood. As I said your current visitor is no lady of the night, but rather a *lady*." The young man's voice slipped to a whisper, like the latter was the more scandalous of the two possibilities.

And in a way, it was.

"A lusty widow then?" Wingrave snapped.

Color set the other man's cheeks aflame. "I . . . would not know, m-my lord," he stammered.

Wingrave smiled coldly. "Oh, you'd know." From their state of dress—or undress—they were easier to identify than a whore in church.

"I . . . She is young. A very *young* lady."

A young lady seeking him out in his familial residence? Curious, that. Not curious enough for Wingrave to care—especially for some innocent miss who'd made the mistake of visiting his doorstep. For all his well-earned reputation as society's most notorious rake, he'd never been so caddish as to bed a virgin.

He did a slow walk about the table. All the while he lazily contemplated the billiard balls scattered upon the green velvet surface.

He'd little interest in virgins' simpering and tears, and he had even less interest in training those creatures for the future use of other men, who'd benefit from the largesse of Wingrave's efforts.

No, he wanted the women he took as lovers to be skilled and possessed of as insatiable an appetite as him—though that invariably proved a rare feat.

Leaning an elbow against the rose, Wingrave launched another effortless shot that ricocheted off the back center of the table and landed in the opposite pocket.

"You're still here," he said, infusing a steely warning into that observation.

The servant cleared his throat. "Y-yes."

The fool didn't say anything more than that.

"Get rid of her," Wingrave snapped.

"Y-yes, my l-lord. It is just . . . the lady is not here to see you, my lord."

It took a moment to register that the butler not only remained but that he did so and continued to speak about the nighttime visitor at Horace House.

At last, Wingrave looked up at the annoyingly tenacious servant.

"The lady is here to see the Duke and Duchess of Talbert."

Ahh. "You should have led with that. I care even less about the chit's identity and presence here. The duke and duchess have retired to Bedford Manor, so direct her there."

The servant's face turned a deeper shade of crimson. "Yes, but there is a storm brewing, my lord."

Still poised to spring his next shot, Wingrave looked across the table and winged an eyebrow up. "Which is something you believe I care about?" he drawled mockingly.

"No, my lord?"

"No. That is the first right thing you've said this evening." He lifted his glass in a jeering salute to the stammering fellow and took a welcome swallow of the subtly sweet brandy.

The butler beamed like he'd been given a raise for good services rendered.

"Do you know what you *should* care about?" Wingrave asked the grinning hireling.

Even the huge shake the butler gave of his head couldn't dislodge the brown hair he'd combed to the right and heavily slicked with pomade.

"Your employment. *That* is what you should care about—"

"I believe she is a ward of His and Her Grace," the servant beseeched.

Good God, the man wouldn't quit. As Wingrave saw it, he had two options before him: one, sack the servant, but then he'd be without a head of the household staff and, for that matter, required to expend energy to find a new one. And two, handle the man's job for him, so he could enjoy his goddamned game and brandy.

"Where is she?"

"In the foyer," the butler said quickly. The man's previously tense shoulders sagged with a visible relief.

Wingrave returned his cue to the wall mount and went and collected his snifter. He thought better of it, grabbed the nearby decanter of brandy, and set down his half-empty glass.

With bottle in hand, Wingrave quit the billiards room.

As he strode the wide, red-velvet-carpeted halls, the butler trotted behind him like a small, obnoxious, obedient pup that tried to keep up with its master.

"Does she have a name?" Wingrave asked, without breaking stride.

"Not that I'm aware of. That is . . . I'm certain she does have a name, just not one—"

Wingrave's low growl cut off the remainder of that damning admission. "Let me see if I have this correct."

He stopped quickly and his slow-witted servant caught himself just before he would have stumbled into Wingrave. "You allowed some stranger, whose name you did not collect and whose identity is unknown, into the ducal residence on the basis of her claims that she has some connection to the duke and duchess?"

The man's pallor turned a deathly shade of white. "I . . ."

"What proof did she give you? What official papers did she provide?"

"None," the nervous servant whispered.

"None," Wingrave repeated flatly. For centuries, the legacy, power, wealth, and influence that came with a dukedom dating back to William the Conqueror had ushered in all manner of graspers who sought whatever scraps they could through the family's benevolence.

Every last one of them had learned the Blofields didn't possess a shred of munificence in their cold-blooded bodies.

This latest parasite would be no exception.

Wingrave approached the foyer. He found her in an instant.

Diminutive and swallowed up by a too-big, tattered cloak, the lady stood in the middle of the black-and-white checkered floor. She'd tilted her neck so far back to view the fresco overhead, she'd knocked her hood loose, which left Wingrave an unhindered view of his *visitor*.

He did a cursory examination.

The young woman's titian hair hung in a messy tangle down her back. What must be a thousand freckles or more smattered naturally plump cheeks, a dimpled chin, and a straight nose.

5

Yes, she was certainly no woman he'd ever kept company with, nor ever would. Furthermore, a bedraggled waif such as she certainly held no connection to the selective duke and duchess.

"*This* is the trespasser?" Wingrave drawled. His voice echoed in the cavernous three-story entryway and brought the lady whipping around.

She looked at him, and her pathetically revealing eyes flashed with recognition that quickly sapped the blood from her cheeks.

Yes, his reputation as a rake preceded him.

When his bumbling butler failed to form a response, he pinned his focus on the trembling creature before him.

Fear flashed in her eyes. "I'm nah a trespasser, my lord," she whispered.

He leveled her with a look. "Do I know you?"

She dampened big, pillowy, soft lips made for a man's cock. "N-nay?"

"Is that a question?" he jeered.

The long white, freckled column of her neck warbled. She drew in a breath. "*Nay,*" she said. "It was not a question but an answer. I do not ken ye."

Wingrave did another assessment of the lady. She'd more courage than his servant, though that was hardly a feat for even the smallest babe.

He turned his attention away from the trembling chit. "She's a wide-eyed *miss*. You couldn't throw a damned slip of a woman out?"

"I . . . could not," the head of the household staff said, his features as strained as his tone.

Wingrave let free a sound of disgust. "I should sack you."

His butler appeared one utterance away from dissolving into tears.

Wingrave had opened his mouth to see it so when, out of the corner of his eye, he caught a rustle and flash of skirts.

The brave—or stupid—chit placed herself between him and his butler.

If he were a man given to humor and laughter, this waif defending a grown man, more than a foot taller than her, would certainly have moved him to mirth.

The fool brought her palms up as if in supplication. "Please, do not punish him," she pleaded.

His lip drew back in a reflexive sneer. He despised little more than those pitiable souls who cowered and beseeched.

"Why *shouldn't* I?" he demanded silkily.

As if the wench realized too late she'd drawn the attention and wrath of a dragon, she retreated a step.

Of course she did. Wingrave had yet to meet a soul unafraid of him or having his anger turned on them.

"It is not his fault."

So unaccustomed to people uttering a single contrary word in his presence, it was a moment before Wingrave registered that faintest and most defiant of whispers.

Wingrave turned all his undivided, wrathful attention on the one most deserving of his displeasure—the woman who'd dared force her way inside his kingdom.

"No, it isn't, is it?" he purred. "Then tell me, who *should* bear the blame for my anger this night?"

The freckled place between the lady's brows came together into a fear-filled little furrow.

Ah, she'd realized too late then that silence had been her safest course.

His butler, on the other hand, wisely dissolved into the shadows and allowed the braver one who'd defended him to take on Wingrave's wrath.

Wingrave didn't suffer cowards.

He suffered fools even less.

The waif before him retained eye contact. The noisy whir of her skirts and cloak, on the other hand, betrayed her attempt at intrepid warrioress.

"You demanded to see me," he said coolly. With a flourish, Wingrave spread his arms wide. "Well, you have my full, undivided attention."

Chapter 2

Do you believe your heart to be, indeed, so hardened, that
you can look without emotion on the suffering, to which
you would condemn me?

—*Ann Radcliffe, The Mysteries of Udolpho*

The Marquess of Win*grave*—icy as the dead and devoid of a heart. The
nobleman's name couldn't have suited him more had it been hand-selected
by the bean-nighe, that Scottish messenger from the Underworld and
bringer of death.

Everyone had heard the dark tales of the Marquess of Wingrave.

Those forbidding and wicked stories had even found their way into
Miss Helia Wallace's corner of Scotland. Lord Wingrave, notorious rake.
Vied for by women upon whom he scattered his attentions but never
his affections. Fighter of duels—and winner of each of them—and yet
unpunished because of the power he and his family possessed.

No warmth on the outside, no warmth on the inside . . .

Such were the words familiarly uttered about the stonyhearted
Marquess of Wingrave, who according to all, came from a long line of
cruel, callous dukes.

The duke possessed a reputation for browbeating his wife and anyone and everyone around him.

The marquess, on the other hand, was known for being cold as ice and as depraved as Caligula.

As such, Helia would take a malevolent, vainglorious lord over a Lothario.

In fact, so salacious had been the stories surrounding the marquess that Helia's ma, dear friend to the Duchess of Talbert, had barred any papers mentioning Her Grace's son, and threatened to remove from their employ anyone who spoke ill of Lord Wingrave.

But ripping all that fodder from Helia's fingertips several years earlier and silencing servants and guests had not and could not erase everything Helia already read, heard, and knew about the infamous marquess.

Now standing in the sinister shadow of this pitiless gentleman, Helia discovered that, for once in her late mother's life, the countess had been so very wrong.

The gossips had gotten everything written, whispered, or spoken about Lord Wingrave correct.

Desperation, however, left Helia no other option.

Burrowing deeper into her cloak, she drew the garment more tightly closed.

Ah'm no simpering lass, though. Ah'm a stouthearted, proud, hearty Scot.

She'd been raised to believe so and grown into that which her parents insisted she was, and now she dragged forth that mantra as a reminder.

It helped.

Some.

"Come all the way from . . . Scotland, I take it, by that ghastly accent," Lord Wingrave cheerfully remarked, "and you don't have a word to speak?"

"I've learned to speak like an Englishwoman, but when I'm . . ." She stumbled.

He arched a cool brow.

"There are times I slip in my speech," she finished.

She'd not admit to him that nervousness or emotion brought out her Scottish.

"And it is a brogue," she murmured. A man such as he wouldn't care about the distinction, and yet as a proud Scot, it felt so very important to educate him on the difference.

The marquess stared at her.

"'Tis just," she explained, "Scots have a brogue, *not* an accent, my lord."

He looked at her with a palpable disdain. "Thank you for that *fascinating* lesson."

Helia took her cue from his nasty response and met the marquess with silence.

Lord Wingrave folded his arms at his chest and proceeded to walk a predative path around Helia.

She kept her gaze forward and made herself remain motionless.

All the while Wingrave walked around her, he assessed her with that wintry, opaque stare.

Her garments did nothing to mute the marquess's incisive gaze; it sheared through the fabric of her cloak and riding dress and cut all the way through her.

And here these past weeks, Helia had thought there could be no greater peril than the threat posed by Mr. Damian Draxton, the dastardly cousin who'd inherited after her father's recent passing.

It hadn't been enough Helia's beloved father had died, passing the title of earl on to him. Cousin Damian was determined to wed Helia, bed her, all in the pursuit of her dowry.

That isn't altogether true, a voice at the back of her mind pointed out. *When you fled to London to meet the duchess, you feared Mr. Draxton might be here, too.*

But Helia had been so desperate, and so fixed on escaping one threat, she'd not considered *this* danger until the moment she came face-to-face with the infamous Lord Wingrave—dark rake, feared by all, and possessed of a reputation as the very worst libertine.

Like a shark who'd got a scent of its prey, he continued his slow circle around her.

Her hands instinctively curled into balls and uncurled.

You will not be here alone with him.

The Duke and Duchess of Talbert resided here. Someday this stark, austere kingdom would belong to the inveterate rake. But for now, the current duke and duchess ruled over this place.

After this exchange, that could—and would—be the last she'd see of him. This residence was big enough to house all of London's poor and, as such, certainly was big enough to avoid a hateful man like the Marquess of Wingrave.

That reminder should bring some solace.

It brought none.

Not until Helia found herself free of his company—and in that of the warm, kindly woman her mother had spoken of often—would she breathe easy.

After a full, threatening rotation, the marquess stopped so he stood face-to-face with Helia.

How was it possible for one man to ooze such malevolence, contempt, and indifference, all at the same time?

A derisive grin formed on lips as hard as this palace. "I most certainly do *not* remember you."

He wouldn't, because they'd never met before now. And thank the good Lord for it.

She was too relieved by his indifference to be insulted by his disparagement.

The sooner she could speak with the mistress of Horace House, the sooner she could be free of Lord Wingrave's malevolent company.

Helia reached for the clasp of her cloak.

"Making yourself comfortable, are you?" he jeered.

She immediately dropped her arm to her side. "No doubt yer wondering my reason for being here."

"You're wrong," he said flatly. "I would have to be curious or interested. I am *neither*."

That brought her up short. She found her voice.

"I'm here to see the Duchess of Talbert," she quietly explained.

"Are you?" he drawled, taunting, mocking, playing Helia as though she were the mouse to him, the cat.

"Aye, my lord. Ah ken ah've arrived at a late hour and Her Grace is surely abed, my lord."

Which was why Helia found herself in the unfortunate position of explaining her presence here to a man who clearly did not wish to be having this exchange.

"The Duchess of Talbert retired to the country, more's the fortunate for me."

So emotionless in his reply, it was a moment before she registered what the marquess had said.

Helia blinked. Nay! She could not have escaped Cousin Damian, braved the long, arduous journey from Scotland—on her own—only to finally arrive and discover the duchess gone.

Her ears buzzed like a hornet's nest had been knocked loose inside her head. Through the incessant hum, Lord Wingrave's apathetic voice came—but from a distance.

"Now, *Humphries*, if you care to continue your employment, I'd suggest you work up the nerve of handling this person . . ."

Helia came rushing back to the horrifying moment.

"The duke," she rasped, pulling both men's attention back to her. She'd heard the current duke was a monster, but desperation gave her no other choice.

Helia's breath came in quick, noisy bursts. "Then ah'll see His Grace."

"I am even more pleased to share the duke worked himself into a small apoplexy—even more fortunate for me—and was encouraged to recuperate in the country."

Ah'm going to throw up . . .

"Your sister?" she whispered. Even as Helia asked, she knew she merely grasped at air, that dream as elusive as the help she desperately needed.

"My sister? Most days I forget I have one," he said with a glib casualness that somehow made the horrifying admission all the uglier.

"Ye cannae throw me out," she entreated.

Lord Wingrave frowned. "Of course I'd never do something so uncouth as to personally escort you outside. My butler will do that."

Dismissing her like she was some street urchin he'd sullied himself by speaking to, the marquess lifted his hand and waved it in a circular motion.

The butler dashed over.

Helia blanched and moved beyond the servant's reach.

The callow fellow cast a desperate look in his master's direction.

"What is it?" the marquess demanded, and there was a steely warning layered into those three words. "I'm growing tired of this exchange."

"My ma," Helia begged. "My ma, she spoke often of ye."

"Yer ma," he said in a perfect rendition of a brogue that would have impressed her, were he not making a mockery of her speech. "You think I know *your* mother?"

She faltered. "Aye?" Unease tipped her response into a question. "She spoke often of ye *and* yer ma."

The ghost of a grin iced his lips. "Your ma spoke of me?"

Hope stirred in her breast.

She nodded frantically. "Often. She regaled me with tales of ye."

His smile became salacious. "Did she now?" he purred.

Helia gave another nod.

At last, she had managed to reach him. Relief swept through her, so profound it nearly brought her to her knees.

The marquess caught his obdurate chin between a thumb and forefinger and contemplated her with actual interest this time. "A Scot," he murmured to himself. "I do not recall a Scot among my long list of former lovers."

Helia strangled on her spit. "She was most certainly nah one of yer bed partners," she whispered, filled with equal parts horror and indignation at the thought that her loving, beautiful ma would ever debase herself so.

"More's unfortunate, that," he said, with a trace of real regret. "I've never tupped a mother *and* a daughter, and I confess that prospect does hold *some* appeal."

He'd have allowed her entry into his household if he'd been interested in bedding her.

All the horrid stories and whispers had not done proper justice to the marquess's wicked ways. For Lord Wingrave proved even more dissolute than the world knew.

Helia's fingers scrabbled with the sides of her skirt, until she caught the marquess's knowing gaze on those movements.

She made herself stop and tried again, with slightly different words. "The storm has picked up and promises to be a mighty tempest, and I have nowhere to go."

"Among those other 'nowheres' to go, you'd be wise to include this residence."

Dread tightened her belly. She couldn't have come this far only to find herself tossed out onto the London streets, in the middle of an unforgiving storm.

Helia, desperately yearning to see that kind soul her late ma had described, scoured the vast foyer and interconnecting halls.

Panic doubling in her breast, Helia looked past Lord Wingrave and raised her gaze some three stories.

Alas, there came no benevolent duchess sweeping forth to rescue Helia from both the storm and the lady's son. No formidable duke and censorious father to chastise Lord Wingrave over his reprehensible behavior toward a lady.

"Yer certain Her Grace is not in?" she implored, directing that question at London's most feared and revered gentleman.

"What, are you not equally interested in meeting with the duke?" he taunted. "That detail does not escape me."

She pressed her lips together. For she wasn't. She had absolutely no wish to meet an all-powerful duke whose wife had clearly hidden a dear friendship from him.

Wingrave arched an eyebrow. "Perhaps you've heard scintillating tales of how he's destroyed the reputations and social standings of fellow peers because of even the slightest offense?"

Wingrave's pastimes included bedding beauties. His sire, on the other hand, enjoyed playing with—and destroying—people's lives to appease his own moments of boredom.

Helia tried and failed to swallow.

"Or," Lord Wingrave continued, with apparent glee at her disquiet, "then there are the young debutantes who became spinsters because the duke has blacklisted their families. And do you know why he did that, my dear?"

When she didn't answer quickly enough, he prodded: "Hmm?"

She managed to shake her head.

Wingrave leaned close and whispered, "He thinks nothing of destroying lives, because it brings him great amusement to do so."

Helia gasped. She raised her fingers to bury her exhalation of horror—too late.

Cruelty for cruelty's sake was something she could not understand.

And this is the family to whom you've turned, a voice in her head jeered.

Except . . .

"What of your mother?" she asked softly. "What stories do you have of her?"

A muscle rippled along his powerful, square jaw.

"It brings me the utmost pleasure to say neither the duke nor the duchess are in town," he declared, with the first hint of true mirth she'd spied from him—something she'd believed impossible until now.

It did not escape Helia's notice he'd not a nasty thing to say about his mother, and she felt hope rekindle in her breast.

That sentiment, however, proved short lived.

Lord Wingrave nodded. Like an obedient pup, his butler trotted over and immediately opened the door.

Wind whipped inside. Snow piled up in a growing mound around the foyer floor.

She looked from the marquess to the threshold, then back to the marquess again.

"Ye would send me out in *this?*" Only the knowledge that if she were turned away, there'd be absolutely nowhere to go kept her pleading with him.

"Not only am I sending you out in this, I'm doing so happily." He glanced down the length of his aquiline nose at Helia. "I've already shown you greater generosity than this situation merits."

Never before had she known a soul could be so dark and empty as Lord Wingrave's. What made a man this way?

"You've said enough mocking things about me being Scottish," she said, needing to know why he detested her so. "Is that why ye'll so easily turn me out and let me die on the streets of London?"

"My dear," he drawled, sounding faintly amused. "I'd have to work up the emotion to care that you are a Scot. I couldn't care either way whether you were Mary, Queen of Scots, returned from the dead or Bloody Mary herself."

"Helia Mairi Wallace," she whispered.

He stared blankly at her.

Maybe if he knew her name, he would see her not as a bothersome thing on his doorstep but a living, breathing woman.

Och, my lass, with yer jolly smile and happy spirit, ah couldn't have picked a more perfect name for ye.

Those long-ago murmurings of her mother flitted through her mind, and in this instant, that remembrance was a bittersweet one.

"My name is Helia Mairi Wallace," she repeated thickly. "Daughter of the late Laird Kilmarnock and Earl of Buccleuch."

"Irrelevant," he muttered coolly under his breath. "The only bearing your name has on the matter is it indicates you are not in possession of any connection to the duke, who despises and detests the Scottish and all things associated with that land and their people."

"What will ah do?" she asked, the question as much to herself as to him.

He flicked a piece of lint from his sleeve. "My dear, since you were so irksome as to invade my household, I've not given a thought to you or what you should, could, or would do—that is, aside from showing yourself out."

Wingrave turned to go.

"B-but . . . but . . ." Helia lifted her palms up at his back. "It isn't *yer* household."

As soon as it slipped out, she knew she'd said the wrong thing.

He wheeled around.

"The brazenness of you," he snarled.

Good God. She was making a mess of all this. "I dinnae mean to—"

"You did not mean to what?" he whispered. "Insult me? Question my ownership of this place and everything I deem mine?"

Helia struggled to swallow. "I'd never insult ye." At least, not to his face. Alone, she'd let spew every last hateful thought she had of him. "What ah *m-meant*—"

He took a slow, deliberate, predatory step toward her, and it briefly stalled the rest of her words.

"What ah meant," she repeated, this time in a steadier tone, "is that the duchess is my godmother, and the residence belongs to the Duke and Duchess of Talbert—"

Wingrave narrowed his eyes upon her. "Finish it."

She wavered.

"Say whatever it is you intended to say, wench."

Even as saying nothing was wiser, his low, resonant baritone compelled her to speak. "Yer their son," she finished weakly.

"I am the Marquess of Wingrave." His gravelly, low-pitched words had the same effect as if he'd shouted.

"Ah dinnae mean any disrespect, my lo—"

"I am next in line to the dukedom of Talbert. All of this, everything around you"—he tossed his arms wide to display the powerful kingdom around them—"belongs to me. The current duke is merely holding on to it a short while more. He is a mere guardian of what is mine and what will belong to me and mine."

For God's sake, what had she done?

"I am set to inherit any number of great things from the duke and duchess," he said, this time conversationally. "Vast land holdings. A fortune to rival Midas's. Power to surpass the Savior and Satan combined."

Lord Wingrave curled his lips in a jeering grin. "My parents' goddaughters, however, are fortunately not bequeathed to me."

"Goddaught*ers*?" she repeated dumbly.

"Thought you were so very special, did you? My mother has any number of goddaughters. She is soft. Weak. Easy prey for one such as you. It is why countless gentlewomen seek to form advantageous connections with the duchess. They hope that such an association will pay dividends to their homely daughters. Let me spare you from wondering: it *won't*."

Her stomach dropped. Something in knowing the duchess had served as godmother to any number of young ladies made Helia's connection to Her Grace both less significant and special.

"Humphries?"

The butler immediately clamored out from behind the enormous hall clock, where he'd taken shelter from Wingrave's ire.

"Give the lady some coins and show her the door."

She blinked wildly.

Then Lord Wingrave's crisp directive penetrated Helia's misery.

"I don't need to be shown the door," she pleaded. "One night. Please, and then ye have my promise I willnae ask for anything more."

The duke spun so quickly he knocked the rest of that thought from Helia's mouth.

"You're dismissed," Lord Wingrave murmured.

She stiffened, and for a moment, she believed that terse order to be directed at her.

In one rapid move, the butler brought the doors closed and then bolted from the foyer, leaving Helia and the marquess.

Alone.

The penetrating chill his presence wrought proved a greater cold than even the tempest raging beyond those panels.

His silence was ominous, savage.

Finally, the marquess spoke. "All right, you may stay."

A relief so profound went through her, it brought tears to her eyes, blurring his harshly beautiful visage.

Her joy died a swift death.

"Do you know, Miss Helia Wallace of Scotland," he said silkily. "For a virginal young lady on her own, with only your virtue to barter for your existence, you seem very willing to throw it away by sharing the same household with a dastard like me. No companions or respectable figures about to shield your reputation and honor . . . just me."

He sought to scare her . . . and it was working. "Snow will soon blanket London. It is but a night." She reminded herself of that as much as him. Tomorrow she would be off for the country, with the world none the wiser.

"Ah, but it is not just any night, Miss Wallace." Lord Wingrave stroked his index finger along the curve of her cheek. "It is a night with *me*."

She trembled—not with a deserved fear or disgust but for reasons unknown to her. He glided that long, lone digit in a haunting caress that stirred . . . something, something unfamiliar deep in her belly.

An arrogant grin slashed his lips up.

"And when you are ruined," he murmured, "you can rely on one truth—I will never marry you. At best, you'll be my mistress, and then only if I can rouse enough interest to want a place between your legs."

With a scathing smile and only that cruel reminder of a different threat Helia faced by simply being here, Lord Wingrave stalked off.

The quiet tread of his footfalls, measured enough to match a soldier's precisive march, faded into nothing, so all that remained was the echo of his portentous words.

Helia stood there, shivering, long after he'd gone.

That previous sense of deliverance was no more.

For she'd done it; she'd managed to persuade a callous Lord Wingrave to grant her a place to stay.

And yet, this night, in putting forth her need to survive a storm, she'd imperiled her reputation—and in that, her very future.

Chapter 3

She immediately withdrew from the casement, and, though much agitated, sought in sleep the refreshment of a short oblivion.

—*Ann Radcliffe, The Mysteries of Udolpho*

The mournful east winds wailed and drummed upon the crystal panes like Badb, the deathkeeper, knocking at the window to claim those slated for death.

The fire blazing in the hearth did little to warm the guest chambers Helia currently inhabited. Instead, those wildly snapping flames merely cast grimly black shadows over the darkened room.

The unforgivable storm continued to rage, the tempest as cold as this palace made of limestone on the outside and garishly gilded throughout.

Horace House was as pitiless as the gentleman who'd ruthlessly stated his claim to the portentous place.

Tucked into the mahogany gadrooned and upholstered four-poster bed and with a heavy silken coverlet drawn close to her chin, sheltered from that violent tempest, Helia should have drifted off to sleep the moment her back hit the billowingly soft mattress.

Instead, just as she'd done since she'd climbed into bed hours earlier, Helia squirmed back and forth in a bid to get comfortable.

It didn't help.

Restless, she stole yet another glance at the table clock on the nightstand beside her bed.

Three hours. It'd been three hours since she'd first been shown to her rooms, bathed, and changed into her modest nightshift.

Three hours thinking about how she danced with ruin by being here. Now she counted down the moments until the storm abated and she could sneak off, with the world none the wiser about her having spent the night alone with London's darkest, most dangerous rake.

Only, if you're truly being honest with yourself, that isn't all you're thinking about . . . a voice in Helia's head silently—and worse, *accurately*—taunted.

It's that you've never seen a man as finely crafted as the marquess.

Nay, she hadn't. She'd known men as big and broad of muscle, but no one like *him*.

A man as fiendish as Lord Wingrave should be an exact likeness of a storybook villain—sporting a thin black mustache that curled at the corners and pockmarked skin.

Certainly, he shouldn't have the face and form of Adonis and the soul of Satan.

Some three or four inches past six feet, and with broad shoulders and finely defined arms, he was as well put together as the brawniest Scots she'd watched partake in the caber toss at the annual Highland Games.

Lord Wingrave possessed a preternatural beauty that marked him untouchable and dared mere mortals to approach him.

He was like a tall, unbending, cold marble statue. With his ruggedly handsome features—sharp cheeks, square jaw, and aquiline nose—he possessed an air of masculine perfection that only those artists could have managed to create. Hard, thin lips and nape-long jet-black hair, with cool, subtle blue undertones, only further lent the marquess an air of icy detachment.

Not that it mattered either way whether he was as bonny as a man could be.

He was a lout. At that, a rude, condescending, mean, surly, impatient lout.

Why, then, did he fascinate her so?

Perhaps it was because she'd never known an enigma such as Lord Wingrave. Why, he was no different from the complex puzzles she'd delighted in solving as a lass but also as dangerous as the games of snap-dragon which had left her fingers burned so many times.

Helia rolled onto her side and stared absently at the windows as they shook from the force of the storm outside.

She'd wager the virtue she desperately needed to guard that becoming too close to Lord Wingrave would not only burn but consume a woman in a mighty conflagration.

Helia unthinkingly brushed the place upon her cheek Lord Wingrave had stroked.

Virgin though she may be, when he'd caressed her, she'd had a small taste of just what it was that made ladies tangle with a devil such as he—for the gift of his powerful, bold, yet shockingly warm touch.

An uncomfortable sensation built between Helia's legs and she shifted in a bid to bring herself some relief.

Stop, this instant. Ye are nah one to lose yer head over a handsome gent.

Helia slunk deeper under the blankets, drew the covers high over her head, and forced herself to recall the vulgar things he'd said, all of which should have made her hate him to the core.

For a virginal young lady on her own, with only your virtue to barter for your existence, you seem very willing to throw it away by sharing the same household with a dastard like me. No companions or respectable figures about to shield your reputation and honor . . .

Icy snowflakes hit the windows like punctuation points to each of his wicked statements.

She continued to let those thoughts slip in.

. . . when you are ruined, you can rely on one truth—I will never marry you. At best, you'll be my mistress, and then only if I can rouse enough interest to want a place between your legs . . .

His rake's vow plagued and repulsed and, paradoxically, tantalized.

What made a man jaded as Lord Wingate had become? Why, when he'd been granted every gift of wealth, power, and influence, and a set of devoted parents who both lived, and a houseful of servants, should he be so very miserable?

And there must have been something so very wrong with Helia that she possessed a yearning to unlock the mystery around the grim stranger.

Not that you need wonder or worry about what gave Lord Wingrave reason to be so hateful and guarded. You'll be gone soon enough, and in the safe folds of the Duchess of Talbert's care.

Letting out an aggravated sigh, Helia lowered the heavy coverlet and abandoned her futile attempts at sleep.

Rolling onto her belly, she swung her legs over the side of the mattress. Her toes danced about in the air as she searched for—and found—the leathered top bed steps.

Shivering, Helia sprinted over to the pink, green, and yellow armoire and drew the lacquered doors open.

She fetched her serviceable white wrapper from within, and quickly shrugged into the garment. Next, she collected a pair of stockings and headed for one of the floor-to-ceiling windows that overlooked the rear of the duke's properties.

Edging back the heavy gold velvet curtain, she perched herself on the wide white sill, and as she drew her hosiery on, Helia attempted to take in the scene beyond the windowpanes. Since she'd last looked outside some hours ago, a thick, heavy frost had grown over the glass, making it near impossible for Helia to discern the previously visible grounds.

After she'd donned her white, worsted stockings, Helia straightened; her skirts fell noiselessly back into their proper place.

She rested both palms against the freezing glass; the bite of cold stung her hands, and still she kept them pressed there several moments.

Then she scraped away at the melted ice until she'd fashioned a small peephole, and leaning close, she peered outside.

Alas, heavy snow came down hard and fast, worse than any Scottish rain, so that she couldn't make out anything beyond the violent whorl of falling flakes and the blanket of white they left upon the vast stone terraces and even vaster gardens.

The ice-coated windowpane reflected back her sad smile.

In the not-too-distant past, there'd been a thrill and joy when wild storms ripped across the Highlands.

As a wee lass, such a gailleann had been one she'd welcomed and relished. After the tempest abated, she was always the earliest to rise the next morn. All so she might sneak outside and be the first to leave her footprints upon the fresh fallen snow. Her ma and da would invariably join her, lobbing a snowball her way to alert her of their presence. They'd all frolic in that snow until their cheeks were red and numb from the cold, then race to the kitchens, where they'd sip hot chocolate and eat oat porridge mixed with jam and sprinkled heavily with sugar.

Her smile dipped.

Now, alone in this dark, imperial mansion, that tempest battering the impregnable fortress cast a sinister cloud over this place and all who dwelled within.

Helia's heart pounded. To get to this point, she'd braved the harshest Highland winter she could recall in all her eighteen years. Recent storms that'd passed through weeks earlier had left the old Roman roads already nearly impassable, all the muddier and more treacherous. Along the way, she'd managed to evade Mr. Draxton, twice. But in order to do so, she had been forced to remain at an inn, alone, unchaperoned, and had gone through too many of her dwindling funds.

She'd finally reached the duchess's residence only to find a different, but no less grave, peril—sharing a roof with Lord Wingrave.

In remaining here, alone with Wingrave, she risked ruination. But to return to Scotland would mean she'd be raped by Mr. Draxton, forced to wed, and by society's standards, then she'd belong to him in name and body.

The frescoed ceiling and walls began closing in on her.

Her breath came in hard, fast pants.

Leave.

Now!

Helia, with shaking fingers, grabbed the bronze candlestick beside her bed. She clutched the elegant triangular base so hard the metal left marks upon her palm as she sprinted for the door.

Helia pressed the delicately cast-brass handle, and as she let herself out into the hall, the well-oiled hinges didn't emit so much as the softest of squeaks.

Helia paused with one foot on the threshold and the other hovering in the air, about to trade inanimate foes for the living, breathing dragon who'd declared his eminence over everything and everyone who set foot inside his kingdom.

He is out there . . .

Another gust of wind howled its concurrence.

He'd also had Helia set up in the main suites, in rooms directly opposite his. All he need do was cross the hall, insert a key he absolutely would have, and let himself into Helia's chambers.

And suddenly, being anywhere else in this household, as long as it was far, far away from wicked Lord Wingrave, won out as the far safer option.

With that, Helia hurried from her temporary rooms, drew the door panel closed noiselessly, and tiptoed away.

The minute she'd put that hall behind her, she broke out into a full run.

Click.

His left ear may have been useless, but Wingrave never allowed that particular organ to face a door or person he spoke to. Following his illness, however, his right ear, not unlike Wingrave himself, had found an even greater strength.

It was how he heard the minute Miss Wallace opened her door. She'd escaped.

If he had a soul worth wagering, he'd have bet the Devil himself Miss Wallace intended to fleece him and, at last, be on her way. Likely with his mother's silver.

Another man may have raised a hue and cry or raced after her out of fear she intended to take something of his.

Not Wingrave.

Naked as the day he'd been born and lying at the center of his four-poster bed, he smiled with a hunter's delight.

When he'd agreed to let her spend the night, he'd known what she intended. As poor as any waif in the streets and bedraggled like one, too, she was no more the daughter of some dead earl than Wingrave was God himself.

No, the prospect of catching Miss Wallace in that willful act of taking something that belonged to him had titillated and left him filled with an insatiable lust.

For one so young and so innocent and chaste, she'd displayed a temerity and resolve that tantalized.

No one had ever dared challenge him. But she had, and instead of being incensed with rage, he'd been inflamed by a fierce desire to lay claim to her, to dominate her.

He relished the chase; it made the eventual capture all the more satisfying.

Wingrave stood.

He didn't bother with a shirt, just grabbed his trousers from the floor.

After he'd jammed his legs inside, he drew the garment up, tugged at his cock, and adjusted himself so he could properly close his placard.

Then Wingrave set out in pursuit.

He didn't bother to collect a candle to light the way—his eyes no longer needed adjusting to the inky black of Horace House at night. No, to carry a flame would alert her of his approach and spoil the hunt.

He allowed her to expand her lead.

All the while, he trailed along the halls at a leisurely pace, and envisioned the delicious moment when he caught her.

Perverse in every way, the idea of the innocent woman, so out of her depths, thinking to take something of his made him hard. Merciless as the day was long, he'd meet that affront with an eye for an eye.

And he knew, from the way her breath had hitched when he'd caressed her cheek, she'd be hot for him. There'd be no taking. Miss Wallace would happily spread her legs and give him what he wanted.

Wingrave would find her, and quickly.

On a silent tread, he continued along the eastern corridor. Nor was it a gamble on his part.

He'd ordered the servants who'd escorted her to her rooms to do so along a specific route.

As sure as the sun set in the west and rose in the east, Miss Wallace would follow the same path she'd taken to reach her rooms earlier this evening. For no other reason than the familiarity and predictability of that path would give her a false air of security and self-control, she'd continue on as unsuspecting as a witless bird for whom he'd dropped crumbs, all to lead her where he wanted.

Which was when he'd pounce.

He reached the end of the west hallway and took a step down the adjacent corridor, which led to the silver cabinet, when a flicker of light snagged his attention.

Wingrave tunneled all his focus on the pale glow coming from a nearby doorway and grinned coldly.

Caught.

He took a step—

"She is in the Portrait Room, my lord."

The bewigged footman, John Thomas, stationed at the front of the hall, spoke quietly and as proudly as if he himself had saved the silver Wingrave had been so very certain she'd been making after.

Wingrave gnashed his teeth.

Goddamn it. "Not a word more," he said on a lethal whisper.

The man's ridiculously large Adam's apple bobbed wildly. "As you wish, m—" He caught himself too late.

John Thomas promptly lowered his gaze to the floor, wisely made himself as small as possible, and said nothing more.

As you wish, Wingrave thought acidly. If wishes were a thing and he were granted them, he wouldn't have a useless ear.

Gritting his teeth, he made for the Portrait Room.

Draped in a flowing, high-necked nightdress, the lady stood with her back to him, examining one of the familial portraits.

"Never tell me you are so stupid as to filch a framed portrait and not the silver," he said coolly.

Miss Wallace's gasp echoed through the empty room. She whipped around to face him.

From across the room, they studied one another.

Wingrave took advantage of the light cast by her candelabra to consider her with a rake's gaze.

Those flames cast a glow that penetrated her modest white shift and wrapper and put on display the hint of pale-pink nipples; the tips of those small mounds puckered against the fabric of her garments.

She wasn't his usual type . . . nor would she *ever* be.

Titian hair he'd once considered garish. Though the flaming red and coppery hues burnished within Miss Wallace's bright auburn curls suited the fiery minx's temperament. Distinct brown freckles stood out, vivid specks upon her sharp, stark white cheeks.

Possessed of long legs, a sinfully narrow waist, and even narrower hips, she didn't have a body to tempt a man, and yet . . .

He was a man of *many* tastes.

Under his debauched study, fear radiated bright in her pathetically expressive eyes.

With an unbreakable courage, she continued to hold his stare.

His randy shaft stirred with renewed interest at this latest display of the lady's strength.

Miss Wallace broke first.

As if there'd ever been a doubt.

The lady sank into a flawless curtsy no street thief could feign. "My lord," she quietly greeted.

That subservient gesture paired with her bold gaze sent another bolt of lust through him.

"I'm not a thief. I've not come to take anything from ye."

"And yet," he murmured, and started for her on deliberately menacing steps, "I find you not in your bed, where you belong, like a good girl, but rather here."

A sinful image whispered forth. Of her, this lady no more than eighteen or nineteen, lying in the ghastly virginal robes she wore now, draped upon a bed and parting her legs as Wingrave lowered himself between her sweet thighs.

"Is there a question there, my lord?"

No, there was no question. He absolutely wanted to fuck her.

"Why have you left your rooms?" he said. Desire left his voice graveled.

"I couldn't sleep," she confessed. Fear sparked in Miss Wallace's eyes. "Am I your prisoner?"

Oh, God. The images this innocent painted continued to come. This time, the thought was of her stretched out with her arms and legs tied to the four posters of his bed so she lay helpless and wide open to his attentions.

"Would you like to be my prisoner?" he asked thickly. He'd be all too happy to serve her wishes.

She scoffed. "If I'd wanted to be *anyone's* prisoner, I would have remained in Scotland with my devious cousin."

Not *anyone's*. *Wingrave's*. Ah, God. Had he ever known one as innocent as she? Perhaps he'd had it wrong all these years. Perhaps the fellows with a taste for wide-eyed, untouched innocence had discovered a perverse pleasure he'd been denying himself.

"How can you be a prisoner," Wingrave purred, continuing his feral approach, "when you begged to stay with me?"

He stopped before her.

"Ah dinnae beg to stay here with ye—I begged for shelter for the night, from the storm," she said, with a husk to her contralto that further aroused him.

"Ah, but isn't that the same thing?"

She swallowed wildly. "I dinnae believe so," she whispered.

"Ah, but I do. Tell me, is it fear of ruin that has robbed you of sleep? Have you realized too late that, with my black reputation, even breathing the same air as me will see the whole world believing I've had you in my bed? And"—he dangled that—"with no choices available to you, that would be your only course—becoming my mistress. I believe you'd love that, Miss Wallace," he purred. "Nay, I know you would. And not for the diamonds I'd drape you in but for the endless pleasure you'd find in my arms."

She retreated a step, so quick she stumbled over her feet.

The lady righted herself.

"You said you dinnae desire me," she reminded him, her voice pleading.

He'd been wrong.

Once.

There was always a first time for everything. And that saying clearly applied to carnal interests in a virginal miss.

"Ye said ye'd only offer me a role as your mistress if ye can rouse enough interest t-to . . . to . . ." Her blush deepened.

"To want a place between your legs?" he supplied all too happily. "I've had time to reconsider my initial assessment." He glanced pointedly down at Miss Wallace's demure white nightshift.

The lady followed his stare and automatically folded her arms around herself . . . as if she could shield herself from his gaze.

With those slim, delectable limbs folded, she bit the corner of her index finger.

Wingrave's gaze homed in on lush, berry-red lips—the most volup-
tuous part of her painfully trim frame—and another wave of desire
filled him.

He'd not last this night without the efforts of his own fist.

"Why are ye saying these things?" she whispered.

Truth. Truth was the reason he uttered each word he did.

"I am a lady," she continued, with ravaged eyes. "And yet, ye dinnae
think anything of speaking to me so."

"I speak the same way I do to my lovers who are ladies amongst the
ton as well as the most skilled ladies of the night."

She drew back and stared at him like she stood in the presence of
a monster.

And she did. The sooner she realized that, the safer she'd be. "Where
is your conscience?" she demanded, with the greatest strength to any of
the words she'd yet spoken to him.

He snorted. "I don't have a conscience."

She stared confusedly at him. "But *everyone* has a conscience."

"Not I." He'd destroy a man as easily as he'd fuck the same man's
wife and never look back.

Miss Wallace continued to peer at him like one seeking any hint
that Wingrave wasn't as soulless as he, in fact, was.

He'd been a weak bastard only once in his life. From his brother's death, Wingrave had been born anew into a stronger man. He'd
made himself a fortress that allowed no one in, so he could maintain
strength and never again be reduced to a pathetic boy suffering hurts
and mourning losses.

"Ye do have one, my lord," she said softly, more to herself. "Some
are just better at speaking louder over it to drown it out, but it's still
there."

He smirked. "Tell yourself that if it makes you feel better to believe
it, chit."

He flicked an icy glance up and down her person. "Now, may I suggest you return to your chambers and not wander my halls, unless you receive my permission to do so."

Miss Wallace gave her head a slippery shake, then collected her candelabra and walked a wide path around Wingrave.

It appeared the lady did have some sense, after all.

When she'd gone, Wingrave glanced over to the portrait she'd been studying when he came upon her—one of but a handful of bucolic paintings: in it, amidst a meadow, Wingrave and his late brother sat, surrounded by the team of hunting dogs. The artist had caught them in the moment, laughing, and memorialized it for all time.

Steeling his jaw, Wingrave stalked off, quitting the room he'd not set foot in since his brother died, and never would again.

Chapter 4

How strange it is, that a fool or a knave, with riches,
should be treated with more respect by the world, than a
good man, or a wise man in poverty!

—Ann Radcliffe, The Mysteries of Udolpho

The following morning, Helia stared out from the little space she'd
made on the frosted windowpane and took in the storm still raging.

Deep drifts, the kind she'd loved to dive into as a child, blanketed
the duke and duchess's vast gardens. The branches of the lone spruce
tree hung heavy under the burden of several inches of snow that had
piled upon them. The six-foot-tall cast stone fountain of Venus stood
with a bronze tray stretched over her head. From that metal platter, ice
dripped like frozen teardrops that hadn't been free to make their final
descent to the Fiore Pond below.

The sky did cry, and it cried for Helia; the storm made travel impossible for a second day.

The marquess's attempts to petrify her had turned out to be
prophecy.

Helia's eyes slid closed.

I am ruined.

A lady could escape notice in the dead of night, in the dead of winter, amidst a storm, but in the light of day . . . discovery was inevitable.

For secrets didn't live in these streets—or, truth be told, *any* streets. People of every station subsisted on scandal, and inevitably their whispers became roars.

Or maybe, since her parents' death, she'd become so accustomed to living moment to moment she'd merely deluded herself last evening.

What was *more* likely? That Lord Wingrave had been trying to scare her or that he'd known exactly what would happen were Helia to spend the night alone in his household?

Nay, a man of his prowess and reputation knew all too well, she'd been ruined the night she'd stepped through the foyer doors.

He'd taunted her with the idea of making her his mistress.

That offer he'd made had come because he knew she'd wake up with no other choice.

The whole world believing I've had you in my bed? And with no choices available to you, that would be your only course—becoming my mistress.

Helia's breath came in raspy, noisy spurts, matched by the driving winter winds.

I believe you'd love that, Helia . . . Nay, I know you would. And not for the diamonds I'd drape you in but for the endless pleasure you'd find in my arms . . .

She'd be no man's mistress. If she didn't mind whoring herself, she'd have agreed to marry Mr. Damian Draxton and had the certainty which came from being a countess.

What was so very wrong with Helia that thoughts of being bedded by Lord Wingrave didn't repulse her the same way thoughts of lying with Mr. Draxton did?

They were both horrid men.

Why then should so many women throw themselves at Lord Wingrave's feet and, according to everything she'd heard whispered or read, beg to be his lover?

Only, you ken, Helia. You ken.

Shame brought her eyes sliding shut once more.

For fear alone had not kept Helia awake last night, into the wee morning hours, but instead, thoughts of Lord Wingrave.

There was no accounting for it—she found herself equal parts repelled by Lord Wingrave and *fascinated* by him.

The moment young girls stopped being repulsed by boys and became fascinated by romantic thoughts of a sweetheart, they imagined the one who'd be the first to kiss them. Helia was no different. In the dreams she'd carried, she'd share that magical moment with a man who was powerful, bold, confident—one such as the Marquess of Wingrave.

Tall and well muscled, and with an obsidian jaw as hard as his nearly black eyes, Lord Wingrave was more beautiful than any mere mortal man had a right to be. Helia, however, had always prided herself on being able to resist the allure of a rake with raven-black hair and a haughty stare.

Instead, there'd been the whisper of a moment where she'd thought he would kiss her, and God rot her wicked soul, she'd yearned to lose herself in Lord Wingrave's embrace—just so she could be free for a moment of the threat breathing down on her.

Helia, revolted to the core at even contemplating such a thing with such a man, slapped her hands over her face and pressed hard.

Her reputation was ruined, and now she faced another threat—one just as great in its own right, and no less terrifying: staying here until the storm let up and being unable to resist any efforts on the marquess's part to seduce her; that was, should he decide he *wanted* to.

Helia's breathing grew shallow in her ears, and she took in and exhaled breath after shuddery breath.

The wind howled, and that mighty gust sent the thin branch of a nearby silvery birch colliding with the window.

KnockKnockKnock.

That branch continued its incessant beating, as if to drum sense into her clouded head.

Helia shivered; however, that slight tremble had nothing to do with the cold penetrating the thick crystal panes.

She folded her arms at her shoulders and rubbed the chilled flesh.

And yet, if you don't fear him and your body's shameful response to him, a voice taunted, *then why do you remain shut away in your rooms?*

From within the windowpane, she caught sight of her own reflection staring back—with both knowing and disappointment.

"I know what you're thinking," she said to her likeness. "I am not hiding."

She stared intently back, willing herself to believe that.

"I'm not," Helia maintained.

She released a sigh. "Very well, I *may* have been hiding," she conceded. "I was *hiding.*" She gave herself a stern look. "Are you *happy?*"

Finally being honest with herself, Helia acknowledged she'd remained shut away in her temporary rooms to avoid seeing the marquess again.

Which . . . given she'd been on her own these past three months, and faced the cruelty of her distant cousin Mr. Draxton, was *ludicrous.*

Everything was worse in the dead of night; shadows were monsters and groaning floorboards the wails of long-dead ancestors. And Lord Wingrave—a fearsome rake whose reputation preceded him—was no different.

But morning had come and they were both clearheaded.

With Lord Wingrave having offered Helia sanctuary—albeit more as a dare—he'd proven benevolent and merciful. Had he truly been cruel, he would have had one of his many servants toss her right outside, storm or no storm—as he'd initially threatened to do.

The more she considered it, she reckoned her exchange with Lord Wingrave—as well as her response to him—had been the culmination of the fear that had followed her on her flight from Scotland and to Horace House.

Or maybe you're just telling yourself all this to make yourself feel better . . .

She gave her head a shake. It was time to stop hiding in her temporary rooms. She was in trouble, and whether she liked it or not—and she decidedly didn't—the marquess was the only person she could turn to for help.

At last, the incessant pressure at the base of her skull which had nagged her since the moment she left her meeting with Lord Wingrave dissipated some.

Before she let all her earlier doubts and fears win out, Helia walked briskly across the room, and without stopping, she pressed the cast-brass door handle and sailed out into the hall.

When Helia reached the end of the corridor, she found two footmen, one stationed on each side of the passageway.

Each man wore a white powdered wig, and the two stood facing one another, their inexpressive gazes directed like the King's Guard outside St. James's Palace.

As neither servant paid her any notice, she cleared her throat.

Still, they remained motionless and numb to her presence.

"Excuse me," she finally said, when it appeared they'd absolutely no intention of looking at her. "I was wondering if you can help me?"

The pair blinked in a like slowness. Only the bewigged fellow to her left, however, glanced at Helia—and, barely, at that.

"His Lordship, the Marquess of Wingrave," she murmured.

The footman remained blankly staring, and she wondered whether her earlier assessment had been correct and the fellow was, in fact, simple.

When no response proved forthcoming, she spoke more gently and with greater clarification. "Do you ken where I may be able to *find* His Lordship, the Marquess of Wingrave."

That managed to crack the composure of not one servant, but both.

A faint look passed between the two men.

"When at Horace House," the footman on her left murmured, "His Lordship does not welcome company, miss."

Aye, she trusted a man so surly didn't . . . except maybe from the wicked women with whom he was rumored to associate.

Both servants went back to their on-alert position, and it soon became apparent they intended to say not a word more.

Again, Helia made a clearing sound—that had no effect. "Ahem," she repeated a third time, more loudly. "I appreciate that . . . information about His Lordship's preferences . . . ?" she urged, when only the slightly more communicative fellow on her left deigned to cast the faintest of glances her way.

A confused glimmer flared in his eyes.

"I trust you have a name?" she asked gently.

The handsome footman glanced back and forth, up and down the corridors, as if he sought the person whose identifier she'd requested.

Helia took mercy on him. "What is your name?" she asked in the plainest way possible.

That directness did not, however, cure the man of his befuddlement. "My name? Is . . . John Thomas?" With that, he straightened into his previously assumed position, clasped his big hands behind him, and stared sightlessly ahead with a blank stare to rival all the marble busts in the hall.

"Mr. Thomas, Lord Wingrave was so good as to make me a guest of Horace House, and I'd like to speak with him. If you would be so good as to share where I may find him at this hour?"

Helia favored him with her most winning smile.

The small, circular, black birthmark at the corner of the servant's mouth disappeared under the grim line his lips formed.

"His Lordship breaks his fast at this hour," he confirmed in a timorous voice.

Her grin deepened. "Splendid! Thank you so much for sharing that."

Helia remained fixed to the floor and awaited further information.

They continued to stare blankly at her.

"Will you be so good as to provide me directions to the breakfast room?"

Both men appeared a breath away from crying.

"His Lordship will be expecting me," she promised.

Their dubious expressions matched her inner self-ruminations, and for a long moment, Helia thought they intended to ignore her request, but then the silent-until-now servant on her right provided taciturn instructions.

Forcing a lightness she didn't feel, Helia gave each servant a little wave and then went in search of the breakfast room.

As she went, she took in her surroundings.

Marble busts sat proudly on display upon French Louis XVI carved pedestals, accented in gold. The lifelike renderings of noble-looking strangers, whose hostile expressions and merciless eyes, frozen in time, dared a soul to do something as foolish as remain in this cold, forbidding place.

She reached the middle of the hall, which led to another like-decorated corridor, and stopped before a bust of a familiar visage—Lord Wingrave.

Bold and unflinching, the man who'd posed for this piece didn't angle his gaze downward as the other subjects had.

The sculptor had expertly, masterfully, captured the likeness of the future Duke of Talbert and committed to stone a clear glimpse of the formidable, unyielding lord.

Helia drifted closer and stopped directly in front of the column. Unbidden, she stretched her fingertips out and traced the rendering of the marquess's stern, perfectly proportioned mouth, lips as hard and unbending in stone as they were on the man himself.

Riveted, drawn in just as the artist had no doubt intended, Helia cocked her head and remained locked in her study.

The bust, not unlike the flesh-and-blood man, possessed a flinty gaze which silently commanded a person to look away, and yet the searing intensity of this marble stare also pulled a person in.

The enmity spilling from Lord Wingrave's stone stare dared the creator of his piece to find a hint of warmth for his work. And yet . . .

Helia traced her fingers along the chiseled planes of his cheeks, lower, and then stopped.

The artist had found and eternalized the one and only softening of his subject—a faint cleft at the center of Lord Wingrave's rock-hard jaw.

How could a man rumored to melt hearts and have women throwing themselves at his feet also be so cold as to abhor company?

How could these two opposing things be true?

They couldn't. It . . . just wasn't possible.

Helia had to force herself to look away from the marquess's likeness and continue on to meet the flesh-and-blood Lord Wingrave.

At last, Helia reached the breakfast room.

Her wide-eyed gaze went to the twelve-foot, crystal-top, gilded-leg table positioned—undoubtedly strategically—at the center of the room, near enough the window that passersby might view the regal occupants breaking their fast, of which, at the present moment, there was just *one*.

From where he sat at the far left end of the table, Lord Wingrave glanced up from his plain toast, a bite suspended near his lips.

His steely eyes locked on Helia; from those cynical depths radiated a self-possession that glittered with some level of surprise.

Only a man so wholly confident in his self-worth and strength could manage such firm eye contact, and Helia, who'd never been without a word at the ready, found herself tongue-tied.

Sharpening that perpetually hard gaze upon Helia, Lord Wingrave set his partially eaten toast back on his pretty porcelain plate.

Say something.

In the end, the marquess took the onus of issuing the first greeting.

"What do you think you are doing here?" His voice rumbled like the violent wind that battered the windows.

Her heart jumped.

In the name of the wee man.

Helia found her voice. "Forgive me," she said, grateful for the steady, solid delivery of her words.

She sank into a deep, respectful—albeit, belated—curtsy.

Aye, she trusted a powerful sort such as Lord Wingrave, a future duke, didn't take well to not being shown his due respect.

Helia turned, and as she did, out of the corner of her eye, she caught the way some of the tension eased from Lord Wingrave's excellently broad shoulders.

Uneasily humming the tune of "Auld Lang Syne," Helia made her way over to the gilded buffet, which was stocked with such a vast selection of breakfast foods, she wondered whether the duke and duchess had returned, and arrived with company for the winter season.

All the while she made the seemingly endless march to that offering, she felt Lord Wingrave's gaze following her every move, boring through her.

When Helia reached the sideboard, she favored the footman standing on duty with a smile. "Good morn, Mr. . . ."

He stared with a blankness identical to that of the two Mr. John Thomases upstairs.

"I trust you have a name?" she gently inquired. She flashed him a gently teasing smile. "Unless all the footmen are known as Mr. Thomas as a matter of convenience for the master and mistress?"

Color splotched his cheeks, confirming just that.

She rocked on her heels. This chilly treatment toward one's staff was not something Helia understood.

"Do you have a problem with that, Miss Wallace?"

That frosty question from over her shoulder brought Helia spinning around.

Lord Wingrave's cold-eyed stare briefly suspended the words on her lips and the thoughts in her head.

You were right in your first assessment of this man and this place. Run. Hide. Flee.

He arched a glacial black brow, daring her to speak.

"N-no," she sputtered. *Except . . .* "Aye."

"Which is it?" he whispered.

Helia's legs trembled and she pressed her knees together to keep them from knocking, lest he see the effect he had upon her.

"My family, we treated our servants as an extension of our family," she murmured in explanation.

"Ah, how . . . quaint." His lopsided grin mocked her more effectively than words ever could. "Now tell me, why did you not seek out the help of your servant family members instead of making yourself a nuisance for me?"

She faltered. "They couldn't . . . They would have—"

"But they didn't because, given their station, there was nothing they were able to provide you, is that not right, Miss Wallace?" he mocked. "That doesn't *sound* like family."

Helia looked him over, and for all the previous dread his presence roused, pity found its way inside her heart. How very sad were the lenses through which he viewed the world.

"On the contrary. What manner of family would *I* be if I let them risk both their livelihood and lives to help me?"

"You'd be as self-serving as the rest of the people in the world," he drawled.

"People all provide different things, my lord," she murmured. "My family's servants were no different. They offered kindness and warmth and—"

"And how *warm* did their warmth keep you when you found yourself in need?" he cut in, effectively shutting down Helia's attempt at enlightening him.

And this is the man whose mercy you find yourself at . . . ?

Her hopeful spirits dimmed.

With a more muted word of thanks, Helia helped herself to the dish between Mr. Other John Thomas's fingers.

Sometimes, as her mother had been keen to say, it was best for one to haud yer wheesht . . . until a later time.

Not even here a single day, holding her tongue proved the cleverer option.

Helia turned her full attention to the well-stocked array of breakfast foods. Simultaneously, her mouth watered and her stomach gave an embarrassingly loud rumble.

Helia went ahead and began making her dish. She plucked a brioche bun and piece of french bread, thought better of it, and added another brioche bun. Moving purposefully down the row of trays and platters laid out, she helped herself to a honey cake, cold pork, liver, and french plums.

Food. Never again would she take that gift from God for granted.

She approached the end of the vast sideboard, eyed her heaping plate a moment, and then spooned a bit of scrambled eggs into the last hint of an open corner on her dish.

The slow scrape of wood striking wood brought her back around.

With a lethal and deliberate-looking slowness, Lord Wingrave unfurled each inch of his greater-than-six-foot frame.

At the raw, unfettered virility of the man glowering back at her, Helia quivered, as did the plate in her unsteady hands.

She tightened her grip.

Quivered? Speechless? *What is next? Blushing?* That third in the threeling signs of a besotted lady?

Helia made the agonizingly long march across the room, to the spot at the head of the table Lord Wingrave occupied.

With each step, she remained keenly aware of the gentleman staring impenetrably back at her.

Male perfection and virility aside—it was Lord Wingrave's darkly enigmatic eyes. He possessed magnetism that alternately compelled a woman to both look away and look her fill, all at the same time.

And then, it happened. She who did not and had not and believed she'd never be so silly as to be drawn by a man's stare alone, felt it—the finisher. Heat bathed her cheeks, in a stinging *blush*.

Aye, apparently she'd gone and completed that triunity of femininity.

At last, Helia reached the white-painted Louis XVI caned chairs nearest the marquess, promptly stopping beside the seat directly next to Lord Wingrave's.

She instantly regretted her choice. Walking into the fire itself suddenly seemed a safer option.

Too proud, however, to retreat, she waited for him to draw her seat out, and when it became apparent he'd no intention of doing so, she set her dish down.

It was as though the slight click of her plate touching the table freed him of the words he'd already shown himself to closely guard.

"You're *here*." He bit out those two words.

"I'm sorry," she said. "I did not realize you'd break your fast so early. Given the late night we—*you*," she swiftly corrected, "probably had." She stole a discreet glance at the servant, whose impassive gaze remained impressively forward in his apparent attempt to make himself invisible. "I didn't mean to keep you waiting."

Another footman hurried over to draw her high-backed chair out.

With a single icy look, the marquess quelled the young man's efforts.

Helia scrunched her nose up. Very well. She could see to her own seat.

With that, Helia tugged out the chair and sat. Desperately trying to avoid the sinister lord towering over her, she snapped a white linen napkin open, placed it on her lap, and then, collecting her fork and knife, began to eat.

While she chewed, she felt his formidable presence hovering over her. Unmoving.

The scrambled eggs on her tongue turned to dust, and she made herself find the courage to look up.

Lord Wingrave snarled: "What do you think you are doing?"

Oh, hell. She'd displeased him again.

Chapter 5

One act of beneficence, one act of real usefulness, is worth
all the abstract sentiment in the world.

—*Ann Radcliffe, The Mysteries of Udolpho*

A madwoman had invaded Wingrave's residence.

Nay, worse. He'd *allowed* a madwoman into his midst.

There was no other accounting for the chit's gumption.

And he, a master of self-control, found the threads of his restraint
frayed. "What the hell do you think you are doing?"

Miss Wallace looked up at him with enormous, plate-size green
eyes. "Eating?" she whispered.

He narrowed his eyes into thin slits. "What was that?" He added
a note of warning to that query, one that, in frosty tones, spelled out
clearly that his was a hypothetical and her silence was expected here.

The minx pressed three fingers near the right corner of her mouth
and spoke, this time more loudly. "I . . . Eating," she repeated. "I am
eating. Or . . . attempting to. Unless you make it a habit of not allowing
guests to dine?" she ventured, with a sheepish smile.

Wingrave's brows shot up, and for the first time in his life, he found
himself taken aback.

Why, was she actually attempting to jest with him?

He flared his nostrils. My god, the brashness. The insolence. People didn't joke in his presence and certainly not over anything he said.

He swiftly found his footing, and latched on to the last foolish thing she'd uttered.

"If you harbor any kind of illusion you're *my* guest—"

"Your mother's guest," she said softly, all seriousness once more.

His *mother's* guest? And wonder of wonders, he found himself capable of humor, after all. No doubt she referred to herself so only because the alternative terrified her—and rightly so—out of her virginal mind. That she kept company with him, London's most notorious rake and womanizer.

"You find that amusing, Lord Wingrave?" she asked, stupidity making her bold as brass.

"If you think that my mother would give so much as a single thought to one such as you, then you clearly don't possess any actual knowledge of or connection to the Duchess of Talbert, or for that matter, anyone in this family."

He may as well have hit her for the pain that contorted her features. "Impossible! The beneficent, warmhearted woman my mother spoke of would never—" Miss Wallace stopped.

Understanding sparkled in her big eyes. "I see what you're doing," she whispered.

What he was doing?

Don't ask. Don't ask. Don't—

"What is it you *think* I'm doing?" A combined annoyance with her as much as himself brought that sharp question past his reluctant lips.

She looked at him like he'd lassoed a star for her. "You seek to protect her."

Protect her? "Who?"

As if energized by the prospect of Wingrave being some sort of protective, devoted son and not the heartless bastard he in fact was, Miss Wallace continued prattling on.

"You said your mother is soft. Tenderhearted, and you wished to protect her from people preying on her."

He snorted. Madness. It was madness that afflicted the lady, after all.

"I *said* she is soft," he snapped. "Weak. Easy prey for one such as you."

"You and I? We are saying the same things."

His mouth moved . . . but no words came out. He found himself . . . thunderstruck.

That was the conclusion she'd come to?

With perfect aplomb, his Scottish visitor resumed eating.

He'd stepped onto the stage of a farce. That was all there was to explain any of this.

Dumbstruck, he glanced around for the other players. His gaze landed on the two footmen stationed near the sideboard; both servants' eyes were wide with wonder and shock.

Good God, she'd even managed to crack the implacable facades of the cheerless staff here at Horace House.

At catching their master's glare, their demonstrative expressions died a swift death. Both servants went instantly stone-faced.

"Get out," he whispered.

The servants scattered at various points throughout the breakfast room all made a hasty retreat, leaving him and Miss Wallace alone.

Wingrave turned his ire back to the one deserving of his wrath.

As the last footman drew the door shut with a soft click, the imp of a lady stared frantically at the panel. She paled to the point that the freckles marked the only bit of color in her face.

He expected tears. He waited for her to flee.

He did not, however, anticipate the way she turned her attention back to him. Then, after looking perfectly unbothered as she slathered her roll with strawberry preserves, she took a big, healthy bite better befitting a man Wingrave's size.

"I'll ask you one more time, Miss Wallace," he whispered. "What are you doing at my breakfast table?"

The minx paused mid-chew, and craning her head back, she met his gaze with an unflinching and astonishing directness.

She didn't quaver. She didn't look away. And she, the first person to do so, unnerved the hell out of him.

Mayhap she was a sorceress, for the otherworldly shade of her green eyes knocked the thoughts from his head.

The lady finished her bite, dabbed at the corners of her mouth with her napkin, and lowered that crisp white linen back to her lap. "I think it should be clear," she said.

Was *anything* clear any longer? Certainly not since she'd stormed his foyer.

"I said I was eating, Lord Wingrave."

And with her succinct explanation, she continued doing just that.

Whatever magnetic pull she'd had over him, that moment of madness, shattered.

Wingrave curled his fingertips into the edge of the mahogany table and leaned forward. "My household, Miss Wallace," he seethed. "Why are you in my household?"

Confusion filled her enormous, expressive emerald eyes. "I . . . You . . . allowed me to remain at least until the storm had abated and you'd confirmed for yourself my connection to your mother."

He gawked at her.

That was the conclusion she'd reached?

"I did no such thing."

The lady's high, freckled brow creased. "You didn't?"

He may as well have kicked a cat for the misery contained within her question.

"No, I most certainly did not."

"You did," she said entreatingly. "You—"

"I did not," he thundered.

Aghast, Wingrave reeled back on his heels.

For the first time in the entirety of his life, he, who'd forever been a master of himself and who'd *prided* himself on not possessing the weak emotions of everyone else around him had lost control.

He'd hand it to the lady. She barely flinched.

Nay, instead, with a calm to rival the sternest tutor the duke had employed to school Wingrave, she dusted her palms together and then stood.

No more than three inches past five feet, but with the regal authority with which she stood and looked down her pert, freckled nose at him, she may as well have soared past the foot in length he had on her.

"I allowed you to spend the night, Miss Wallace. Not a moment more. I wasn't suggesting you remain indefinitely," he said.

"And I'm not looking to stay indefinitely." She paused. "Please, when the storm lets, allow me a carriage to seek out Her Grace."

This again.

Her insistence on some manner of connection to his family.

It was an impossibility.

Her staying with his mother also meant the minx would, in fact, be remaining indefinitely with Wingrave.

Briefly setting aside his annoyance, he gave her another look.

Attired in a drab brown dress that did nothing favorable for her trim, slim-hipped figure, in the light of day, Miss Wallace certainly wasn't the manner of woman to appeal to him and certainly not to earn a place in his bed.

Wingrave stared at the dauntless lady before him. "Given your insolence and brass, I trust your mother possessed a like disposition."

A wistful smile stole across her features, momentarily transforming her from ordinary chit to fetching fairy and, in the process, transfixing Wingrave.

"Aye, she did," she said with an affection and warmth he'd never before known where his own mother was concerned. "She also had the biggest spirit and biggest heart."

Her lilting musings proved as hypnotic as her physical metamorphosis.

As from the far fringes of the furthest corner of his mind, a long-ago memory whispered forward.

Wingrave, racing across the paved stone between the neatly trimmed boxwoods, heading for the three brick steps that led to a grass terrace above and the wrought iron bench that sat there.

Then, tripping on those same steps, coming down so hard on his knees that he wore the faint scars of that innocuous tumble all these years later.

And then, his mother, swiftly scooping him up and holding him close to her chest, softly singing. Those strains of a forgotten-until-now lullaby echoed in his head.

"Lullay, mine Liking, my dear Son, mine Sweeting,
Lullay, my dear heart, mine own dear darling."

Miss Wallace gave her head a shake, and it was as though that slight twitch of her head cleared his own and freed his words.

"My father would never allow my mother any connection to a woman with spirit," he finally said.

"Och, but don't you ken, women are possessed of all manner of secrets *and* courage."

Not all women. This stalwart minx, yes.

His mother, absolutely not.

"Not my mother," he said with absolutely certainty. "The duchess does what the duke wishes and orders her to do."

A twinkle set her eyes aglow. "I trust *he* believes that and you think it."

"Trust, I know that," he said flatly. The duchess hadn't fought the duke when he'd at last had need of Wingrave, and demanded his new heir's every hour be spent with him and devoted to learning the workings of the dukedom.

Wingrave thumped a hand against his leg. "We are at an impasse, Miss Wallace."

"Aye." That deservedly worried glint returned to her eyes. "But if you agree to allow me to stay, at least until the snaw relents, then the impasse would cease."

He could.

Just as he could easily throw her out.

And it *should* be easy.

"Lord Wingrave?" she ventured.

"Quiet," he said inattentively. "I'm thinking."

He was heartless and hardened and unmoved by *anyone*.

So why didn't he toss her on her pear-shaped buttocks?

Could it be, she'd been correct earlier? Could it be that all men—even soulless ones, such as him—possessed . . . a *conscience*?

Wingrave shrank. Impossible.

The remorseless wind howled and battered against the windowpanes.

From the corner of his eye, he caught sight of Miss Wallace as she slipped away from him, and for a moment, he thought she'd at last come to her senses and left of her own volition.

Instead, she wandered over to the winterscape on full display in the wide french windows.

Presenting Wingrave with her back, she gripped the edge of the mahogany and stared at the storm raging outside.

"I always loved the snow," she said softly. "And in the Highlands? There's so much of it."

He'd asked her for silence. Of course she'd been unable to grant that request which had been more of a demand.

Peculiarly, he found himself unable to shoot that retort her way. Strangely, he found himself . . . angling his undamaged ear so he could hear the whole of her telling.

Miss Wallace touched a lone fingertip to the glass, and her index finger left an oval-shaped mark upon the frost. "As a wee lass, my ma and da and I, the moment the storm would let, we would play hide-and-seek. My da was always it first, and would count to thirty."

As she spoke, her speech dissolved into a thicker, more noticeable brogue that swallowed up nearly completely her crisper English tones.

"A wad trudge throuch as quick as Ah coud an' jump intae as many drifts as Ah coud, then race an' hide myself in one. Then, whan he'd come close tae catchin' me, I'd spring oot an' hurl a snowball at him, hittin' him square in the nose, an' ah'd tak aff runnin'. He'd pretend tae howl an' shout, but he let me evade capture."

That bucolic scene she spoke of was something foreign to the Blofield way of life and living. Family closeness and playful moments were not something they partook in.

The crystal panes reflected back the sentimental smile adorning her full lips. "Then, after, we'd return, sit in the Great Hall by the old stone hearth, and sip hot chocolate and sing carols and Scottish ballads."

Her smile wavered, dipped, and then faded altogether, and it was as if the cold breeze had gusted in the room and stolen the warmth Wingrave hadn't even known existed until the woman before him.

She cast a glance over her shoulder, back his way, those big eyes now stricken. "And I'm ashamed to say, I loved the snow and wintry months, but I dinnae give a proper thought to all the people who dinnae have a home and warm hearth. Or food."

As if on cue, her stomach growled, and Miss Wallace reflexively touched a hand to her flat belly. "Until now," she said, with a palpable shame not a single lord or lady of London could have managed to express.

The lady took a step toward him, and he hooded his eyes.

She stopped a pace away. "Until now. Until this very moment"—she pointed a finger at the floor—"I didn't know what it was to be reliant upon the generosity, charity, and kindness of strangers."

"I'm neither kind, nor generous, nor given to charity," he said flatly, determined to disabuse her of the desperate conclusions she'd come to.

Miss Wallace briefly considered her leather boots. "Mayhap you haven't been before." She lifted her eyes to Wingrave's. "You could be now."

She believed that. She *actually believed* that.

A log shifted in the hearth, setting off a noisy hiss and crackle of embers.

Turn her out.

Or . . . let her stay.

What was it to him whether she remained now, or left tomorrow, or the next day? In fact, she'd proven a diversion from the tediousness of London at winter.

Perhaps she could prove an even greater diversion, in more lascivious ways.

"Fine."

In further testament of the lady's naivete, her wide eyes grew impossibly round, and an even bigger smile curled her lips up into her matching and deceptively sweet dimples. Her joy transformed Miss Wallace's elfin features into something . . . almost . . . beautiful.

"Thank you," she said, full of her customary ebullience, and then as if it were the most natural thing in the world, she took Wingrave's hands in her own.

Heat from her silken, soft palms radiated into his own larger ones, and his traitorous fingers curled themselves over hers in a bid to be closer to that tremendous warmth.

"May the scent of the heather and Bonnie blue bell waft a message to you that no words can tell." Her husky, dulcet tones pulled him deeper under her spell. "May the links in our friendship keep steadfast and true . . ."

Friendship? Good God, was that the conclusion she'd drawn? That snapped Wingrave out of his trance.

Her winsome smile deepened. "May good fortune and health be ever with you."

Wingrave sneered. "If I were really enjoying good fortune, we'd not even be having this discussion now."

He attempted to pull free of whatever maddening pull and hold her touch had over him, but even slight of frame as she was, she proved as tenacious with her grip as she did with her words. "Now that we're friends . . ."

How droll. "We are not friends," he said. "I do not have *friends*." He'd people who sought a connection to him for the title he'd one day inherit, but that was it.

Compassion flared in her eyes, and she tightened her hold upon Wingrave's hands, and that deepening heat in their drawing proved compelling. Lust stirred. From a mere touch?

Nay, it wasn't a mere touch, but rather that of an innocent whose hands were unsullied and inexperienced.

Now, in his mind, he envisioned guiding her fingers around his hard cock and teaching her the rhythm he so loved.

"You may not have had friends before, but you have one now," she murmured.

Friends. The half-wit. Had she not yet realized he was not a man who wanted or needed friends?

"I was fine before," he purred.

Miss Wallace scoffed. "No one is fine without friends."

Suddenly, he switched the position of their palms so that he'd hers under his, and his fingers curled tightly around to keep her in place.

She trembled but did not pull away, and that show of courage and strength only fueled the flames of his unlikely desire.

"As I said . . ." He drew her closer and placed his lips close to her right ear. "I have no need of friends, Miss Wallace," he whispered.

Near as they were, he felt her body quiver with a physical awareness he doubted she understood.

With his spare hand, he pushed her heavy titian curls away from her neck and exposed that long, graceful arch. He moved his mouth lower. "What I do have a current need for is a mistress." As he spoke, his lips brushed her skin in an intentional kiss. "Might you be interested in filling that coveted role, Helia?"

Daughter of the sun god, and possessed of an irrepressible aura of light, a more perfect name for the lady couldn't exist if Helios himself had conferred it upon the effervescent, titian-haired sprite.

The column of her throat moved wildly. Her supernaturally lustrous lashes fluttered.

Satisfaction brought his lips curling at the corners.

Hungry to taste of her innocent mouth, he moved to take it under his—and claim their first kiss.

"Helia." Her threadbare name in the form of a breathy exhalation froze him.

He stared at her.

"You called me Helia," she murmured, her eyes heavy with desire and some other soft, sentimental emotion he'd never before witnessed or experienced and as such couldn't put a name to.

"And?" he snapped, annoyed that she'd befuddled him when all he wanted to do was drink his fill of her mouth so he could at last be free of this malignant spell that, in her innocence, she'd cast upon him.

Her long, sooty lashes lifted to reveal glittering green eyes. "That is the first time you've done so."

Impatient, he repeated himself. "And? What is it exactly you are saying?"

"Well," she said slowly, "you've now referred to me as my given name, but I do not have yours."

"Wingrave."

She shook her head. "That is your title."

"You don't need to refer to me as anything else," he said bluntly.

Helia scoffed. "Of course I do, and it can't be Wingrave, because that is a rather grim title that does not suit you."

"It suits me beyond perfectly."

"Aye, with your surly temper, it does, but as Edward Gibbon says, the prediction contributes to the accomplishment."

"The prediction being my name?" he drawled.

"In this case." She gave his fingers a little squeeze, as if to pull the information she sought out of him.

"What proper Scottish lady reads and quotes the great essayist Edward Gibbon?" he mocked.

"The *same* lady whose parents wished her to be well read in many topics."

They stared at one another—again at an impasse.

He'd hand it to her. If he were in the habit of admiring people, with the unswerving way her gaze held his, she'd have been one he admired.

Helia peered up at him, and when he offered only an answering silence, she sighed. "I am going to find out your name, Lord Wingrave. And not only that, I wager the very generous offer of hospitality you tendered that you're going to freely give it."

"You shall be waiting until the cow comes home," he said dryly.

She waggled her eyebrows. "Ah, a Highland cow, unlike a Sassenach one, is a friendly sort. They never fight, and also enjoy the company of humans."

She was making that up. He wanted to say so, but the twinkle in her eyes indicated she both knew and waited for that retort.

He grated his jaw. God, what was it about this minx that got his thoughts all topsy-turvy?

The lady sighed, and then with her two hands, she took his right palm in her own and forced a shake. "I'm so very happy to be growing our friendship."

Growing their friendship?

He flashed a cool smile. "I thought you'd already declared us friends, Miss Wallace."

"Ah, wishing to be friends is quick work, but friendship is a slow-ripening fruit."

Quoting Gibbon and now Aristotle. He sought to mask his surprise.

The women he kept company with had many years on Helia Wallace. They favored the baubles he bestowed, in exchange for an emotionless connection where he sated his baser urges. Every last woman he'd had any association with read the gossip pages, and not a thing more.

And others? His mother and sister indulged in tawdry, melodramatic gothic novels, certainly not Gibbon and Greek philosophers.

All the while, through his quiet shock, Helia stared at him with warm, friendly eyes.

This was too much. *She* was too much.

Growling, Wingrave anchored an arm around her waist and drew her close so she could feel the stiff line of his cock.

She gasped, but did not pull away.

"Do you feel that, Helia?" he whispered jeeringly against her ear.

Wingrave rubbed his shaft in a slow circle over the flat of her belly. Her eyes went wide, and her cheeks flushed a pretty shade of pink.

"Feel how hard I am for you, sweet?" He pressed himself against her stomach. "Does this put you in mind of friendship?"

At her silence, he licked at her neck and lightly nipped that damp spot, marking her.

A little moan spilled from her lips and Wingrave grinned.

She wanted him.

Of course she did.

His smile faded.

Her body's surrender to him somehow proved more potent than that of any of the other women who'd come undone in his arms.

"You are now on your second day alone with me, Helia, and as such, ruined." He scooped her by the buttocks and pressed her more tightly against his cock. "You may as well allow yourself the rapture that comes with your ruination."

Her eyes grew stricken.

Then, like a hellcat, she struggled in his arms.

Wingrave released her in an instant.

Her chest heaved, rising and falling furiously.

And without a word, Helia turned on her heel and fled.

Chapter 6

But a terror of this nature, as it occupies and expands the mind, and elevates it to high expectation, is purely sublime, and leads us, by a kind of fascination, to seek even the object, from which we appear to shrink.

—*Ann Radcliffe, The Mysteries of Udolpho*

Run. Flee. Hide.

Though she'd ignored the warnings her subconscious gave before, this time Helia heeded them well.

She ran from Lord Wingrave's suggestive stare.

She ran and didn't look back.

Except, no matter how fast she flew, and how much distance she put between herself and Lord Wingrave's dangerously seductive offerings, they remained, ringing as loud and clear as the carillon of bells struck at the Collegiate Church of St. Giles.

Do you feel that, Helia?

Helia bit her lower lip. The pain didn't help; it offered no distraction.

Feel how hard I am for you, sweet? Does this put you in mind of friendship?

Nay, it certainly hadn't. What was worse and most shameful was that the furthest thought in her head that moment had been of friendship with him; instead, she'd felt a yearning to know his embrace.

Helia took a turn too quick at the end of the hall; her boots slipped along the marble floor, but she managed to right herself and kept on running.

The place between her legs ached still, in a way she'd known only on occasion when she ran a washing cloth over herself.

But that frustrated sensation dissipated quickly the moment she ceased touching herself so.

Lord Wingrave's seductive words, however, had an even more powerful effect than any caress. They remained in her mind, on repeat.

You are now on your second day alone with me, Helia, and as such, ruined. You may as well allow yourself the rapture that comes with your ruination.

And God forgive her, she'd wanted that.

She'd wanted a taste of what he'd tempted her with—*nay*, taunted her with.

And most shamefully, she hadn't cared that he'd mocked her with his desire and, worse, *her* desire for *him*.

Helia reached the back northernmost point of Horace House, and a row of windows, thirty feet from floor to ceiling, marked a crystal end to her flight.

She stumbled to a stop. Gasping and fighting for breath, Helia bent over her knees and struggled to fill her lungs with blessed air.

In the light of a new day, Lord Wingrave had proven no less horrid, no less vulgar.

What was wrong with her that she should want him so?

You are now on your second day alone with me, Helia, and as such, ruined . . .

Ruined . . . ruined . . . ruined.

Ruined.

Helia's head pounded as that one word drummed into it, again and again. Over and over.

She'd managed to escape and evade Mr. Draxton, but in the end, Helia had failed in a different—but no less damaging—way.

With a sob that echoed mockingly around the cavernous corridor, she took off for the ornate gold handle of a glass doorway out of this place and set herself free.

The sudden blast of winter air slapped her face and stole the breath from her lungs so quickly she dissolved into a choking fit.

And yet, she welcomed the ice-flecked snowflakes that hit her face and the exposed skin on her body. They proved sobering and cooling on her heated flesh, freeing her of the shameful lust Lord Wingrave had roused her to.

She raced forward, stopping only when she collided with the limestone railing. Six inches or more of snow had formed a drift upon the top.

Restless, Helia shoved the small mound over the side, where it silently tumbled onto the untouched blanket of snow below.

What if the friendship between their mothers hadn't been as true and two-sided as Helia's ma had thought? What would happen to Helia, especially now that her reputation would be in tatters?

What if it'd been a brief camaraderie between two lasses who'd made their Come Out and who'd gone on to have their own lives, and in that whole lifetime that separated the women, those remembrances had shifted and changed for Wingrave's mother?

Helia stared desolately.

Surely any magnanimity on the duchess's part would be severely limited now that Helia had spent a night in the same house as the lady's rakish son.

What woman as powerful as the duchess would align her reputation with Helia's sullied one?

And despite the cold wind whipping at her skirts and cutting across the fabric of her garments, perspiration slicked her palms and beaded at her brow. Her fear proved greater than the cold, as her teeth chattered.

If—when—the duchess turned her away, there'd be nowhere to go. No one to whom she might turn.

She'd be forced to return to Mr. Draxton, and—

Her stomach roiled, and a pressure developed at the back of her skull, in remembered pain of the grip he'd had on both her arms. As brawny as any pugilist, he possessed such might there could be no doubting that if he decided—when he decided—to force himself upon her, she'd be powerless against him.

The memory alone of his punishing hold sent pressure building at her temples and the back of her skull.

Helia reached a hand up to rub that ache away. Her efforts proved as hopeless as her circumstances.

Unwittingly, she angled another look back at the soaring stone residence where Lord Wingrave remained shut away.

Helia continued to assess that handsome, three-story townhouse. She touched her gaze upon each frosted windowpane, wondering which room now held the occupant of her thoughts.

He struck her as a man in desperate need of a friend. Och, she kenned all too well, the marquess didn't want one and thought he didn't need one, but he did. And in Helia? He saw only a potential mistress.

What would it be like to be possessed by a man such as he?

"You're a d-damned numpty, H-Helia Mairi Wallace," she spat, hating herself for that wicked wondering.

With her previous efforts to escape Lord Wingrave futile, Helia resumed her flight. She stomped along the terrace. The hems of her skirts grew damp and heavy, and at the top of the stairs, she hiked her dress up and took the stairs as quickly as the elements permitted.

Her raspy breath stirred clouds of white upon the air, while whorls of flakes swirled around her face.

The moment she reached the base, Helia resumed her trudge through deep snow. As she went, she looked past the small shrubs and bushes whose leaves and limbs bent under the remorseless wind, those poor, already burdened branches heavy with snow.

Once again, Helia continued her march, until she reached a row of tall, proud oaks that ended her flight.

The arborist who'd planted these trees had been strategic in his design. He'd staggered a variety of them, offsetting them in a way that they appeared natural in their placement; all the while they provided cover nearer the back of the grounds for the tall brick wall—unnoticed until now—that framed the immense gardens.

Tears filled her eyes, and yet even the cruel winter cold refused to allow Helia any control of her body and decisions; the wind erased those drops before they might fall.

She blinked and blinked until a warm tear slipped down her cheek, and she welcomed the winding path it wove.

It was the faintest and yet most profound victory.

And yet, it was a victory.

With the smallest of smiles, she opened her eyes.

Helia trembled. She wrapped her arms close around her middle and vigorously rubbed through the fabric at her shaking limbs.

Even so, a bead of moisture slipped from her forehead, and she wiped back the drop of perspiration her efforts had wrought.

And then she saw it.

Helia stilled.

Her gaze locked on a flowering tree, with crimson berries. That graceful, narrow deciduous one stood shorter than the others, making it one she couldn't look away from.

Smaller than the birch or planes or sycamores and tucked in the far left corner of the gardens, this tree managed to prove still more vibrant for the vast swell of red that adorned its branches. Each cluster of berries sported the newly fallen snow, wearing it like a crown upon its mass.

A sob ripped from her throat, and enlivened for the first time in too long, Helia dashed as quickly as the snowfall allowed toward the solitary little tree.

Her heavy hems slowed her down, and then the weight of them pulled her forward.

She landed hard in the snow, and alternately laughing and crying, Helia struggled back onto her feet and resumed her unsteady tromp.

At last, she reached it.

Breathless and dizzy from the importance of this very moment, of this very find, she stopped and tipped her head back.

A *rowan* tree. Amongst the Scottish, it'd long been a sacred symbol of wisdom, courage, and protection. Each year, Helia and her mother would plant another so that those gifts continued to flourish for all.

Here in the duchess's gardens, in this flawless, English-plant-packed Eden, there existed but one.

But it was a rowan tree.

A stirring so very soft and small and faint, but profound enough that everything inside tunneled into that slow-building sensation—*hope*. That realest, pervading, intoxicating emotion where the impossible seemed possible, and the darkness which had gripped her these past months gave way, ceding its previously tenacious hold to a fervent, all-powerful light.

Helia moved closer, then rested her weary head against the thick, cold bark, finding only warmth.

Home.

This tree and its branches filled with berries harkened to the wild, untamed, majestic Highlands. That this glorious mountain ash, steeped in folklore and tradition, had been planted here was surely a sign that all would be well.

Then, placing a kiss upon the smooth, grey-brown trunk, Helia reached for the tree.

Her hand trembled and shook from the fervency of this moment, and she wrapped her gloved fingers lovingly around the nearest narrow branch.

Ever so gently, Helia bent it sideways. Back and forth.

As she worked, little puffs of white escaped her lips and joined in the cold of the winter air.

Snap.

Reverently, Helia looked upon the twig of berries she'd separated from the rowan tree, and with a murmur of gratitude for its offering, she carefully tucked the twig inside the pocket of her dress.

Helia reached for one more bundle of berries.

After she'd availed herself to one final twig, she examined this last crimson cluster she'd take.

The bright pomes, vibrant harbingers of good, appeared even brighter upon Helia's white leather gloves.

For the first time since her parents had gone on to heaven and she'd been left behind with a grasping relation to contend with, and an uncertain future, Helia laughed. That joyous resonance spilled from her lips and filtered into the Duke and Duchess of Talbert's gardens, filling the previously barren grounds with gaiety.

It felt so very glorious . . . to have hope. To laugh. To not live with fear.

I am alive. In this moment, I am safe.

She'd let fear become her constant companion, but maybe, just maybe, instead of bemoaning and lamenting her fate as a ruined woman, Helia should accept that it had happened and live her life to the fullest.

An indescribable emotion swept over her, so profound and great it left her lightheaded, and Helia swayed once more, nearly overwhelmed by the mightiness of that feeling.

She caught herself against the rugged, steadfast trunk of the rowan tree, and found the solace and support it provided.

For she knew in that instant, it was going to be all right.

She was going to be all right.

Chapter 7

How then are we to look for love in great cities, where selfishness, dissipation, and insincerity supply the place of tenderness, simplicity and truth?

—*Ann Radcliffe, The Mysteries of Udolpho*

Seated on one of the leather wingback chairs, with his elbows on the arms of his seat and his fingers steepled, Wingrave stared absently out the center panel of the wide bow window to the pristine white snow blanketing the vast gardens below.

Wingrave had always possessed an affinity for the library.

As a small boy, Wingrave had considered the immense, coffered-ceilinged room, lined with wall-to-wall bookshelves, each shelf filled with an endless number of leather tomes, a place of magic and wonder.

Then, as the forgotten spare to the duke's ever-precious heir, Wingrave had been unencumbered by the same constraints placed on his late brother.

In time, he'd realized the inherent silliness in the stories he'd once eagerly read in the early hours of the morn. The ridiculousness of the Greek legends and Roman ones, which he'd believed wholeheartedly to be real.

For it hadn't been long into his rigorous edification of his role as future duke that Wingrave realized his father avoided books the way a sinner steered clear of church.

The only reason Wingrave'd come and read here, and the only reason he continued to do so, was because it had become a habit.

Not because he was in search of a distraction following his caddish behavior, which had sent intrepid-until-now Helia fleeing.

He'd have to possess a heart and conscience. Fortunately for him, he had neither.

What he'd not, however, anticipated, was how intolerably retentive past memories were, sitting in the library, while a storm brewed outside.

. . . but it is snowing, Evander! Snowing!

Wingrave drew back in his seat.

When was the last time he'd thought of that day? In fact, when had thoughts of his late brother last slipped in?

Not because it hurt to do so. Wingrave was no longer a man capable of puling emotions.

In short, he couldn't be hurt.

Which was mayhap why those faraway remembrances whispered forward.

In Wingrave's mind's eye, he saw himself in this very spot, a book on his lap and silence his only company, until he'd snapped whatever title he'd been reading shut and gone in search of his brother.

So many times, Wingrave had caught sight of his sad-eyed sibling, elder by but a year.

That hadn't always been the case. Before Evander's studies as future duke commenced and their sire severed the connection between them, Wingrave and Evander had been inseparable.

But then Evander had been all but locked away in His Grace's office, with the duke and the army of stern-faced, monotone tutors who'd hammered away at all Wingrave's brother needed to know about the duchy and the responsibilities that accompanied it.

In contrast, Wingrave had found himself blessed with free rein to explore, to pursue whatever curiosity fascinated him in a given moment, and each and every one of those many moments had involved losing himself in the pages of the books shelved here. They'd been a poor substitute—inanimate companions—but companions nonetheless for a then newly lonely Wingrave.

Wind wailed and gusted, sending flecks of ice-mixed snow pattering against the windows like little crystalline teardrops the skies had stirred to life from memories of long ago, and Wingrave sat motionless, his unblinking gaze riveted on the whorl of flakes whirring outside those frosted panes.

In his mind, the past mingled and mixed with the present, a kaleidoscope of images and words and sounds.

The duke responding to an urgent summons that had arrived from London.

Evander's tutor choking on his ink-filled tea and running from his employer's office.

And Evander. All the while, a fifteen-year-old Evander, home for winter recess from Oxford, put to work on the Blofield books. Through that sudden and intrusive chaos that had drawn both duke and tutor elsewhere, Evander remained with his head bowed, his pen scratching away at the open pages before him. Evander . . . a changed figure, now a shadow of the boy, brother, and friend he'd been.

"Come," he urged. "The lake is frozen, and it won't be long before the duke realizes there's no emergency requiring his attention."

Evander finally looked up, with clever—and stunned—eyes. "You did this?"

He flashed a proud grin at his big brother, then sketched a flourishing bow.

Evander frowned in return. "I cannot leave. I've the books to see to," he said, his pen flying across the page once more as he returned to work.

He came around to the space left between the duke's desk and the imposingly heavy and ornate desk adjacent it that his brother occupied.

"We always used to skate, Evander," he said quietly.

"I don't have time—"

"I miss you."

The frantic and fast strokes of Evander's pen slowed, then stopped. His serious features, so very like his own, made seeing his face like looking into a mirror.

After a seemingly endless quiet, a smile built slowly on Evander's lips.

Evander snapped his book closed and jumped up so quick, his mahogany Hepplewhite armchair flew back and landed with a loud clatter on the floor. "I'll race you there."

Before that final word had left his mouth, Evander took off, running from the office, and he set after him, racing in swift pursuit.

The sounds of their laughter—the final laughter they'd ever shared as brothers and the final expression of stupid mirth Wingrave had ever known—rang in the chambers of his mind.

Emitting a sound of annoyance, he gave his head a firm shake.

Good God. He couldn't recall a time in recent memory when he'd thought of his late brother.

What accounted for *those* maudlin thoughts?

Maybe this was his penance for scaring the young lady?

Wingrave's lips twisted in a mocking grin. Or, as she liked to refer to herself, his new . . . *friend.*

His wry mirth faded.

She was the reason for the remembrances now plaguing him. He, who didn't think about the past, and who'd long ago ceased to care about anyone or call a person a friend, since his brother's death.

Wingrave growled.

Why, she was the reason the word "friend" had reentered his consciousness.

She who'd come in here like a whirlwind, with all her bold defiance and innocent eyes.

Well, it wouldn't be for much longer. Soon enough, she'd be on her way, and he'd be free of her and the lust *for* her that consumed him.

After propelling himself to his feet, Wingrave stomped over to the window and, planting his feet wide, clasped his hands behind him and glared out.

Nay, the lady was nothing but a blasted bother. A titian-haired nuisance with as bountiful a number of freckles on her face as there were illimitable words on her big, bow-shaped lips.

She was . . .

Outside.

Wingrave frowned.

Impossible. The chit was driving him to madness, or . . . she'd already done so, because he was seeing her everywhere.

Nothing else accounted for why, after she'd persuaded Wingrave to offer her shelter from the elements, in the midst of this raging storm, she'd chosen to go traipsing about his family's snow-covered, wind-battered gardens.

Wingrave jammed the heels of his palms against his eyes and pressed hard.

Only, when he let his arms fall to his sides, the sight of her remained.

A mere speck on the horizon, distant and faint but decidedly there.

"What in blazes are you doing?" he lashed out, amidst the quiet . . . as if she could answer him, as if she could even hear him.

It appeared she'd gone out into the storm, all so she could— Wingrave pressed his forehead against the cool windowpane so quickly, and so hard, it was a wonder he didn't shatter the glass—hug a tree.

Aye, she'd gone mad. There was nothing else for it.

Another growl built deep in his chest. It climbed and climbed until it emerged from his lips, a low and feral sound.

And it appeared madness was contagious, because he'd descended into delirium right with her.

For Wingrave shouldn't care either way what the hell happened to her. If she wished to venture out into a storm and catch the ague, then so be it.

"All the better for me," he muttered.

With that reminder, he marched back over to his leather chair and fell into its comfortable folds.

He steepled his fingers once more and drummed them together, the pads of those digits colliding and then separating. Over and over again.

I do not care . . . I do not . . .

With a black curse, he jumped up once more and strode for the door.

He was going to wring her neck.

As he pounded along the corridors, he thundered for his cloak and hat.

Two footmen were stationed nearby. Each took off running; the *click-click-click* made by their slightly heeled shoes echoed as they went.

He still didn't care whether she went and got herself ill. The absolute only reason he even went to find her now was so that he could rail at her for being a daft ninny and remind the lady that if she wasn't at all fearful of the elements, perhaps she could take herself elsewhere sooner rather than later.

Wingrave's frown deepened.

Nay, she'd likely meet his challenge, and then she'd definitely get herself killed of the cold and would absolutely delight in haunting him. He'd never have a moment's peace again—a moment's peace, which was beginning to look like an unattainable fate.

He reached the south hallway that led out to the terrace and his mother's prized gardens.

Lined with floor-to-ceiling windows and two crystal doors at their center, this portion of the residence emitted more light than this family deserved.

Even with the grey storm clouds that hung over the household, the snow which had piled up high outside added a blindingly bright whiteness Wingrave had to squint against in order to see.

He blinked furiously to accustom his eyes to that vision, adding yet another thing to be annoyed with, which only reminded him that he now waited for his belongings.

Wingrave turned and bellowed, "Where—"

He nearly collided with a pair of out-of-breath, bewigged footmen, who'd just reached him.

Letting out another curse, Wingrave grabbed his greatcoat first. He drew the garment on and then, with furious movements, promptly fastened himself up. "And my—"

The other servant proffered Wingrave's beaver hat.

He snatched it from the younger fellow and jammed the high, straight-sided, flat-topped article on his head.

This time, before Wingrave could open his mouth and utter an impatient query, the same footman who'd given him his cloak extended Wingrave's leather gloves.

Wingrave took the set and made to tug them on.

Furious energy, however, made the ordinary task a sloppy chore.

"Damn it all," he muttered, continuing to fight his fingers inside their respective slots.

The demure pair of servants each drew open a door.

Straightaway, wind gusted inside; at the same time the bitter east breeze sucked the breath from Wingrave's lungs, a mixture of ice, snow, and rain slapped him square in the face.

"Dead," he growled. "I'm going to kill her."

That was, if the minx didn't perish before the upbraiding he intended to rain on her ears.

Ignoring the nervous looks exchanged by his servants, Wingrave gritted his teeth against the sting of cold and stomped outside.

The petrified pair instantly brought the doors closed behind him.

At least someone feared him. Albeit the *wrong* someone.

He looked off to see whether the *right* someone had at some point sprouted a brain and begun her return to the damned residence.

Alas . . . in addition to family, friends, resources, and funds, the lady appeared to be equally lacking in common sense.

Wingrave glanced down at the blanket of snow, but for the sprite-like footprints made upon the thick, otherwise untouched, white path.

He set off in pursuit. As he walked, in an attempt to bring warmth to his already cold digits, Wingrave rubbed his gloved hands together vigorously.

With every heavy step he took through the snow-covered gardens, Wingrave's ire spiraled with a ferocity to match the storm that held London in its grip.

When she'd arrived last night, he'd been determined to throw her out on her delectable buttocks.

He took another furious step, grinding up thick, wet snow as he went.

But she'd pleaded to stay.

She—a temerarious woman with her courage, pluck, and mettle—had begged him.

The wind sent the hem of his greatcoat snapping in an angry consensus.

All the while, he glowered at that very still, unsuspecting figure at the vibrant tree.

Why, it was as if she'd been determined to find the farthest place to venture and now sat under the tree as though it were a summer day, and she a fine lady partaking in a picnic under those colorful branches.

He'd let her stay.

"What in blazes are you doing?" he lashed.

With all the grace, calm, and aplomb of two people meeting in a London drawing room, Helia stood and turned about, slowly.

The chill of the winter's day had left an entrancing crimson hue upon her cheeks, a shade so bright it'd engulfed those tiny specks of freckles.

"*You!*" She smiled as she greeted Wingrave, briefly taking him aback.

Had anyone smiled at him? Or for that matter, even near him? Certainly, never *because* of him.

And yet, this woman's green eyes . . . glowed.

Unnerved, Wingrave dusted his palms together. "You know, if you'd been determined to get yourself killed from the cold, we could have avoided all previous arguments and exchanges we had prior about your seeking out shelter."

"W-we haven't argued."

"Haven't we?" he drawled.

The lady gave a wave of her spare hand. "Mere differences of opinions. And you n-needn't worry about me—"

"I'm not worried."

"I'm not afraid of a little c-cold. I'm—"

"Scottish. Yes, I believe we've ascertained as much."

A little laugh bubbled from her trembling lips.

Frowning, Wingrave drew back. Any and all previous fear she'd shown in his presence was no more. What accounted for this absolute cheer?

"I was *going* to say," she stammered through her shivering, "I'm not at all cold. In fact, I'm feeling quite w-warmish."

Warmish?

Wingrave eyed her dubiously.

"Yes," he drawled, giving her bundled and shivering frame an up-and-down look. "You look like the *epitome* of summery."

"Aye, well, you were the one to point out that I a-am S-Scottish." Her eyes glittered with more of her mirth, a sparkling in her irises that proved as captivating as it was unnerving.

He wasn't a man to be taken in by a pretty pair of eyes. With that reminder fresh in his head, he sharpened his gaze on the shivering woman before him.

"First, claiming a connection to the duchess," he jeered. "Now, professing to be warm in the midst of this storm? With those two yarns you've spun, I'm led to wonder what else you may have lied about. Certainly, the invented Gothic-romance tale of a nasty guardian determined to steal your virtue and your dowry."

A frown chased away her smile, and damned if in her doing so, the air around them didn't go several shades colder. "Cousin."

Wingrave just stared at her.

"H-he is not a guardian. He is my cousin, and h-he inherited after my da passed."

"Forgive me," he said drolly. "Of course. Your nasty cousin. Never tell me? He locked you in your rooms and denied you meals until you consented to be his bride."

"He didn't d-deny me m-meals on a-account—"

She swayed slightly, then steadied herself. "O-on account, he—"

Helia tottered on her feet once more.

Wingrave frowned. "What—"

He shot an arm about her waist just as she would have this time fallen.

His words trailed off as he took in the specks of perspiration at her damp brow, the inordinate red of her cheeks he'd previously taken for stamps made by the cold, the glazed look in her feverish eyes.

"You are ill," he said sharply, those three words an accusation.

"N-no. I do not g-get ill." Her assurances came so threadbare, the north wind nearly swallowed it whole. "I g-got you this."

Puzzling his brow, he followed his gaze to the twig of berries she proffered. "A stick," he said flatly. "You came outside to fetch a stick with berries."

"Aye. And it isn't a stick. And n-not just any branch. 'T-tis a rowan twig."

"Oh, forgive me. Not a stick, but a twig," he said, keeping his face expressionless.

Yes, she was decidedly mad, after all.

But then again, *he* was out here debating over the terms "stick," "branches," and "twigs." What did that make *him*?

Helia frowned. "I-I can detect sarcasm, you ken. As I was saying—"

Another sharp wind whipped around them, sending whorls of snowflakes spattering against their faces.

"Might you say it later, when we are safely indoors?"

That elvish glitter in her eyes deepened. "Afraid of the cold, are you, Wingrave?"

"I'm not afraid of anything."

"Everyone is afraid of someth—"

"Your s-stick, Miss Wallace," he snapped, his own teeth beginning to chatter incessantly in the cold. "Y-your stick." He ground those two words out.

"Och, forgive me. Ye see, in Scotland, burning the *twig* of a rowan tree is a tradition during the festive s-season. The l-lore has it that in doing so, a-any bad f-feelings of m-mistrust between f-friends will be cleared away."

She smiled widely, looking so very pleased with herself and her story.

"Really?" he finally said.

The imp nodded.

He stared incredulously, searching her cherry-red cheeks for a hint of a jest. And found . . . none. Since his brother's death, Wingrave had subsisted on a diet of logic and sharp rationality. He'd apparently found the one person, however, who made hogwash her main course.

"Miss Wallace," he said, looking down the length of his nose, "that is the silliest thing I've ever—"

"Helia," she corrected him.

"Very well. That is the silliest thing I've ever heard, *Heli*—"

She pressed a palm against his chest. Not just any palm, but the one filled with that rowan twig and berries.

Wingrave stared in befuddlement at the snow-dusted branch against the vivid blackness of his overcoat.

"'Tis for you," she said softly.

"For . . . me."

Helia nodded. "For you," she repeated, in a confirmation he'd humiliatingly spoken those two halting words aloud.

And yet . . .

"I've never received a gift," he said gruffly. He didn't even know why he'd made the reluctant acknowledgment.

Helia looked up at him with sad eyes. "Surely you've received something, through the years?"

"Don't you know, madam, it is improper for lords and ladies to exchange gifts." He strove for aloofness but remained strangely unable to pull his gaze from the branch of red berries she still held against his chest.

"Och," she scoffed. "I'm well aware of the rules of decorum. Friends and family are permitted to bestow a g-gift upon one another."

Yes, she was right in that regard. Decorum and social rules dictated that social equals such as friends and family may exchange or accept gifts. The Blofields, however, were a power cut above the rest. Though Wingrave's tenderhearted mother would have likely been all too happy to give gifts, her husband didn't allow it. For the current duke considered no one his friend. And as for family? They may as well be strangers who happened to share a name and the same dwelling.

"I've already told you," he finally brought himself to say. "I do not have friends." And he preferred it that—

"You do now," Helia said softly, and unlike every other word she'd uttered thus far, which had been lent a quaver by the cold, these three emerged strong and unwavering.

Wingrave stood there dumbly, uncertain for the first time in his life, his mind addled at her lack of nervosity about him.

He'd become so accustomed to people being daunted by him that he didn't know what to do with this intrepid, tiny slip of a woman who smiled at him and absurdly declared herself to be . . . a friend.

To him.

When still he made no move to take the slender twig, Helia folded the right lapel of his jacket back a fraction, and with an unflinching boldness, she reached inside and tucked her present to Wingrave within his pocket.

And strangely, as she edged away from his arms, and with the wind and sleet battering at him, Wingrave felt the most peculiar . . . warmth.

A muscle twitched irritatingly at the corner of his right eye.

Warmth? It had absolutely nothing to do with a ridiculous and inconsequential offering.

"You're w-welcome," she said.

"I did not say thank you," he snapped. To do so would have to mean he appreciated or even wanted her *gift.* Which he didn't. He didn't need *anything,* and most certainly he neither wanted, nor needed, Helia Wallace's friendship.

"What should I be thankful for or about?" He gave her a frosty look. "That you're out here risking your foolish neck to bequeath me some rowan bra—"

Her eyes twinkled brighter than the North Star, momentarily distracting him from his error.

"Stick," he gritted out through his teeth. *"Some stick."*

"Y-you needn't worry about me. Remember, I'm a Scot."

"How can I forget? You keep reminding me," he muttered. "As if I needed any reminders."

"I'm h-hale and hearty."

Another sharp wind gusted, making a liar of her, as she swayed slightly on her feet.

This time he caught her at the elbow to keep her from falling. "Oh, yes," he said drolly, giving his gloved palms another vigorous rub. "You look like the *epitome* of stalwartness."

The tiniest of snowflakes peppered the lady's eyes, and her coppery lashes fluttered. "I-I'm really quite . . ." Her voice faded. "F-fine."

And then, with that tangible *third* lie she'd given him, Helia pitched forward.

Wingrave caught her about the waist once more and drew her against him. Were it any woman other than this tart-mouthed minx, he'd have believed her actions deliberate, and her intention to snag his notice.

"Yes," he said ironically. He knew Helia Wallace hardly at all, but he knew enough to gather she wasn't the swooning-and-fake-fainting sort. "You appear most hale and . . ."

His words trailed off.

Even through the layers of their garments, a spectacular heat poured from her trembling frame. A heat as unnatural as the captivating chit herself. A heat that defied the logic of a bitter winter's day. A heat that could only come from . . .

Wingrave reeled as it hit him.

"You're feverish," he barked.

There was no quick retort or witty rejoinder, only a stark silence, made all the grimmer by its rarity from the lady, who challenged him at every turn.

He glanced at the woman tucked against his side.

Sure enough, her eyes remained closed, as if she'd fallen asleep standing up and been frozen that way by the unforgiving northern wind.

A dangerously childlike panic settled in his bones.

For he, who prided himself on fearing nothing and no one, had one Achilles' heel. It was one that he never readily acknowledged, even to himself, but that had lingered in the far corners of his mind since his brother had died all those years ago.

"You would be the one to bedevil me by acknowledging my own aversions," he muttered into the unnatural quiet. "You are a witch, madam. An infuriating, extraordinary, titian-haired witch."

In one fluid motion, Wingrave swept her up into his arms. For one who snacked and feasted with the gusto he'd observed, she was remarkably as insubstantial as the flakes.

Still, even with her slight form and following the same path he and she had traveled separately in the garden, the heavy, wet snow made Wingrave's journey back inside agonizingly slow.

His breath came fast and hard as he stomped through the gardens, those quick inhalations and exhalations a product of his exertions and certainly not any fear on his part.

Absolutely it wasn't fear.

As he'd told her, he feared nothing and no one.

He certainly wasn't going to worry about an insolent visitor who didn't have a brain in her—

"What possessed you to go outside in the middle of a bloody snow-storm," he railed.

Her head wobbled against his arm, bouncing about like that of a child's doll, and Wingrave quickened his pace.

She was burning up.

"Quite fine, are you," he bit out. "Oh, yes, as I said, you are the epitome of hearty and hale."

Once more, no cheeky response or dauntless reply met his jeering. The always loquacious chit remained unnaturally still and silent.

An odd sensation, something that felt very nearly like panic, beat away in his chest.

Not because he cared about her either way. Nay, the only fear he did possess was that she'd perish here and her ghost would remain to haunt him. He merely sought to send her on her merry way.

In the greatest hint of irony, the snow at some point had stopped, and only the occasional whisper of wind filled the landscape. That and the crunch of snow under his lone pair of boots.

Helia whimpered, and he glanced down.

Her auburn lashes lay vividly bright against her stark-white cheeks.

Wingrave quickened the already fast pace he'd set, breaking into a near run.

"Y-you had to go out so b-bloody far," he said into the quiet, his breath coming quick.

Only more of that unnatural silence met his livid assessment.

Cold little puffs of white gusted forth from his swift exhalations and inhalations, those little breaths having absolutely nothing to do with fear.

He'd have to care to be afraid.

He didn't.

"I-I don't. I-I don't." That mantra came from his lips over and over, until, at long last, he arrived at the snow-covered limestone steps leading to the terrace above.

Wingrave readjusted his hold on Helia and took the steps quickly.

The moment his feet touched the patio, the double doors were thrown open and two servants rushed out.

One of the strapping footmen reached for her.

Wingrave reflexively drew her closer. "Now you'd come," he taunted. He'd not hand her over to either of the inept pair who'd allowed her to go out and not immediately reported the lady's whereabouts to Wingrave. For if she died, Wingrave would be the one she haunted—not them. "Fetch me a damned physician!"

One of the men immediately dropped a bow and bolted in the opposite direction, while the other servant kept pace at Wingrave's side.

"And you—see that a hot bath is readied this moment," Wingrave ordered.

"Yes, my lord. Immediately, my lord."

Wingrave shifted the woman in his arms. "It's not 'immediate' if you are still walking with me and talking."

"Yes—"

Wingrave's low growl ended the remainder of the footman's affirmation.

The tall fellow with an enormous Adam's apple nodded, then took off racing.

Spared of that unwanted company, Wingrave shifted his focus back to the sickly woman in his arms.

"You couldn't have fallen ill before you came from wherever it is you hail," he said tersely. He glanced down and then promptly regretted it.

Beads of sweat dotted Helia's brow. She whimpered and shivered, burrowing against him like a cat who'd escaped a drowning and now sought warmth.

This marked a first: the first time anyone had looked to Wingrave for comfort.

"You'd be best to find a different heat source, madam," he warned. "I've not a hint of warmth in my body, and my soul is even colder."

Except, despite his own warning, Wingrave tightened his hold upon Helia, drawing her even more snugly against him. His legs ached, as did his lungs and arms, from the onerous task he'd put to them.

Out of breath, he reached the massive staircase that led to the guest suites and stopped at the bottom. Wingrave slumped against the hand-carved oak stair rail with a wide-mouthed ogre fashioned into the wood.

As a boy, after his mother had commissioned a new staircase, Wingrave had avoided it because of that menacing rendering. Now he borrowed support from the railing; he sucked in a breath, and another, and attempted to get his lungs back to proper working order.

And then he felt it—the quaking tremor that racked Helia's slender form.

You foolish, foolish chit . . .

A young servant stepped forward and reached for Helia.

Wingrave quelled the liveried footman with a single black look, and then forcing his tired legs to resume their forward movement, he proceeded to take the marble steps two at a time.

As soon as he reached the guest quarters, he found the head house-keeper, Mrs. Trowbridge; a trio of maids; and a pair of footmen sta-tioned outside one of the rooms.

Wingrave promptly headed for them.

"My lord," Mrs. Trowbridge greeted at his approach.

The three maids stepped aside and let him past, while one of the footmen drew the panel open.

A black cat immediately darted from the room, bolting around Wingrave's legs.

The maids all gasped and crossed themselves.

Wingrave looked to that thick creature, ambling down the hall as quick as its corpulent frame might allow.

"What the hell is that creature doing here?" he demanded as the stout animal darted off, surprisingly quick for its size.

"A black cat, my lord," one of the girls whispered.

"I know what it is," he snapped. "Why is it . . ." *In Helia's rooms.*

The terrified maid's whisper cut over the remainder of Wingrave's actual question. "A bad omen, it is."

The maid beside her nodded. "If a black cat walks into the room of an ill person and the miss dies, it will be because of the cat's powers."

An odd sensation squeezed at his chest.

If the miss dies . . .

It'd be her fault. Not some damned cat's. Why did that not drive away an emotion that felt more like fear than annoyance?

"Enough of your silly superstition, you stupid girls!" As unaffected as the only servant who ever resided in this miserable residence could be, Mrs. Trowbridge, who also happened to know everything about this household, had the answer. "It is one of the mousers, my lord."

"Keep that vexatious creature away from these rooms," he demanded. Not because he was superstitious. Just . . . because, rather.

Several servants stationed near the end of that hall promptly took off, chasing after the thing.

Black cat forgotten, Wingrave stormed into Helia's rooms and focused on his *current* vexation.

The source of all his woes and miseries.

The group converged on him, with a servant reaching to take Helia from him.

Wingrave glared sharply back, and just like the previous footmen had, this fellow, too, fell back.

Mrs. Trowbridge took charge of the room and began calling out directives and orders. "If you will, place the lady over there." She pointed to the big tester bed.

Wingrave headed swiftly over—and then stopped.

His arms, of their own volition, tightened about the slight figure in his arms, and he glanced down.

A vicious tightening centered somewhere in his chest and gut.

"My lord?" Mrs. Trowbridge's no-nonsense voice broke him from his musings.

He immediately set her down and fell back, feeling an unfamiliar sense of gratitude as the housekeeper took full charge.

Mrs. Trowbridge stepped between Wingrave and Helia and went back to calling out orders.

While servants set to work all around him, Wingrave's unblinking gaze remained fixed on a frail and still Helia.

She looked so very small and delicate upon that big feather mattress. Helia, so slight of form, did not so much as leave an indentation upon the soft bedding.

Her cheeks, flushed from fever, had taken on a shade to rival the deepest crimson found in her auburn tresses. Those curls that now spread damp and limp about her pillow.

Past merged with present as distant and long-buried memories danced with the moment.

You are now my heir, the future duke . . . Your brother proved himself weak, after all. He did not survive.

She will not survive. She will not survive.

Fevers ravaged bodies, and if a person managed to triumph over the ague, then they were forever transformed, left shallow, hollow, empty versions of their former selves—as Wingrave had been.

He reflexively balled and unballed his hands at his sides, his fingers sinking into the sodden fabric of his gloves.

I do not care. She is nothing to me. No one is anything to me . . . certainly not—

"My lord." That sharp, authoritative utterance brought him rushing back to the chaotic moment.

Mrs. Trowbridge pointed over his shoulder, and he followed that gesture over to the door, just as a team of footmen bearing a copper tub and bucket of steaming water poured inside.

Wingrave found his feet and hastened from the room.

The moment he stepped into the hall, the stalwart team of footmen came rushing out.

Wingrave looked past them, stealing one more glance to where Helia lay, but managed to catch but a sliver of a glance of her before a maid pushed the door shut, and then she was gone from sight.

Chapter 8

In death there is nothing new, or surprising, since we all
know, that we are born to die; and nothing terrible to
those, who can confide in an all-powerful God.

—*Ann Radcliffe, The Mysteries of Udolpho*

Helia was cold, so very cold.

No matter how deep she burrowed into the soft mattress and under
the blankets, the chill racked her from the inside out.

She tossed and turned, bringing her knees close. She wrapped her
arms about those quaking lower limbs in a bid to find any hint of
warmth, but there was none to be found.

The world had gone ice cold, and that same numbing gelidity
had invaded every corner of her body, until there was no escaping the
unadulterated, bleak misery it wrought.

If only she could get warm.

She wept and wailed.

"You are going to be fine. Do you hear me?" a distant voice called.
"You're too stubborn and strong to die."

Whoever uttered that assurance sounded deuced angry about it.

"I . . . I can't," she wept.

"You're a hale and hearty Scot, remember?"

A hale and hearty Scot? Only, she didn't feel either of those things.

Another tremor overtook Helia's frame.

She whimpered.

And then she saw them. Her ma and dad. They stood side by side, their arms linked, and Helia's mother's head rested so serenely against the laird's shoulder.

They smiled and gave her a little wave.

"P-please," she implored, through chattering teeth. Why would they allow her to hurt this way? "W-won't you give me more b-blankets?"

Why were they smiling? Why, when she was racked with agony?

An inky darkness crept in, swallowing their smiling visages.

And then, the blankets she did have were removed, and she was forced back to this horrid place of suffering. Only, someone was determined to torture her. For they now mocked her earlier pleas for warmth by casting her into an inferno.

"Noooooo," Helia wailed. Tears stained her cheeks.

"I'm sorry." That apology came ragged and harsh.

"Make it s-stop," she begged, flailing and thrashing in a bid to escape the heat.

Why would her parents . . . ? Only, they wouldn't. They loved her.

And then she recalled . . . they were no more.

Helia wept all the harder.

Mr. Draxton's loathsome visage materialized, mocking her, taunting her.

He'd found her.

And there was no escaping.

She was trapped.

She was going to die.

Wingrave had reached that conclusion two days earlier, even before he'd set Helia down on the very mattress she now writhed upon.

The ague killed, and spunky of spirit though his Scottish guest may be, the fact remained, she wasn't so strong that she could defeat such an infirmity.

His brother hadn't.

Wingrave almost hadn't.

And the only reason he'd managed to survive was because the Lord hadn't a use for his rotted soul and the Devil didn't want a wretchedly imperfect fellow with a useless ear.

Standing over Helia, his hands clasped behind him, Wingrave stared down at the feverish woman so very still in the bed.

But this woman?

She was a delicate, diminutive fairy, possessed of a wholesomeness that couldn't be feigned, and such souls were not destined to last long in this world.

With the fever's hold, she'd thrashed and writhed so much these past two days, she now lay motionless and limp under the thin white cotton counterpane.

A light rapping at the door brought his attention from his musings about the minx who'd upended his life and his household.

"Enter," he barked, his gaze fixed on Helia's still form.

"My lord," Mrs. Trowbridge said. "Dr. Hembly has arrived."

Another doctor.

The floorboards groaned and shifted, announcing the approach of the latest physician to visit Helia.

He stopped beside Wingrave. The man, younger by a decade or so than the previous ones who'd come and gone, was near in height to Wingrave.

"My lord," the doctor greeted. He set his black medical bag down on the Louis XVI bedside table with its butterfly veneer. "If you would—"

"I'm not leaving," he snapped.

The last time he'd done so, one of the more contumelious fellows had stuck several of those bloodsucking leeches on her wrist.

This latest physician proved just as insolent. "It would be best—"

Wingrave leveled Hembly with a single black look that managed to effectively quell those objections.

Dr. Hembly flushed and cleared his throat. "Very well."

Through this latest examination, Wingrave stood as the same silent sentry he'd been during the six others she'd endured.

The young doctor gently lifted Helia's flaccid hand in one of his and touched two middle fingers to the place at the center of her wrist.

All the while, Wingrave stared intently at her. Against his better judgment, he'd allowed the minx to remain until the storm broke. And what had she done? She'd gone out in that blasted storm, and would now get herself killed for that carelessness.

His fingers curled tightly into his palms, his nails leaving familiar impressions upon the flesh.

After an infernally long examination, Dr. Hembly made a clucking sound with his tongue and shook his head regretfully.

Sparks of red rage dotted Wingrave's vision. "For the love of God, man. You aren't a damned chicken. Words. Use words."

Wingrave had never been known for his patience, and with Helia Wallace of Scotland dying in his household, he'd even less of that *virtue* now.

The physician flushed red and lowered Helia's palm back to her side. "The lady is weak, my lord. By everything reported to me by your housekeeper at my arrival, and based on my own evaluation here, I do not expect she can last much longer."

Wingrave knew as much, and had been expecting such a prognosis from the doctor. And yet, even so, the muscles of his gut clenched like he'd taken a fist to them.

"She's not to die," he said on an icy whisper. He had the loss of his brother on his soul; he'd not add the chipper, cheerful Miss Helia Wallace to the list of his blacker sins. "I don't care what you do, but you are to save her."

A somber Dr. Hembly inclined his head. "In speaking to Mrs. Trowbridge, I understand you are opposed to bleeding the young lady."

Opposed? More like, he'd cut off the hand of the man who thought to employ that useless medical technique upon her and inflict a different type of bleeding upon a person.

"However," the doctor went on, and that single word quelled Wingrave's last hope of a physician being able to help her, "I am afraid the only course is to ble—"

"Finish the thought, and I'll finish you." Wingrave issued that threat on a deep, velvety purr.

The doctor frowned. "My lord," he persisted. "I understand you are opposed to bleeding the young woman; however, it is the only course of treatment that may save her."

"And you finished the thought," he said, with a cheer to rival Helia's.

Paling, Hembly took several quick steps away, proving himself not a complete lackwit. "My lord, it is a tried-and-true method we employ for all number of illnesses and ailments."

"Sucking the lifeblood from a person hardly seems like it would be bolstering to their health."

Dr. Hembly pounced on that. "On the contrary. The illness is in her blood, and the only way to draw out the illness is by drawing out the poisoned blood."

"By that logic, wouldn't all her blood be poisoned and the only way to rid it of illness would be to remove all of the sickened blood?"

That gave the other man pause. Several lines creased Hembly's brow in a palpable confusion. "I . . . It is the only way," he finally said. "The hope is that we may draw out enough of the poisoned blood so that the healthy fluid might then, in turn, exceed the pois—"

Wingrave growled. "Say the word 'poisoned' one more time."

This time, more wisely, the other man shut his demmed mouth.

Hembly bowed his head. "Forgive me, my lord. If I am not allowed to perform the treatment I believe the lady requires, I cannot be of any further assistance to you."

"You have been *no* assistance to me," Wingrave said nastily. "You are right about one thing, however."

The physician brightened.

"Something is poisoned in these chambers," he hissed. "The time I've given of my life, listening to your ancient, half-witted drivel."

Clearing his throat, Hembly drew his shoulders back. "There is a reason they are anci—"

Wingrave narrowed his eyes into thin, unforgiving slits.

This time, the young man took proper warning. Swallowing noisily, Dr. Hembly packed up his bag. When he'd snapped it closed, he avoided Wingrave's eyes, dropped a bow, and made a hasty retreat.

And Wingrave and Helia were alone once more.

The moment that fraudulent pretender to medical skill closed the door behind himself, Wingrave whipped his attention back over to Helia.

She lay there, so very still and, but for the flushed red splotches on her cheeks, pale as a ghost.

A ghost is what she will become . . .

Wingrave forcibly shoved the thought aside.

"You've continued to make a bother of yourself, Helia," he growled. "Forcing me to entertain fools."

As an afterthought, he muttered, "More fools, that is."

After all, the whole reason she lay in that bed and Wingrave met doctor after incompetent doctor was that she'd been daft enough to hie herself outside, in the midst of a bloody snowstorm.

A snowstorm which ironically had ceased, started again.

Wingrave picked up a neatly folded white linen cloth and dunked it into the long-cold washbasin water.

"I'm not happy with you," he snapped.

He wrung the towel out and pressed it against Helia's forehead. Before, when he'd done so, she'd thrashed and turned. Now it was as if the fever had left her too weak to do anything other than whimper.

That only added to his crossness.

"How dare you go from strong, spirited, indefatigable she-devil to weak kitten."

She remained still as death.

He deepened his glare on her. "And do not think you're going to get off so easily and do anything like *die* before I've had the chance to take you to task for running outside like a ruddy idiot."

Her silence was his only response.

"Oh, forgive me," Wingrave taunted. "I should be a better host, you say? Well, I've far greater burdens to attend . . . namely, the one involving looking after you."

He yanked the towel from her brow. Her fever had turned the previously cold fabric lukewarm, an unnecessary reminder of the fact that she lay feverish, dying in her bed. Worse, dying in *his* bed. Because even after the servants carted the bodies off, the reminders lived on. They dwelled in this house and one's mind, until a man managed to wrestle his demons and squash those weakening thoughts.

Only, a different thought now intruded.

May good fortune and health be ever with you.

Thoughts not of death but of a different exchange between Wingrave and this insolent imp, who lay still before him.

You may not have had friends before, but you have one now . . .

And despite himself, despite the misery of these past days, and despite the fact he never smiled, a wry grin dusted his lips.

A friend.

God, he'd never believed there existed a guileless, optimistic innocent such as this one.

Wingrave contemplated her still form.

Perhaps that naivete accounted for why she'd defied his orders and why, when no other man would dare to, Helia, despite the fact he clearly intimidated her, met Wingrave's gaze and did not back down in speaking her mind.

And in the end, no matter how mighty of spirit, it didn't matter.

His smile withered.

For the inevitable outcome remained the same.

Nor, for that matter, are your musings altogether accurate. Didn't the lady flee your presence . . . ?

An emotion dangerously close to guilt slithered around, unwelcome and unpleasant, inside him.

Snarling, Wingrave tossed the lukewarm fabric into the brass bowl. Water pinged over the edges and dotted the floor like tears the washbasin shed for the impending fate of its temporary mistress.

Like tears the washbasin shed?

He recoiled.

Good God. Insane. I am going utterly insane.

The lady's madness had proven contagious; she was turning him into a demmed bedlamite.

Angrily squeezing out the cloth, he wrapped the fabric about one of her wrists and then, fetching another, repeated the same for her other hand.

Determined to remain with her until the end, Wingrave dragged the chair he'd stationed at her side closer and dropped his tired frame into the thick upholstered folds.

Slouching into the chair, he sank his palms upon the mahogany arms of the throne-like seat and stared from veiled lashes at the lifeless miss.

"What manner of witch are you, Helia?" he murmured. First, she'd managed to wheedle her way past the butler, and then him. She'd convinced Wingrave to let her remain the night, and now, having fallen sick, he couldn't make himself leave her side.

Now he'd taken on the role of damned nursemaid.

Granted, he'd done so out of the absolute incompetence of everyone else. But that was neither here nor there.

Either way, he wished that she'd get on with it . . . live or die. That way, Wingrave could get back to living as he'd been since his brother's death—alone and unbothered by anyone.

Chapter 9

It is wrong to give way to grief.

—Ann Radcliffe, The Mysteries of Udolpho

A faint grizzling made by an unidentifiable beast split across the quiet.

The creature called out. Its disconsolate mewls came and then went. Over and over.

Wingrave struggled to open uncharacteristically heavy lashes and look about for the fretful creature responsible for that forlorn sound.

When he did, only silence met him. That and inky-black darkness left by the night's hold.

Somewhere behind him, a soft fire crackled quietly in the hearth.

Groggy, he fought to clear his thoughts. All his muscles ached. Only when he overindulged in spirits did he awaken in this nebulous state.

Wingrave scrubbed a palm over his face.

But . . . it'd been years. He'd been a mere boy at university. Nay, he'd come to *detest* those puling, weak men who imbibed on spirits.

He blinked slowly as he registered his palms resting on the arms . . . of a chair. Not even a comfortable chair, at that. What in blazes . . . ? Why, he had fallen asleep . . . in a chair.

Meowwwwww.

Wingrave went absolutely still, and his suddenly alert gaze went to the big black cat burrowing contentedly upon his lap.

And why in hell did he have a *cat* on his lap?

The big creature stared at Wingrave through direful yellow eyes.

His brain was still clogged by sleep and confusion, but then recently spoken words whispered forward.

A bad omen, it is . . . If a black cat walks into the room of an ill person and the miss dies, it will be because of the cat's powers.

Then it came back to him.

She came back to him.

Helia Wallace.

A feverish Helia Wallace.

At some point, Wingrave had fallen asleep.

An eerie silence hung over the room.

With a hiss to rival the black beast who'd appropriated Wingrave's lap for his nap, he scooped up the cat and stalked across the room. He held the squirming fellow in one arm and opened the door.

The servants on sentry all jumped.

Wingrave tossed the mouser down. "I said to keep this goddamned cat away," he thundered.

The beastie bolted.

"Yes, my lord," one of the footmen said. "We'll see to it immediately." Two servants set off in quick pursuit.

Cursing, Wingrave returned to Helia's sickroom and pushed the door shut.

Wingrave clasped his hands behind him, leaned back against the oak panel, and glared at the quiescent woman, so still, so silent.

"A cat that has the same nerve as you, Helia Wallace," he muttered. "It is only fitting he try to keep you company."

Try. Wingrave's jaw worked. The hell he'd let that beast anywhere near this room.

His fury and determination had nothing to do with any ridiculous superstition imparted by some maid.

Absolutely nothing.

Wingrave pushed himself from the door and rejoined Helia's bedside.

And staring down at her, his ever-present anger, so twined with the fabric of his soul he believed it could not be separate, drained out of him.

He worked his gaze over her.

She lay motionless, her chest barely moving. At some point, she'd shed her blanket and her modest nightskirts had climbed above her knees to reveal a pair of well-turned limbs.

Wingrave swallowed hard as he stared, briefly transfixed by muscular calves that bespoke a woman who took well to the saddle. Her legs were the manner of which a man dreamed. Ones that had been so fashioned to wrap about a man's—

A sardonic laugh, rusty from ill use, exploded from his chest.

Had he entertained any delusions that he was anything other than the bastard he was, ogling deathly ill Helia Wallace put to bed any worries there.

She shivered; a little tremor racked her frame.

Wingrave carefully drew Helia's garments back into their place, preserving her dignity . . . and his honor.

He gave his head a wry shake. And here he possessed more principle than he'd previously jeered, after all.

———— ⚬❧⚬ ————

She was dying.

And she fought herself, both wanting to get on with it, so she could end this suffering, and wanting to fight forever, if need be, so that she might live.

"Don't hurt me," she pleaded.

"I won't hurt you," he gruffly promised.

"You must have a name . . ."

"Anthony . . ."

"Who are you?"

"A friend . . ."

"I don't have any friends."

"You have many friends. The servants. Their children."

He was right. This Anthony. This stranger.

She had friends. But what of her family?

And then she remembered, and wished she hadn't.

For this anguish . . . hurt far more than that wrought by the heat burning her up from the inside out. This was the pain of loss and heartbreak that couldn't go away. That would never go away.

Helia proceeded to weep. She wept for the loss of her beloved parents. She wept for knowing she'd never again be held in the secure, loving folds of their embrace and for knowing that they'd never join their laughs together.

They'd never dangle their grandbabes upon their knees as they'd always longingly spoken of.

And for the fever tearing her apart, she felt herself racked by a chill that would not quit.

Sobbing, Helia flipped onto her side, drew her knees close to her chest, and hugged herself in a forlorn, lonely hold, which was all she'd ever again know.

Because there was no one.

There was no mother or father.

She—

Suddenly, Helia found herself scooped up and drawn into the fiercest, most protective embrace. Strong arms clasped about her, and she instantly ceased her flailing as those limbs wrapped around her. They conferred a welcome and wondrous heat and . . . strength. They slipped about her being, chasing away the sorrow, and left her warm where she'd previously been only cold.

She didn't want this moment to ever end. She didn't want whatever this was, whoever this was who held her, to draw away.

Helia burrowed her cheek against a soft, warm linen shirt, the softness of that fabric a sharp juxtaposition to the hard muscle that provided stability and strength. It wasn't enough.

She wanted to get closer to it; she wanted to climb inside and borrow more of that strength and heat.

She turned and twisted in a bid to do so.

Then she heard it.

Faint and distant—a song.

> "Should auld acquaintance be forgot,
> and never brought to mind?"

The strains so very familiar and soothing.

> "Should auld acquaintance be forgot,
> and auld lang syne?"

That song of her childhood, and of her family.

> "For auld lang syne, my jo,
> for auld lang syne."

Only, it wasn't her father's deep voice now singing. Rather, this deep, sonorous baritone belonged to another.

> "We'll tak' a cup o' kindness yet,
> for auld lang syne."

And then, her pain and heartache somehow . . . forgotten, replaced by that deep, distant, melodious voice, Helia slept.

Chapter 10

The refreshing pleasure from the first view of nature, after the pain of illness, and the confinement of a sick-chamber, is above the conceptions, as well as the descriptions, of those in health.

—*Ann Radcliffe, The Mysteries of Udolpho*

Helia opened her eyes, then promptly wished she hadn't.

Her father had often said the moment she'd been born, she'd chased away the dark clouds that had gripped the Highland skies, and the first sun after a winter of gloom had marked her a daughter of the sun.

And yet, with the bright rays streaming from that great orb through the crack in the curtains, she'd far prefer a darker sky to the blinding brightness.

With greater care, Helia tried again.

This time, she turned her heavy head away from those windows, and toward the other side of the room. She blinked remarkably heavy lashes and sought to make out her murky surroundings.

Her gaze locked on the ornately carved, unfamiliar oak door . . . and with an uncharacteristic lethargy, Helia forced her stare away from that intricate panel and took in the other surrounding details: the Louis XVI bedside table with its butterfly veneer. The ornate, polished brass ewer and basin. The damask rose wallpaper, just a faint shade away from being too garish.

These weren't her rooms.

Ma favored bright, cheerful shades and less elaborate decor.

Her head thick from the fog of sleep, she tried to make sense of her surroundings.

Where am I?

Panic built at the base of her skull, knocking away, and Helia, sluggish as she'd never been, raised her hands to the back of her head.

"You're awake, dear child."

Dear child?

Helia looked about for the owner of that cheerful pronouncement.

A kind-eyed, regal-looking older woman, dressed in the attire of a housekeeper, smiled at her.

Helia tried desperately to place her identity, but that, too, remained as futile as sorting out her surroundings.

The woman hastened over to the opposite side of the room. Helia attempted to follow her steps, but all the muscles of her neck ached, making it impossible to keep up with the quick pace the servant had set.

Helia raised her right hand and began to rub at the tight muscles along her neck and the bottom of her skull.

What in blazes happened to me?

But the answer to that remained as unclear as the one pertaining to her whereabouts.

Suddenly, the smiling woman reappeared at her side, with a carved crystal goblet filled with water.

Then, for the first time, Helia registered past her discomfort and achiness to her unbounded and terrible thirst.

She struggled up onto her elbows.

The servant instantly set the glass down upon the nightstand with a little plink and looped an arm about Helia's waist. "Slow as you go, my dear."

She helped guide Helia back several inches so that the Venetian, painted, gilt headboard provided a steady surface on which to rest her weary frame.

"Who are you?" Helia asked, her voice thick and hoarse and dry as it had never been.

"Mrs. Trowbridge," the kindly servant offered. "Now, here," she continued, reaching for the elegant glass she'd previously set aside. "I trust after the time you've had of it, you're more parched than our Lord himself had been in that desert he once wandered."

Mrs. Trowbridge slid an arm about Helia's shoulders and then, with her free hand, began to proffer the drink as if Helia were a babe.

In actuality, Helia felt as weak as one of those helpless creatures.

The moment the water passed her lips, she gulped and swallowed, welcoming that glorious cool liquid as it slid down her throat.

"Slower, my dear," Mrs. Trowbridge gently admonished. "You do not want to choke."

Choking might in fact be the preferable fate to this insatiable thirst.

Still, she made herself sip more slowly from the goblet the servant held to her lips.

When she'd downed its contents, Helia collapsed into the headboard. After Mrs. Trowbridge deposited the glass back on the nightstand, she bustled over to the opposite side of the room.

Helia ran a tired hand over her eyes and tried to sort out where—

And then, with all the force and enormity of a headfirst collision with a stone wall, it hit her.

Her parents' death.

Mr. Draxton's arrival.

Her desperate flight to London and the godmother she'd never met.

And the son who'd been there to greet her instead.

Lord Wingrave. Surly and menacing and unsmiling . . .

And then she recalled the terms under which he'd allowed Helia to remain.

Suddenly, the heavy brocade curtains were drawn wide, sending so much of that blindingly bright and cheerful light streaming through the thin, gossamer undercurtains that Helia shielded her eyes.

When she'd managed to accustom them to that great, torrential luminance, she looked fully at the window.

Sun.

So very much of it.

She'd always loved the sun and had first entered the world at the highest point of a Sunday, no less.

And yet . . .

This time proved different.

For at some point, the storm had stopped, and the skies had turned a vibrant blue . . . which meant . . .

"I have nowhere to go."

"Bah, you are not fit to go anywhere, my dear."

Helia looked dumbly at the still-smiling housekeeper.

It was a moment before she registered she'd spoken those five words aloud.

Panic began to clamor and build inside her chest, and it was all she could do to keep from saying both she and Mrs. Trowbridge had been right: Helia must leave, while at the same time, she wasn't fit to go anywhere.

Wingrave, who'd been clear in his annoyance with her from the start, had only been further inconvenienced by Helia falling ill and burdening him with her presence.

She felt the familiar prick of tears at her lashes.

"He is going to throw me out," she whispered.

A man of Wingrave's reputation would hardly make a mistress of a bedraggled waif.

Worse, what did it say about Helia's circumstances that becoming the marquess's lover was the best option available to her—only, it wasn't even available.

"His Lordship?" Mrs. Trowbridge scoffed. "Hardly. Why, what would be the sense in that . . . ?"

As the kindly housekeeper continued, Helia's head had already begun to swirl with her deepening dread. She couldn't return to Mr. Draxton.

"I understand he's quite menacing," Mrs. Trowbridge went on, her voice shifting in and out of focus.

A shudder racked Helia's frame. If the insults and threats Mr. Draxton had doled out before had been bad, what would they be like when she showed up on her family's doorstep after having outmaneuvered him and run away?

She shook her head, already dispelling the thought. She'd sooner starve on the streets than turn herself over to that miserable, hateful bounder. She might have nothing, but she did have her strong Scottish pride.

". . . but as they say, timid dogs bark worse than they bite . . ." The housekeeper's consoling managed to penetrate Helia's blinding panic.

Timid dogs . . . ?

Through the fog made by fear and her recent illness, it was a moment before Helia registered that the motherly housekeeper in fact spoke of . . .

"Lord Wingrave?" Helia's voice, still rough from lack of use, emerged as a croak.

Mrs. Trowbridge nodded. "The same. And he'll be most glad to know you're up and talking."

And despite the foreboding future awaiting Helia and her desperate circumstances, a laugh spilled past her cracked and dry lips.

"Lord Wingrave?" Helia repeated, because it really did bear repeating and clarification.

The housekeeper gave an even more energetic bob of her head. "The same."

His Lordship, who wouldn't even share his name with her.

Something pricked at the corners of her mind. A murky remembrance danced just out of reach. Hallucinations she'd wailed and moaned through.

Anthony . . .

Through the process of trying to sort out where figment ended and reality began, Helia registered the other woman's absolute seriousness. "You are *serious*."

"Very much so. I know it is hard to believe—the rest of the staff has had a hard time reckoning His Lordship's actions with his usual temperament." Color singed the housekeeper's thin, lightly wrinkled cheeks. "Not that anyone would ever speak ill of His Lordship or any in the duke's employ," she added hastily.

"Of course not," Helia demurred.

And then, as if she feared she'd said too much, the housekeeper cleared her throat. "You must be famished."

Mrs. Trowbridge didn't allow for an answer and had already headed for the bellpull.

In an instant, a light scratch sounded at the door. A maid ducked her head inside.

"Please see that a tray is readied for Miss Wallace," Mrs. Trowbridge said in a no-nonsense way. "And do not tarry."

The small young woman stole a glance in Helia's direction, then dipped a curtsy and hurried off.

The moment she'd gone, a now silent Mrs. Trowbridge proceeded to right Helia's already nearly tidy chambers.

Helia studied the housekeeper as she flitted about the room.

Though Helia would never break the housekeeper's confidence, she'd known Mrs. Trowbridge but a couple of days—most of which, Helia had been unconscious for—and as such, she understood why the other woman would be wary of being heard speaking ill, or allowing other servants to speak poorly, of a forbidding master such as Lord Wingrave.

In fact, being on her own in the world now, and with her security stripped away, she understood on a level the fear Mrs. Trowbridge would have at the prospect of being turned out.

Desperate to know how a man like Wingrave *became* Wingrave and something about his life, she looked to the kindly housekeeper.

"Have you been in His and Her Grace's employ very long?" Helia asked.

Over at the walnut recamier chaise longue, Mrs. Trowbridge paused mid-plump of an already perfectly plump gold silk pillow. "I've been head housekeeper for nearly twenty years." Pride shone in her silvery eyes.

One could tell much about a master and mistress's kindness by the length of service and loyalty of their servants. Between that affirmation and the marquess having let her recuperate here, Helia found hope that maybe, just maybe, the members of this household weren't so cold and unfeeling as their son had made them out—

"I'm the longest-employed member on the staff, I am," Mrs. Trowbridge informed, effectively quashing Helia's earlier optimism.

"Many have left?" Helia ventured.

"Many have left," the housekeeper confirmed, and went back to her task of arranging the trio of pillows along the back of the chaise.

Which was hardly a testament to any kind of magnanimity from those who lived under this roof.

Pathetically fatigued from the herculean effort it took to prop herself up, Helia rolled onto her side so she could face the housekeeper.

Mrs. Trowbridge dropped the pillow in her hands and hurried over. "Now, now. I've warned you that you are not to tax yourself. His Lordship will be most displeased if you fall ill again."

"Yes," she said tiredly, as the beneficent servant straightened Helia's coverlet and then gave it a firm tug up to her chin. "I trust Lord Wingrave would be most cross at my further illness. Not when it would further delay my departure."

More like my eviction.

Mrs. Trowbridge frowned. "I see why you're of that opinion, miss. And . . . several days ago, I myself would have been of a like one, but the marquess? He's been quite distraught at your condition."

Distraught?

Helia snorted. "*Impossible.*"

"I assure you, it is not only possible, but in fact, the truth." The housekeeper stole a glance about, as if to check for possible interlopers, and then returned her focus to Helia. "Lord Wingrave did not leave your side, Miss Wallace."

Had Helia not already been lying down, the servant's words would have knocked her square off her feet. "He didn't?"

"He surely didn't. Even cared for you himself, he did."

Helia reeled. He'd *cared* for her himself? "He *did?*"

Mrs. Trowbridge nodded. "Toweled your brow and wrists and dripped little amounts of water into your lips so you had something to drink."

And a terrific heat spread through her chest; this warmth was a tingling one, caused not by any fever but by the staggering breadth of Lord Wingrave's benevolence. "My goodness," Helia whispered.

"Never thought I'd see it myself," the housekeeper confessed. "Not after—"

The woman abruptly stopped, catching herself from sharing something, and Helia held her breath, wishing she would, wishing she'd finish her unspoken thought.

"After?" Helia quietly urged, desperately wishing for her to say more, wanting to know whatever secret she held about the enigmatic marquess.

Mrs. Trowbridge grunted. "That's neither here nor there. What matters is that you are well and are going to get stronger with each day."

"Which is undoubtedly why he cared for me," she murmured. That was the only thing that made sense. "Once I'm well, he can send me on my way."

The head servant scoffed. "If he *didn't* care, he may as well have left you to die." Mrs. Trowbridge shook her head. "But he didn't. He summoned doctor after doctor, and time after time, he showed them the door because he deemed them incompetent."

A small smile formed. She'd known the marquess but a very short time, and yet, with Wingrave's imperturbable sangfroid, she could both hear and see him taking on a team of doctors so. Where Lord Wingrave was concerned, his self-assuredness extended to all matters and things.

Mrs. Trowbridge wasn't done with her stubborn and faithful defense of the marquess. "After he learned one of the doctors bled you, he refused to leave during any further examinations. He wouldn't let a single one of those men bring even a single leech near you." An obstinate glint lit the old woman's eyes. "Threatened to do each one of them harm if they so much as put a leech on your wrist."

Ah, he'd refused to allow customary bloodletting as part of her treatment. Now, *that* made sense.

A twinkle sparkled in the older woman's eyes. "I know what you're thinking, my dear."

She couldn't.

"He didn't disallow them to bleed you because it was the easiest way to be rid of you."

Heat exploded on Helia's cheeks. "I did not—"

"Say so?" The stouthearted housekeeper smiled. "You didn't need to. You do not know His Lordship, Miss Wallace. You do not know who he was before. But if you'd seen how afeared he was during your illness, you'd see a different man than the one he lets you believe he is."

Floored by Mrs. Trowbridge's revelations, Helia lay there. Her mind spun.

Lord Wingrave had challenged an army of doctors he'd let in, for *her*.

For that matter, what nobleman would ever take on such a grim, effortful task as to play nursemaid for a sick woman? No less, a woman whom he did not personally know and denied any connection to?

Aye, recover she would. And apparently she'd do so not because of any miracle or intervention from any doctor's part, but rather because of . . . *Wingrave.*

The housekeeper spoke, drawing Helia from her racing thoughts. "In fact, I've not seen His Lordship so shaken since—" Mrs. Trowbridge caught herself once more.

Too late.

Helia's ears immediately latched on to that incomplete thought. She waited a moment for the faithful servant to speak again.

"Since?" Helia gently prodded when no further words were forthcoming.

In response to that urging, Mrs. Trowbridge pressed her lips closed and shook her head.

"Please," Helia implored, somehow desperate to know the secrets Anthony kept. Mrs. Trowbridge herself had confirmed he'd not always been this way. Each detail shared offered another piece of a puzzle, which once completed would paint a picture of why he'd become the guarded man he had.

The housekeeper remained silent, then spoke reluctantly. "You know," she whispered, as if the marquess were within earshot. She pointed at her left ear.

Helia puzzled her brow. "I do not understand."

Her expression grew serious once more. "One winter, the former Lord Wingrave fell ill and died. Those lads . . ." Tears filled Mrs. Trowbridge's eyes; she fished a kerchief from her pocket and dabbed the moisture from the corners. "They were as close as two brothers could be, until—"

The older woman stopped to collect herself. "After Lord Wingrave's brother died, His Lordship hid away in the library and pored over books. I'd bring him tea and biscuits throughout the day. He'd mumble his thanks but never so much as picked his head up from his research."

Helia hung on the woman's every word. There'd been a time when Lord Wingrave mourned a brother, and researched books, and thanked servants. It was anathema to everything she'd read, heard, and herself witnessed about the marquess.

"One night, His Lordship burst from the library and went running through the halls, shouting for the duke. His Lordship demanded the surgeon be removed as the family physician for having killed his brother."

"What did His Grace do?" Helia whispered.

An chilling and out-of-character rage darkened the older woman's face. "For having awakened the household, the duke beat His Lordship."

Anthony's father had beaten him? *Oh, my god.* The stories surrounding the Duke of Talbert were true, and even worse. Sorrow and anger filled her breast.

Mrs. Trowbridge must have seen horror reflected in Helia's eyes.

The older woman grunted. "Forget that," she said, in a stern directive.

"Of course," Helia lied. She'd never break the woman's confidence, but neither could she forget everything the housekeeper had revealed about the marquess.

"All you need to know is His Lordship remained by your side until the fever broke, and he was certain you'd recover." Mrs. Trowbridge grunted. "Anyway, His Lordship is not a bad man. Or he wasn't." Sadness slipped into her voice. "An angry one, yes. But angry men are angry for reasons, and only if one cares for that person do they take time to understand why."

Questions swirled and sprang to Helia's lips, demanding to be asked.

"Uh-uh," Mrs. Trowbridge said, and patted her shoulder. "That is enough talking for now. You need to rest so that you can heal up right quick."

Helia opened her mouth to protest, her hunger for information about the marquess far greater than even her long-overdue need for sustenance, when there came another light scratching at the door.

The one person in possession of, at the very least, *some* information about the gentleman brightened and turned toward the door. "Splendid!"

Helia wanted to rail at that untimely interruption that kept her from asking more questions about Lord Wingrave.

The housekeeper whisked across the room and drew the door open for a quartet of maids who stood in wait, each holding trays and pitchers and linens.

The moment the young women came pouring in, Mrs. Trowbridge offered Helia another smile, dipped her curtsy, and left.

While the servants gathered about Helia and proceeded to care for her, she contemplated all the words the head housekeeper had spoken . . . and found herself gripped by the need to know more about the future Duke of Talbert.

Chapter 11

How short a period often reverses the character of our
sentiments, rendering that which yesterday we despised,
today desirable.

—*Ann Radcliffe, A Sicilian Romance*

Seated upon the gilded, throne-like chair his father had commissioned
upon his ascension as the latest Duke of Talbert, Wingrave sifted
through the old bastard's mahogany desk. Wingrave searched for some
sign, some hint, some word, or anything in the duke's records, notes,
or files about Miss Helia Wallace.

He'd committed himself to finding out whether the woman he'd
taken for a charlatan was, in fact, just that, or whether, by some extraordinary, outrageously unlikely chance, she was actually a ward or goddaughter or something to his parents.

Thus far—unsurprisingly—Wingrave had discovered absolutely
nothing.

Having already inspected the entire contents of the right-side ped-
estal of drawers, Wingrave turned his attention to the remaining ones.

The lady hadn't died, after all.

Funny, that. Wingrave had been so very certain the good died
young, and then the Lord took them by fever.

Only, she hadn't.

She'd lived. Recovered. And . . . remained here in his bloody residence for nearly a week. In all, she'd been here ten days, which was ten days longer than he'd ever wanted his saucy bit of company to remain.

Granted, since her fever had broken and he'd ceded his place at her bedside to Mrs. Trowbridge, he'd not had to see her. That, however, was neither here nor there.

She was here, sharing the same roof.

He knew it, and that was enough.

There was no escaping it.

And since she hadn't died, that of course left him to ascertain for himself that he'd been right all along.

That woman was a witch of sorts, and he, who didn't give a bloody hell about anyone, had found himself worried about *her*. Wingrave cringed.

She'd wheedled her way into his household, and somehow left him . . . *weak*.

Wingrave yanked out the very bottom drawer and delved a hand inside, extracting a pile of notes with a brownish-red, velvet ribbon about them; the shade of that neat tie nearly matched the shade of Helia's freckles, a detail Wingrave only knew because of the length of time he'd remained at her side, staring at those tiniest, unpatterned specks dotting her cheeks and nose.

He gave that blasted fastening a tug and freed the notes for his search.

My god, what is wrong with me? Wingrave silently railed as he sifted through correspondence after correspondence belonging to others, and not any Wallace family, but rather the Bradburys. These letters had been written between his mother and the marchioness, the duke and duchess's former friend, whose daughter had left Wingrave at the altar—and not even figuratively.

That should have bothered him. Not because he'd had feelings for her, aside from those about his betrothed marrying another. He hadn't and didn't.

Rather, if he were to care about or worry about *anything*, it would be the abasement of his pride, in being thrown over and made a laughingstock by Lady Alexandra Bradbury, now McQuoid.

But it wasn't. Instead, he sat here, preoccupied by thoughts of Helia Wallace, and how very close she'd come to death.

Sweat slicked his palms, and his gut clenched, those muscles tightening in an unwanted reminder that Wingrave was human.

He stared blankly down at the random notes he held in his hand.

It'd been the fever. That was why. That was the absolute only reason he'd behaved so uncharacteristically.

A shadow fell over the desk, startling Wingrave. He yanked his head up so quick, his neck muscles screamed their protest, and the papers slipped and rained down about his lap.

He stared at the serene and unapologetic woman standing before him.

His heart thumped strangely in his chest.

Helia.

Helia, with her freckled cheeks no longer flushed with fever and her pretty green eyes perfectly clear, gave no indication to the precarious battle she'd fought for her health and life.

"Hullo," she said softly. Hers was the sweet voice of an angel, and something in her husky tones only further unnerved the hell out of him.

"Don't you knock, Miss Wallace?" he snapped.

"I did and quite *loudly*." Helia glanced meaningfully at the double-door panels she'd opened and walked through, all while he'd remained oblivious.

A dull flush climbed his neck.

"You didn't hear m—"

Wingrave shot a dark glare upon her, daring her to finish that sentence.

She didn't, but that didn't matter, just as it didn't change anything. He hadn't heard her entry.

But then, why would you? You'd your bloody left ear to that goddamned panel. This, when he never left his unhearing ear vulnerable that way. He never kept his head anything but directly toward any and all doors.

Feeling left open, defenseless, he wanted to flee.

Flee? This was his damned household. In fact, this room she'd invaded would, in fact, belong to him after his bastard of a father kicked up his heels and went on to where all the other miserable souls went to rot.

He grunted. "You're awake, then." He'd known as much. He'd known the minute her fever broke days earlier, just as he'd learned from Mrs. Trowbridge of the lady's improving health.

A wistful smile teased at her full crimson lips. "Never say you missed me while I slept."

"I meant from your fever, Miss Wallace. You've awakened from your fever. Furthermore, you didn't sleep," he said flatly. "You were unconscious."

Which begged the question . . . "What in hell are you doing here, Miss Wallace?" When she should not be here but resting or sleeping instead.

Meowww.

Wingrave narrowed his eyes. Nor had Helia entered this lair alone.

The lady made a familiar clearing sound with her throat, one he recognized as a telltale sign of her unease. "I—"

"You," he seethed.

Helia faltered.

That fat cat, on the other hand, took Wingrave's warning as a welcome and wandered into the room. In a display of feline challenge, it promptly collapsed at Helia's feet.

Wingrave flared his nostrils. "Oh, no, you don't." He'd kept the goddamned beast away until Helia healed. He didn't need the damned creature anywhere near her now that she'd begun to recover. "Go," he barked.

Helia's auburn eyebrows came together into a troubled little line, and she took an unsteady step to go. The bloody beastie matched the lady's steps.

"Not you," he snapped, freezing the pair of them in their tracks. *"You!"*

Helia glanced about the room, like there could possibly be someone *else* he spoke to.

Wingrave jabbed a finger in her direction. "Him. *Her*," he snapped. "That *thing*?"

Helia followed his impatient gesture downward. "Thing?" She frowned. "*This* is a cat."

"I know what a damned cat is," he bellowed.

Her eyes went wide.

Or was that his own?

Perhaps it was the both of them.

He inwardly recoiled. Good God, in the whole of his thirty years, he'd never lost control more than he had with this woman.

Wingrave took in a slow, deep breath. "I know what a cat is," he repeated frostily and with a greater calm. "I want it out of this room."

"But—"

Wingrave slapped his palms together with such force that the mouser took off through the opening in the doorway, leaving Helia and Wingrave . . . alone.

The young lady shut the panel.

An uncomfortable silence filled the air.

"I understand," she said softly.

He gritted his teeth. Here she went again with her fearlessness, speaking to Wingrave when the absolute *last* thing he wanted to do was talk to her or anyone.

"What exactly is it you think you understand, Helia?" he asked brusquely.

"You are afraid of cats."

"I most certainly am *not* afraid of cats," he exclaimed, exasperated. "I am not afraid of anything."

A wise person would have demurred and said nothing further.

Only the most lionhearted one would continue to challenge Wingrave.

"Everyone is afraid of something," she said in a gentle voice, *clearly* nonplussed by his explosion.

If he were being honest with the minx, he'd admit he was fast approaching that sentiment for infuriatingly stubborn Scots. Scottish women, to be exact.

"What do you want, Helia?" he asked impatiently.

Despite his curt tone, Helia's eyes revealed none of the unease they'd held before. Now she looked at Wingrave with wide, trusting, and tender eyes.

He resisted an unprecedented urge to squirm. It was as if Helia had sprung a dauntless comfort in Wingrave's presence.

"Mrs. Trowbridge said you remained at my side, my l—"

He swiftly cut off the remainder of her words. "Mrs. Trowbridge said too much."

"Too much, as in the truth, my lord?"

Yes, too much as in the truth.

He charged to his feet, knocking free the papers he'd previously searched; this time, they fell to the floor.

Unfazed, Helia continued to meet Wingrave's gaze.

His frustration mounted and led to an increased swiftness of his steps, as he at last plucked forth the reason for his unrest. He forced himself to stop at the side of the desk and kept several paces between them.

"You are better," he whispered in steely tones.

"Aye." The lady ran her palms along her skirt, drawing his gaze to the light tremble of those long, freckled digits, and also the first indication of her disquiet.

Oddly, that did not make him feel better. It should have. Only, strangely, it didn't.

Helia caught his focus and instantly stopped her nervous movement— that surprising pridefulness and strength gave him pause. Ladies were not so proud as this one. At least, none of the women he'd known or met. Maybe that was why he'd found himself spellbound by her.

"I am in good health," she continued in her almost lyrical tones, which didn't know whether they wished to be a crisp English accent or husky Scottish brogue. "Thanks to you . . . *Anthony.*"

Anthony . . .

Wingrave recoiled.

No one used his Christian name. Not even his parents—certainly not his parents. Certainly not anyone, and yet this woman, this insolent slip of baggage who'd invaded his household and his thoughts, took possession of a name he'd tendered as she'd tossed and turned, had somehow recalled it despite her fever, and now used it with all the familiarity of an old friend.

"My name is Wingrave," he whispered, adding an additional layer of ice to his declaration of war.

"Wingrave is your title." Hers was a gentle reminder that set his teeth to grinding. "Anthony is your name." She paused. "Is it not?"

He could deny it.

On instinct, that declination sprang to his lips, begging to be spoken.

Helia's eyes were all-knowing. Those captivating green irises called for—no, demanded—Wingrave's focus.

Of their own volition, his legs moved, carrying him the remainder of the way.

The moment he stopped before Helia, unlike days prior, she did not retreat. This time, she tipped her head back and continued to boldly meet his stare.

He dusted a palm along the curve of her cheek, the same cheek he'd washed the sweat from, now like cool satin under his palm.

The lady's eyes fluttered.

Wingrave fought himself; he battled a jeering voice that told him to yank his hand away—and lost.

Wingrave swallowed, his throat working spasmodically. "What manner of enchantress are you, Helia?" he demanded on an angry whisper.

"I'm nah enchantress," she returned, her voice having given way to more of that delicate brogue.

Her lush mouth beckoned; her lips invited a man to explore them.

His fingers curled reflexively upon her cheek, and he made himself gentle his touch.

Nay, not any man. He'd sooner kill a bounder who dared to avail himself of that treasure before Wingrave. After he'd claimed Helia as his own, he wouldn't care. But not until he himself plundered them. And after he'd kissed her, he could purge her from his blood.

He palmed her cheek.

Helia trustingly turned herself into his touch; her endlessly long auburn lashes fluttered.

Such guilelessness, he'd never before known. Maybe that accounted for his inexplicable fascination with this woman who'd invaded his household.

"If you were wise, you'd run now, little kitten," he taunted in a bid to resurrect the previous fortress he'd made himself into.

Go. Leave. Flee. Run.

Though his muddled mind sought to sort out to whom he gave those silent orders. Himself . . . or her?

A thread of fear and a greater husk of desire lent a warble to the lady's voice. "Wh-why?"

Both her responses pleased Wingrave and pleased him mightily.

Wingrave curled his lips into a cold, hard grin. "Because if you don't, little kitten, I'm going to kiss you."

Chapter 12

Tremblingly alive to a sense of delight, and unchilled by disappointment, the young heart welcomes every feeling, not simply painful, with a romantic expectation that it will expand into bliss.

—*Ann Radcliffe, A Sicilian Romance*

Because if you don't, little kitten, I'm going to kiss you . . .

Helia's heart, it pounded.

When Helia was a wee lass, her ma had told her the tale of Little Red Riding Hood, who befriended a wolf. In her trustingness, a deceived Red had allowed him to lead her into the bed, where he'd eaten her whole.

And in this instant, she understood all too well: How Red's judgment had proven so weak. How that unsuspecting, trusting girl had found herself confronting the grisly fate she had. And that inexplicable draw possessed by the wolf, which had left the hapless Red unable to pluck herself from the danger awaiting her.

Go, leave, flee, run, a voice in Helia's mind screamed. This place she'd run to in search of sanctuary couldn't possibly offer safety, when this man posed a peril of his own.

Not because she truly thought Wingrave might do her actual harm. Nay, it was because she feared the overwhelming feelings he wrought— ones she'd never experienced and ones she didn't understand.

For Helia prided herself on being rational, certainly not the sort of ninny who'd carry a tendre or, for that matter, feel *anything* for a man who at every turn sought to unsettle and scare her.

So how to explain any of this?

That scornful grin on his lips deepened . . . as if he'd sensed her inner turmoil and relished in that disquietude.

"You look about ready to faint, sweetheart."

His breath bore the sweet hint of vanilla and mint, like he'd been sucking upon a peppermint candy stick. That innocent aroma had a dizzying effect; it clouded her senses and left her with a shameful yearning to know his kiss and taste of him.

Lord help her.

"I'm n-not the fainting sort," she rejoined, wishing her voice had been as steady and unaffected as his own.

With a ponderous slowness that both allowed her and dared her to pull away, Wingrave—nay, Anthony—reached out the same hand that had stroked her cheek moments ago and cupped Helia, this time by the jaw.

His gently unbreakable grip bore an unexpected tenderness.

"You haven't run, little kitten," he said in silken tones that bore an underlining of steel and mockery.

His dark-blue eyes slipped to her mouth. "Dare I take that to mean you *want* my kiss this time?"

Her belly quickened.

I do. She did. She'd wanted it before, when the storm had raged, but she'd been too afraid of this pull he had over her.

Belatedly, Helia compressed her lips, in a bid to hide their tremble.

The glitter in his shrewd eyes silently mocked her for thinking she might have any secrets from him. He stroked the pad of his right thumb along her bottom lip.

It was just a touch. She'd absently rubbed her mouth any number of times, not even giving it so much as a passing consideration. And yet, his amazingly sure, bold caress choked out logic and chased away all thoughts. Helia found herself hypnotized by that back-and-forth glide of his finger across her lip.

Her lashes fluttered, bringing his coolly knowing visage in and out of focus.

"I will take your lack of denial and that hungry little way you're biting at that flesh as an 'aye,' Helia," he murmured.

Helia.

She drew in a shaky, breathless inhalation. There it was again, her Christian name uttered upon his beautifully hard lips. The sound of those three syllables huskily spoken was like a wonderfully warm caress.

And still, he did not kiss her. He did not ravage her lips, or take them in a punishing possession that robbed her of choice and put his own desires to the forefront.

"Nothing to say?" he taunted. "Do you intend to flee again, so I can't take your body and mouth the way I wish?"

His words liquefied her, and surely she should possess horror that she responded to him so, but strangely, she didn't. Existing in its stead, however, was a thrill born from the lamentations about her reputation.

Helia lifted her gaze to his and held his stare. "You can't take what I freely give, Anth—"

With a savage growl, Wingrave brought his mouth down hard on hers.

Nay, *Anthony.*

And this, her first kiss, was not the tender, gentle meeting she'd always thought she would know. Rather, there was a primal rawness to Anthony's claim.

He slanted his lips over hers again and again, plundering, punishing. Her? Or himself, for wanting her?

She rather suspected it was both.

He caught her wrists in one of his larger, powerful hands, and stretched them high above her head. Using them as if to steer her, he guided her so her back collided with the wall, so that his punishing grip and muscle-hewn frame kept her upright.

"Like that, do you, sweetheart?" he purred between each kiss.

Words failed, and she could offer him nothing more than a whimper in return.

A pleased-sounding, triumph-filled, husky laugh rumbled in his chest.

"Let me in," he demanded, and she did as he bade, knowing intuitively what he sought.

She parted her lips.

"Very nice, kitten," he praised. With his spare hand, he caressed his palm hard over her hip, then swept his tongue inside; that silken, hot flesh lashed against Helia's like a brand.

He kissed her like he wanted to possess her, and she ached to belong to him, in this way.

In this way, or in other ways, too . . . a voice at the back of her mind murmured, sounding that alarm.

Helia thrust that uneasy and unwelcome reminder aside and gave herself fully over to his embrace.

His tongue danced around hers in a fiery pirouette that left her dizzy and struggling to keep up.

She touched the tip of hers to his, experimentally at first. Enlivened as she'd never been, Helia grew bolder in her movements.

Anthony's chest rumbled, and Helia swallowed that primitive growl of approval and sagged under the power of it.

He kept her anchored between his strong body; the hard, punishing wall at her back; and his even harder erection at her belly. Anthony moved his hips in a circular motion so she could feel all of him. His rod, thick and long and rigid, prodded her belly.

For—before now—Helia may have been untouched, unkissed, and innocent in every way, but she'd grown up around livestock. She knew the act that occurred between the mounts and dogs they bred, all in the name of breeding, was no different from what transpired between a husband and wife.

She'd been wrong. So very wrong.

For this? This sinful but beautiful act wrought pleasure and a need that had nothing to do with babes and everything to do with the feelings this embrace stirred inside Helia.

Anthony drew her lower lip into his mouth and suckled that flesh.

She dropped her head back on a low, agonized moan.

A restless ache settled between her legs.

He tossed his head back in masculine delight, then filled his hands with her breasts. "You love that, don't you, my pet? You like when I palm your breasts?"

He nipped lightly at her lip. "Or is it my violent kiss?"

She lifted her hips against his.

Anthony stilled his ministrations; he hovered his mouth over the spot right where her pulse pounded. "Or," he dangled, sin and temptation incarnate, "do you like when I rub myself over you?"

His words were naughty, his tone somehow a jeer and a silky caress all at the same time.

All of it, she silently screamed.

She loved it all. She wanted all the things he did and spoke of . . . and more. Whatever *more* was.

Suddenly, Anthony stopped.

Helia cried out; her breasts heaved from the force of the breaths she drew; her respirations came in fast spurts.

In a bid to ease that hot pressure, of their own volition, her hips began to move against Anthony.

He chuckled. "Uh-uh." Anthony drew himself back so that she was denied the feel of his body against hers.

Helia whimpered.

"Tell me what you like, kitten," he demanded with a harshness that should have scared her but only sent a further wave of white-hot heat to Helia's core. "Which one of those?"

"All of them," she cried out. Her desperation-tinged voice rang around the room and pealed from the rafters. "I want you to do them all to me."

"All you had to do was say it, Helia."

With that, Anthony gave her everything she sought. Simultaneously, he devoured her mouth, toyed with the swollen peaks of her breasts, and rubbed his erection over the flat of her stomach. Until it was too much.

She shifted and swayed and stretched.

Helia didn't know exactly what it was she sought; she knew only that this man was the one to help free her of this sharp yearning.

"Please," she begged between each meeting of their mouths.

Wordlessly, Anthony yanked her silk skirts up about her waist in a noisy rustle.

The cool air slapped at her exposed limbs, in a welcome balm.

That relief proved all too short lived.

Anthony pressed a hand between her legs, and she cried out from the surprise and deliciousness of that forbidden caress. He cupped her in that most special of places, which she touched only—and only quickly—during her baths.

Never, however, had her touch felt like *this*.

Suddenly, Anthony slipped a finger through the curls shielding her womanhood.

Helia whimpered.

She shouldn't do this. She shouldn't want this. Her body, however, cared nothing about what it should not do, and only about what it wanted.

She wanted whatever wicked, wonderful gift he promised.

Anthony continued to stroke her, moving that long, powerful digit in and then out of her channel. The slow, deliberate glide coaxed a pleasure so deep it crossed over to pain.

Panting, she lifted her hips, in search of some surcease from the unrelenting, urgent ache.

Anthony's breath came quick and hard, as if he, too, were somehow a beneficiary of the gift he now conferred.

"Please," she implored, unsure what she begged for, knowing only this man could show her.

Anthony took her mouth in another forceful, possessive kiss that only further deepened the persistent ache between her legs.

Helia angled her head to better receive him. She matched each lash of his tongue, swirling hers around and against his.

He groaned. "You learn quick, love."

That praise should rouse shame. Except . . .

Love . . .

Uttered in the heat of the moment, that endearment certainly didn't mean what she wished it would, but Helia sighed anyway.

Anthony added another finger and stroked her channel harder, faster.

Perspiration beaded at her brow. Helia found herself soaring toward some peak. Higher and higher Anthony took her, on a seemingly ceaseless climb. She bit her lip hard.

Close. I am so close . . .

To what?

And then . . .

Helia's body tensed as she approached some invisible but gloriously brilliant peak.

"Come for me, Helia," Anthony demanded; that rough command sent Helia tumbling over that precipice.

Yes! Yes! She'd follow wherever he led.

She wept his name and screamed, incoherent, desperate cries. All the while, she pressed herself against Anthony's fingers, still buried in her channel until her body was replete with every last bit of pleasure he'd wrung from her.

Helia's legs went limp.

Anthony swiftly caught her about the waist with an arm. His other remained firmly tucked between her legs, until she shivered and trembled in that place he'd touched.

Ever so slowly, Anthony withdrew his fingers. The shine of her fluid on those long digits gleamed in the sunlight.

Alternately shy and embarrassed, Helia buried her cheek against his shoulder and just remained that way, soothed and comforted by the feel of his arms about her.

With an aching tenderness, Anthony stroked his hand in a smooth, soothing circle over the small of her back. "Enjoy yourself, kitten?"

She gave a small nod against him.

Ever so gently, Anthony caught her chin in a delicate grip and angled her head up so their gazes met. "There's nothing to be ashamed of, Helia," he murmured.

Helia. There it was again. Somehow his saying her given name moved them to a deeper plane of intimacy. This man, who a short time ago had been a stranger. And yet, how quickly everything had changed. Reluctant friend though he may be, the care Mrs. Trowbridge said he'd shown Helia revealed a warmth he fought desperately to hide.

Helia examined the man who'd been her unlikely nursemaid and savior. Aye, she expected he did rouse terror in the breasts of most. She'd been no different.

In a short time, however, though gruff and nasty, he'd proven himself good-hearted.

Anthony had shown a crack in the mask he wore, and in so doing, he'd revealed glimpses of the man he truly was underneath his hard exterior.

I want to know everything about him.

She moved her eyes over the harsh planes of his gloriously chiseled face. He was nothing like the man she'd dreamed of for herself. That man would have been always affable, romantic, and uncomplicated. Anthony . . . he was none of those things, and yet he'd bespelled her.

That organ in her breast which had previously found a normal tempo resumed a dangerously erratic beat.

God help Helia. If she were not careful, she could find herself losing her heart to the last man who wanted it.

Chapter 13

For those, who were charmed by her loveliness, spoke with enthusiasm of her talents; and others, who admired her playful imagination, declared, that her personal graces were unrivalled.

—*Ann Radcliffe, The Mysteries of Udolpho*

Helia stared up at Wingrave with a dewy-eyed gaze that bore a tenderness no one had ever before directed upon him, and for good reason—he was the *last* person who either wanted or deserved such warmth.

He had never been in love, nor would he ever give himself over to that puling emotion.

For that matter, he didn't even believe in its existence.

But with Helia still in his arms, and with that look in her expressive green eyes, he saw it plainly.

His mouth went dry. His heart thumped in a sickening beat against his ribs.

He didn't want her falling in love with him. He didn't need it. He wanted only to go back to living his uncomplicated, solitary life without a worry for another person's well-being and safety and—

It was too much.

This situation with Helia . . . it had become untenable. He'd allowed her to share his residence, and in return, she'd also made him share himself with her. It'd been a mistake. *All* of this.

"I am not a kind man," he said sharply.

"I disagree, Anthony."

She wielded his name like a mawkish endearment.

"I am a man of logic and reason," he continued as if she'd never spoken, wishing she hadn't.

Wingrave's words were a reminder for himself.

He hardened his already rock-hard heart and armed himself with the remembrance of his discovery before she'd swept into the duke's office like she was a thousand rays of sunshine and warmth.

"I'll not be taken with you, Helia Wallace," he said grimly.

Confusion filled her guileless eyes. "I-I didn't believe you w-would be."

He took her lightly by the shoulders. "I am a man who takes what he wants." *And yet, I hunger for her and didn't slake my lust.*

"That may be," she said softly, unnervingly reading his thoughts and sending his panic spiraling, "but you didn't take pleasure for yourself, and only gave me . . ." Her cheeks went warm, and she remained unable to finish the rest of that thought.

"I decided I didn't want you," he lied through his cold, hard mouth. Wingrave ached for her still.

He may as well have slapped Helia for the hurt that fell across her features.

I will not let that forlorn little look bother me. I will not. Wingrave steeled himself against the signs of suffering he'd himself inflicted.

Helia moved her gaze over his face. "You're trying to scare me," she whispered. "You're trying to convince me you're an awful man."

Did she speak those words to Wingrave? Or herself? He'd venture it was for the both of them.

He steeled his features, determined to disabuse her of all the illusions she'd erroneously developed about him. "I don't *try* to scare people. I *do* frighten them."

Helia rested her palm against his right cheek and, through her touch, conferred an embarrassingly welcome warmth. "I'm not afraid of you," she insisted.

A short, scornful laugh left his stern lips.

"I'm not," she insisted. "Though I suspect you've gone out of your way to do so, Anthony."

He yanked his cheek from her hand, and silently regretted the loss of her delicate, butterfly-soft caress; all the while he hated himself for that weakness.

"Do not!" he growled. "Do not call me that."

"What?" She merely moved her palms to the lapels of his jacket and smoothed her hands over them. Under her touch, his heart beat frantic and fast. "By your name?"

He glared at her.

Helia continued to pass that probing, searching stare over Wingrave, and he'd never felt more exposed and vulnerable.

"What has your life been, Anthony, that prevents you from sharing that still intimate, but most basic part of yourself? How very lonely. How very sad."

His entire body recoiled. She *pitied* him.

"You cared for me when I was ill," Helia said again.

"Would you stop saying that?" he barked. "I only did so because I did not want you dying in my household."

"You could have allowed someone else to care for me," she said softly, persistent as a dog with a bone. "But you didn't. I *know* it was you who sat by my side."

Fury sent his nostrils flaring. "My servants do not have loose lips. The ones that do, I sack—"

"Oh, hush." She pinched him, and that press of her thumb and forefinger on his arm knocked him off-balance.

Wingrave stared incredulously. "Did you . . . just pinch me, madam?"

"That is what we common people call it." Then, her lips, still swollen from his kiss, tipped up at their corners.

He sharpened his gaze on her mouth.

Unbidden, his mind and body recalled at once the sweet taste of her: apple blossoms and peach, a sweet combination which had made for an unexpected aphrodisiac. Just the memory of that kiss sent another wave of lust through him.

Under Wingrave's scrutiny, Helia's innocent smile remained unwavering.

For a woman who'd just come long and hard in his arms, she remained remarkably wholesome.

How, with the ire and wrath he'd turned on the minx following that very thorough climax he'd coaxed her to, did she still wear that wide, sunny, and *disarming* grin?

"I know what you're thinking, Anthony," she said with a lightness paradoxical to the turbulent nature of his own thoughts and feelings.

She had absolutely no idea the lustful thoughts centered on her. If she did, she'd flee—and fast.

"You're thinking you don't tolerate servants with loose lips or allow people to put their hands on you," she said, completely off the mark, as he'd predicted.

Her lips took a mischievous tilt, revealing a pair of adorable dimples. "Especially as you're a future duke. But I know you will not sack your servants."

Wingrave folded his arms. "And just how did you arrive at that conclusion, Helia?" This he had to hear.

"Because you care about them."

He laughed, and damned if that wasn't a real explosion of mirth.

"Just as they care about you," Helia said, undeviating from her course. "They *do*. They wouldn't speak so highly of you if you were, in fact, cruel and heartless."

God, had he ever been that innocent?

His laughter faded. "You're an unworldly thing if you believe *that* drivel you now speak."

"So what if I am unworldly?" she challenged. "I'd rather be unworldly and optimistic than so jaded by the world that I can't see there are people who care about me."

Why must she persist in seeing things that were not there? To make herself feel better. That was the only reason for her gullibility where Wingrave was concerned.

"I am heartless," he gritted out.

Helia shook her head. "I don't believe—"

Anthony took her by the hips and dragged her closer, pulling a gasp from her.

Her chest heaved, with a modicum of fear . . . and desire.

Good. Both of those emotions were safe. He knew how to handle those sentiments.

Burned by the feel of her, Wingrave released her swiftly and flexed his fingers to forget the feel of Helia Wallace.

"You think I *care* about you," he said flatly. "Why? Because I had my hand up your skirts and your hot quim in my hand?"

Helia flinched. Her perpetually rosy cheeks went ashen.

Until now, Wingrave had never given thought to the words he'd spoken after they left his lips. In this instant, for the first time in the whole of his miserable life, he found himself filled with a profound . . . regret.

He'd let her too close.

"Why are you saying these things, Anthony?" she whispered, edging away from him.

Good, let her go. That was precisely what he wished for. What accounted then for this disconsolation?

Her. Besieged by a wave of self-loathing for having become spellbound by the woman before him, he ran an angry stare over her. She was the root of all these new, unfamiliar, and more, *unwanted* feelings.

"Why am I speaking the truth?" he asked, deliberately dispassionate.

Needing some space and distance between them, Wingrave headed over to his father's desk. All along that deliberate, measured march, he felt her gaze on his back like a physical touch that followed his every moment.

Only after he'd settled himself back into the duke's throne-like chair did he speak.

"The thing about you, Helia Mairi Wallace, with your cheery outlook, despite the supposed death of your parents and a villainous cousin on your trail, and your always smiling face, is that in your naivete, you see good where it doesn't exist. You expect there will be someone there to help and that things will get better. But they won't. Do you know why?" he asked detachedly. "Because the world is a shite place, full of shite things and shite people, Helia. People that lie."

Wingrave placed his hands upon the last folders he'd searched through and leaned forward. "Just as you've done, Miss *Wallace.*" Ultimately, all people lived to serve themselves—even lying about having connections to a family she'd never before met.

The sadness in Helia's eyes gave way to confusion. She shook her head and ventured over. "I don't—"

"Understand?"

Wingrave waited until she'd reached him. "Let me speak more plainly, shall I? I've searched every corner of the duke's office." He spread his arms wide over the piles and piles of papers before him. "Each and every single file, paper, parchment, envelope, journal—anything and everything."

Helia followed his gesture to those stacks.

"Do you know what I discovered, Helia?" he asked, coming slowly to his feet.

She shook her head dumbly.

"As I'd expected, you don't have any connection to this family."

He may as well have delivered a mundane remark about the unseasonably cold winter London enjoyed.

"What?" she whispered.

He nodded. "Not a mention."

"But—"

"The only mention of anything remotely Scottish pertains to the lands my family holds there and—" He stopped abruptly.

Helia stared at him, silently urging him to continue. "And?" she prodded, as if holding out hope that he'd uncovered something linking them and their families.

And in a small part of him, buried deep inside, in a place he'd never before known existed, he admitted . . . he had, too. It would've meant she had grounds to stay and—

"Those matters, Miss Wallace, do not involve you or your family in any way, but rather another family of Scottish descent."

"Oh, God," she whispered. Helia faltered.

Cursing, Wingrave reflexively stood and rushed around to catch her but caught himself at the edge of the desk.

Of course, the spirited Scottish beauty righted herself, no help from Wingrave necessary.

He curled his fingers into tight, hard fists.

"*That's* what this was about." She looked at him with distraught eyes. "*I'm going to be ill.*"

The anger went out of him, replaced by the same panicky dread that dodged him at the mention of anyone being sickly.

Nay, not "anyone." *Her.* For some reason, this cheer-filled sprite elicited a numbing fear he'd never before felt on account of anyone.

A healthy color returned to her cheeks. Nay, the red filling her face was an angry flush.

Steadied by that reminder and realization, Wingrave found himself breathing more easily.

Helia tipped her chin at a gumptious little angle. "You were testing to see if I would make you a suitable mistress," she whispered, her voice cracking with despair.

He started. That was the conclusion she'd come to? But then, why shouldn't she? He'd availed himself of her mouth and the feel of her body and then, after all that, lied through his teeth and told her he didn't want her.

Good, it was better this way. She'd be gone soon. Tomorrow. Maybe the next day. When she was fully recovered, as he'd not have her death on his conscience.

And Wingrave, to whom antipathy had always come so easily, now found himself presenting only a facade of that emotion.

He flicked a mocking gaze over her diminutive frame. "I'm not a man to take an innocent woman as my lover."

She searched his face. "Are you saying . . . ?"

Wingrave looked at her, silently encouraging her to complete whatever inane idea had popped into her head this time.

As shy as she'd grown after climaxing in his arms, Helia bowed her head a tiny fraction. "You are not saying . . . You are not thinking . . ."

He continued to follow along as she fumbled about.

"You're not . . . offering marria—"

Wingrave balked. "Good God, no!" A short, nervous laugh escaped him.

If blushes could burn, the lady would have set a fire to rival the hottest, brightest Guy Fawkes bonfire.

"My mother was many things," she said, her voice unwavering. "Good, honorable, resilient, fearless. Funny. Loving. But she, my lord, was no liar. Every woman has her secrets. I trust, given the man you've described the duke to be, the duchess carries secrets of her own." Helia ran her steady palms over the front of her skirts, rumpled from their embrace. She inclined her head. "I thank you for your generosity and the kindness you and your staff extended me, my lord."

Finally. "My lord" and not "Anthony."

Weird, how hollow a victory that proved to be.

"I will be sure to have my belongings packed."

His heart hammered.

Wingrave jumped to his feet. "You are not well enough to leave," he said gruffly. "You may remain for your convalescence."

Indecision glimmered in her revealing eyes.

The lady warred with herself. Even having known her a short while, he'd discovered her to be as proud as headstrong.

"I . . . thank you, my lord," she said, and once again, perverse bastard that he was, Wingrave found himself missing the sound of his given name on her lips. "I will not overstay my welcome."

He released a breath he'd not even realized he'd been holding.

That relief proved short-lived.

His thoughts raced. What would she do? Where would she go? She'd already maintained she'd no one, aside from, supposedly, a gothic-novel-inspired cousin . . . who, given she'd already told one lie, might very well be another. But . . . there had to be some truth to her being a young, innocent lady on her own.

Helia dipped a curtsy and let herself from the office; she closed the ornate oak panel behind her with the faintest click.

Meowww.

Blankly, Wingrave looked down at Black Bothersome Cat, who'd sneaked himself back inside the office.

The beastie stared up with angry, accusatory eyes, and damned if Wingrave didn't find himself deserving of that feline censure.

Chapter 14

How suddenly one comes to be happy, just when one is
beginning to think one never is to be happy again!

—*Ann Radcliffe, The Italian*

A short while later, along the tideway of the River Thames, the world
lay before Helia, a veritable winter wonderland of snowdrifts and ice
amidst which had sprung a makeshift carnival of merchants and frol-
ickers of all ages.

The frozen waterway found itself a temporary home to peddler
tents; they sat in the distance, a collection of symmetrical forms and
vibrant colors.

From within those booths rose the boisterous voices of peddlers
hawking their wares. The din of that bustling activity melded with the
rollicking laughter of the merrymakers.

For all the joy the Frost Fair had brought to London, Helia moved
along the edge of that revelry, like a lost soul who'd been forced to dwell
amongst the lucky living.

Though there felt nothing fortunate in this anguish sluicing away
at her insides.

Since the moment she'd availed herself of the marquess's carriage
and servants and set out across London to put distance between her
and the man who'd broken her heart, the memory of each cruel word

he'd uttered had played over and over again, like a lash upon her heart and mind.

You think I care about you. Why? Because I had my hand up your skirts and your hot quim in my hand?

Helia quickened her stride, all the while wishing she could outrun each hated utterance that had crossed his lips. The memory of his hateful declaration, combined with the pace she'd set, caused her breath to come in harsh, uneven spurts. They slipped from her lips and left little clouds of white upon the frigid air.

She willed the echo of his voice to cease repeating in her mind—to no avail.

The thing about you, Helia Mairi Wallace, with your cheery outlook, despite the supposed death of your parents and a villainous cousin on your trail, and your always smiling face, is that in your naivete, you see good where it doesn't exist. You expect there will be someone there to help and that things will get better. But they won't.

Helia caught her lower lip between her teeth and bit down hard. Since the loss of her parents, hope had sustained her—hope that there was, in fact, safety, security, and happiness awaiting her. That charity all hinged upon just one woman and her family.

What she'd not anticipated was meeting the duchess's enigmatic and clearly hurting son, Anthony. She'd not anticipated being drawn to a man so cynical and angry and with a thousand fortresses built about him.

You deluded yourself into seeing parts of him that aren't really there. You let yourself believe he cared. And why? Because he gave you shelter from the storm? Because he sat beside you through your illness . . .

Only . . .

Aye. That'd been precisely what she'd thought.

Helia abruptly stopped on a slight rise overlooking the festivities. As the cold winter wind whipped her cloak about her legs, Helia ran a vacant gaze over the fair that existed as a blur down below.

Gentlemen didn't tend to sick young ladies. But Anthony *had*.

Surely those glimpses she'd caught of him were real and—

The world is a shite place, full of shite things and shite people, Helia. People that lie. Just as you've done, Miss Wallace.

Helia yearned to clamp her hands over her ears to drown out the remembered viciousness of his charges and tone.

She blinked slowly, and at once the world came rushing back in an explosion of beautiful sound and color.

What is wrong with me? Melancholy? Woolgathering? That wasn't who she was.

He was trying to scare me. To hurt me. She knew that. He had done so in a bid to avoid presenting himself as vulnerable in any way.

That didn't mean Anthony's caustic words didn't remain like well-placed arrows stuck in her breast, but it also didn't mean she should let her misery drown out the beauty of the day.

Forcing aside her hurtful exchange with Anthony, Helia drew her shoulders back.

After losing her parents, it had been all too easy to see the awful: the sorrow. Uncertainty. Mr. Draxton and his intentions for her.

Aye, her heart would never stop hurting over her ma and da being gone, but since their passing, she'd lost her way. She'd been raised to look for the good. And for all the ways in which life had become harder than it'd ever been, there also remained a whole host of things she had to be grateful for.

In the heart of a storm and illness, she'd been afforded a warm bed, roof, and food. She'd nearly perished but been nursed back to health by the marquess. And even after Anthony uncovered nothing linking their mothers, and believed Helia to be a liar, he'd still promised she could remain until she was fully recovered.

The rousing thrill of joy and excitement that hung over the Frost Fair made it impossible for Helia to feel anything but a boundlessly potent energy that hummed in her veins.

The previously inauspicious chill that had overtaken her on that rise now harkened Helia all the way back to the harsh but gloriously brilliant

Scottish winters. Those heartiest and most loving remembrances of her homeland filled Helia anew with a fresh wave of gladness.

As she'd done as a girl frolicking in the snow with her father, Helia raised an imaginary pipe to her lips and exhaled little puffs of white clouds to the skies above.

While she walked, Helia breathed deep of the pleasing aromas of roasted venison, roasted ox, and the sweeter scents of gingerbread and chestnuts wafting through the air.

As she meandered amongst those crimson, sapphire, canary-yellow, and emerald-green tents upon the frozen Thames, the happy whine of fiddles and violins and throngs of carolers singing along the shore grew louder.

Helia made her way over to a young merchant.

A bright blue, red, and green canvas was draped over the top of the peddler's big wood wagon, offering a splash of radiance amidst the grey that had reclaimed the London sky.

From the hooks along the perimeter of his rectangular cart hung a vast array of objects: silver spoons, handkerchiefs, ribbons which danced in the wind.

When she reached the cart, Helia trailed alongside the clever shelves built alongside the wagon and perused the various items brimming from within.

She skimmed her hand over books, toys, and trinkets—and then stopped as her gaze fell upon a brown, red, and green painted wood ornament of a rowan branch.

Helia gently picked up the crude carving. As she fingered the trinket, the snowy garden exchange between her and Anthony whispered around her mind.

"The lore has it that in doing so, any bad feelings of mistrust between friends will be cleared away."

"For . . . me?"

Helia nodded. "For you."

"I've never received a gift," Anthony said gruffly.

"Surely you've received something, through the years?"

Only, he hadn't.

In one uncharacteristically candid moment, he'd opened up about himself. He, a future duke, and in his own right a powerful marquess, had never received something as simple as a present.

And all because his stonyhearted father forbade the giving of gifts.

An unfamiliar but black, unalterable hatred for the duke she'd not met—and now, never would—singed her veins.

Was it any wonder that Anthony, who'd had such an austere upbringing, became a man so harsh and so hard?

For all the uncertainty and peril she now found herself in, Helia still wouldn't have traded so much as a single day with her parents for the wealth, power, and holdings enjoyed by Anthony's family.

He, however, hadn't a choice in the life he'd been born to.

Absently, she ran a gloved fingertip over the red-painted berry.

Who would you be if your life had been different, Anthony?

But she knew. Gruff though he may be, without a doubt, Helia knew from the care he'd shown her that—

"You've visited the finest wagons, you have."

Helia looked up quickly.

The peddler, who had the dark good looks and olive coloring of a Rom, had since finished with his previous customers and joined Helia.

At her silence, he flashed a wicked, lopsided grin.

Coming back to the present, Helia returned his smile. "Hullo, sir."

Both corners of his lips quirked up and he raised a wood decanter. "Can I persuade you to try a dram?" he asked. A heavy West Country–sounding accent laced his speech.

As a Scot out of place in the heart of England, Helia immediately felt a kindred connection to the handsome Romani. "I dinnae require any persuading. I'd been harkening this way with your rum in mind," she said, before remembering she still held one of his trinkets.

She held the wood ornament up. "Och, and glad I am for it as ah found this beautiful piece, too."

After a short negotiation, Helia turned over five shillings and placed the rowan branch in her cloak pocket.

At that generosity, the young man bowed his head. "It is God who brought you." With a slow, flirtatious wink, he handed over her drink and pocketed his coins.

"Mulțumesc," she murmured.

Those beautiful cobalt-blue eyes flared with his surprise.

"My fowk employed a Rom traveler," she explained, and then took a sip of the smooth, fruity drink.

Welcoming the immediate warming effect of those spirits, Helia lifted her tankard. "Kushti—good," she praised.

The merchant opened his mouth to speak, but another patron came over, and his interest and attention in Helia instantly vanished as he returned to making his coin.

Helia took a step and made to drink from her glass when, suddenly, another forbidding breeze stirred the air around her.

Her skirts snapped angrily about her ankles. With her spare hand, Helia futilely slapped them down.

Her nape tingled and pricked.

Helia glanced frantically over the bustling fair. The frozen Thames brimmed with revelers of all ages. Men and women, lords and ladies, and children, they all mingled in a blur of humanity.

Just then, a black cat darted across her path and Helia gasped; her heart pounded painfully in her chest.

That omen of ill fortune kept Helia frozen to her spot on the ice. Gooseflesh popped up on her arms.

"Good luck, they are." That deep, accented voice snapped across her fearful musings.

Dazed, Helia looked at the handsome Rom presently serving a new customer. "Ah'm sorry?"

"The black cat," he clarified as he poured another tankard.

She mustered a weak grin. "It . . . The Scots have a different view of the cat."

"But what do *you* think, inima?"

Helia finished off her dram. "I have a black cat," she said, and handed him back his glass.

He laughed. "There you are, then." He flashed another one of those winks that would have devastated any other lady.

Somehow, Helia could see only the Marquess of Wingrave in her mind. What was it about a cynical, hardened Anthony that so captivated her while she remained unmoved by the charming, flirtatious attentions of a handsome, smiling man?

As she parted ways with the peddler, another strange, tingling sensation took hold. She did a sweep of her surroundings.

Excited energy thrummed amongst the throngs of revelers. A small cluster of dapperly dressed gentlemen each held drinks of their own. The lofty lords chatted and laughed uproariously. Bright-eyed, giggling children dashed and darted around the slower-moving adults.

"You are being ridiculous," she muttered. Even knowing as much, when Helia resumed walking, she did so at a quickened pace.

Excited screams and trilling laughter filled the frozen fairgrounds.

Helia paused when she reached the portion of the frozen water where wild-looking sled races took place. How many times had her father pushed her in that way so that she'd soared and sailed so fast over Loch Morar, she'd felt a breath away from taking flight?

"Care for a roide, missus?"

Looking down at the tiny owner of that coarse Cockney, Helia smiled. The young boy couldn't have been more than eight or nine.

She paid her fare, and soon she was squealing wildly as two young boys shoved each sled.

She went racing across the Thames, past the twirling skaters and the games of ninepins that'd broken out upon the ice.

Laughing, Helia held tight to the makeshift bar the boy had fashioned onto the sled.

The dizzying speed with which Helia sailed over the frozen river sent her hood whipping back; her curls tumbled over her shoulders. That same frigid air slapped at her face and stole her breath.

Over and over she went.

Time melted away.

All her troubles and worries faded along with it.

The gap-toothed, freckled boys gave Helia a final push, one that went cockeyed and sent them diverging in an uneven line.

As the world sped past, she closed her eyes tight, tipped her head back, and freed herself fully to the joy.

Until, too soon, the speed of her sled gradually slowed, then suddenly came to an unexpected jolting stop.

That abrupt finish brought her eyes flying open . . . and she froze.

A gentleman in a costly deep-blue, fur-lined cloak and a chimney-style, black top hat stood with a black riding boot propped on the edge of her sleigh.

Her stomach churned and fear exploded in her breast, a crippling terror that kept her paralyzed.

"Dearest Helia," Mr. Draxton murmured in smooth, silky tones too hard to ever truly be warm. "My goodness, you've given me quite the chase."

Chapter 15

He loved the soothing hour, when the last tints of light die away; when the stars, one by one, tremble through æther, and are reflected on the dark mirror of the waters; that hour, which, of all others, inspires the mind with pensive tenderness, and often elevates it to sublime contemplation.

—*Ann Radcliffe, The Mysteries of Udolpho*

Hours after he'd searched the duke's office, Wingrave remained seated upon his pompous sire's imperial chair.

He had long since returned the old duke's official records and correspondences to their respective places within the always tidy desk.

Wingrave stared off into nothing and drummed his fingertips along the mahogany arms of his current seat.

Nay, not nothing.

His gaze remained locked on the wall where he'd pinned Helia and coaxed her body to surrender.

Both her embrace and shyness had proven—as if there'd ever been a doubt—the lady was as pure as the snow covering the gardens below.

And what had he done after she'd come undone in his arms? He'd uttered vile, unconscionable things.

Wingrave's gut clenched. The memory of Helia's wounded expression twisted a knife in his chest. The memory of the hurt bleeding from her expressive green eyes would haunt him until he drew his last miserable breath.

Since she'd left the duke's office, Wingrave had found himself confronting the staggering, sobering, and very unwelcome realization that he felt . . . *shame.*

Him!

Wingrave gave his head a firm shake. *Shame. Regret.*

"What is next, Wingrave?" he snarled. His lips curled in a disgusted sneer. *"Love?"*

The moon would sooner fall and the stars rain down upon a darkened earth before *that* happened. Which was not only for the best, but very welcome.

Nay, he'd never love anyone or anything, but Wingrave apparently possessed the ability to know shame. And after everything he'd said to Helia, he found himself drowning in heaps of it.

He scrubbed a hand over his face. This *feeling* of any emotion was deuced unpleasant business.

"Mad," he muttered into the ring of silence when he'd dropped his palms back to the armrests. "I'm going mad."

As if that truth were in doubt, since cheer-filled Helia Wallace's arrival, Wingrave had begun talking to himself.

Bound for Bedlam, he was.

As he'd told himself many times before, the sooner she went, the better off he'd be. Except, that merely served to remind Wingrave of the lady's circumstances.

She'd be all alone.

Furthermore, what did he really know about her *circumstances?* She'd been disingenuous about her *connection* to the Blofield family. If she'd invented those ties between their mothers, it stood to reason she could be lying about every last thing she'd shared with Wingrave.

He steepled his fingers together, and while he drummed the tips, Wingrave stared distractedly over to that place where he'd forever see her trembling, begging, and climaxing.

Only, the stunned little glimmer in her eyes, the shock stamped on her features, and the indignation at his having called her mother a liar couldn't be feigned.

Which meant . . . what, exactly? It didn't matter there existed no evidence of her family's ties to his own; *Helia* had clearly believed it to be true. That notion had come from . . . *somewhere*.

Certainly, prejudiced as the duke was to anyone and everyone who was not the highest, most respected members of the ton, he wouldn't countenance any association with a Scottish family.

As for Wingrave's mother . . . The duchess may be cut of a different, kinder, softhearted cloth than the duke, but ultimately, she fell in line with whatever her husband demanded. After Wingrave'd become the heir, she'd ceased visiting with and talking to him, and turned him over completely to his miserable bastard of a sire. Recently, she'd been a willing partner in the duke's plans to see him wed Lady Alexandra Bradbury.

No, she'd never be brave enough to form a friendship her husband disapproved of.

I trust, given the man you've described the duke to be, the duchess carries secrets of her own.

Helia's avowal whispered around Wingrave's mind.

He drummed his fingertips together.

Her words were so unlikely as to be anything but impossible. After all, where would his mother even begin to hide such information from her . . . ?

Of their own volition, his fingers ceased their tapping.

Wingrave sat for a long moment and then exploded to his feet.

Without breaking stride, he strode through His Grace's office, yanked the door open, and sailed into the hall.

Wingrave moved with determined, purposeful steps down the length of the wide, crimson-carpeted corridors, and then stopped.

He stared at the door, with its carvings of delicate white roses and pink peonies, a moment and then looked down at the brass princess handle.

Clasping it quick, he let himself inside. The hinges, as well oiled as they'd always been, allowed him a noiseless entry.

He did a sweep of this space he passed often but never entered.

That wasn't true.

A lifetime ago, back when he'd been invisible and useless to the duke, as a younger son and spare to the heir, then as a half-deaf son, Wingrave had visited these rooms and often.

Stepping inside was like stepping back in time. His mother's office remained unchanged.

Unlike the dark, somber selection of wallpapering, curtains, and furnishings which adorned the duke's offices, the duchess's door opened to reveal a summery, fairy-tale setting. A pale-pink-and-white floral Louis XV gilt, upholstered sofa set formed a semicircle near the white stone fireplace, adorned in rose and peony carvings which carried the theme of that flower from the entrance and into the whole of the duchess's office.

The white Italian lace curtains were drawn back to allow the vibrant afternoon light to stream through.

The sun, which continued to wrestle for a place in the stubbornly grey sky that day, chose this very moment to peek out from behind the clouds.

Long, dazzling rays brought a brightness shining down upon the gleaming mahogany desk near the floor-to-ceiling windows that overlooked the gardens below.

In his mind's eye, he saw a younger version of the duchess and himself.

Back then, though, when he'd been a small boy, he'd only ever been *Anthony*.

His mother would pull up a special chair she'd kept just for him and drag it over so he could join her. Wingrave had attended his pretend work, while she'd attended her business.

He'd sat alongside her, drafting made-up battle plans for his future as a commissioned soldier in the King's Army. Both that dream and expectation had died the day Wingrave's hearing in his left ear was lost.

He'd still continued to visit his mother here, but he'd stopped with the imagined work he'd eventually do as a soldier and instead sat next to her and scrawled various verses, sentences, and pictures.

The thing of it was that not once in all those years had Wingrave given thought to what kept his mother busy here.

It wasn't until he had landed the unwanted role of ducal heir and been forced to spend time with the ruthless, heartless, menacing figure who'd sired him that he understood the duchess came here to escape her domineering husband.

At once, he contemplated whether she'd done more here, away from the duke's unforgiving eye.

Compelled forward, Wingrave's gaze remained locked on that desk across the room.

He reached the white-painted, rotating, rattan desk chair and stopped in his tracks.

The matching seat of smaller proportions she'd had commissioned remained tucked in the corner, as it had always been when Wingrave was a boy.

How . . . peculiar. She'd kept that unnecessary furnishing designed with a child's measurements in mind. She'd not only held on to the chair, but it occupied the precise spot it had always occupied.

Some strange feeling came over him, a queerness that suffused his chest.

Taking in a shaky breath, he swiftly averted his gaze, returning it to the duchess's workplace.

This won't take long.

He seated himself and then got on with examining the contents of his mother's desk. Wingrave started at the center drawer and moved around methodically.

He'd always taken the duke as meticulous and tidy in the organization of his records and business. The duchess, however, took that skill to an even more impressive level. Not only were her stacks of notes and correspondences, receipts of transactions, and charity work neatly organized, they'd also been each tied with ribbons of differing colors and properly labeled.

As such, Wingrave flew through his search, and then stopped.

He stared at a small pile of letters aged yellow with time. The top identifying label contained but two names—*Angela* and . . . *Anthony.*

Not Wingrave, as she now only ever referred to him as.

But Anthony, his Christian name that only Helia insisted on using.

Wingrave turned the stack over in his hands. Something in reading through his mother's personal notes about him added a level of wrongness to his futile hunt.

He made to return the one with explicit mention of him and then stopped.

Why shouldn't he be knowledgeable of whatever business his mother discussed about him? Frowning, he tugged an end of the intertwined blue and white ribbons. They fluttered to the immaculate surface of her desk.

Setting aside the rectangular scrap of paper bearing his Christian name, Wingrave reached for the top note addressed to him.

He skimmed his gaze over the handful of sentences written in the duchess's elegant scrawl.

> My dear boy,
> If you are reading this, I trust I'm no longer of this world. I also expect your father will not bother examining the contents of my desk. As such I also expect you and your sister, Angela, are the first to come across these letters.
> I wish to begin by saying the duke has certainly not been the warmest, most amiable, or involved father.

Wingrave snorted. A greater understatement had never been put to page.

I oft said the duke loved you as he was able—even if at times, it may have not seemed to be the case.

A bark of laughter burst from Wingrave, and he gave his head a wry shake. Now this was *too* much.

He discovered himself capable of another emotion—pity. This time, that sentiment was directed at his mother. The duke had been born of stone, with a heart of steel and soul of ice that couldn't have thawed under the hottest summer sun.

He went back to reading.

The fault lay not with your father, but rather the generations of expectations borne by the Talberts before him.

Wingrave gave his head a shake and tossed aside the letter, not needing to read another bit of this postlife drivel where his mother, who'd been absent in his adult years, attempted to play peacemaker between the husband and children she'd left behind.

Frustration surged through him, a restiveness that left his muscles twitching. This was what his search of Helia Wallace had yielded. Absolutely nothing other than the duchess's hopeful wishes for the duke and the children he viewed as helpful chess pieces upon the board of His Grace's existence.

He stilled. That was how it *should* be. Wingrave frowned. He himself understood the expectations which went with the Talbert title, and he took pleasure in fulfilling his role—though not for his sire. God rot the old bastard's festering soul.

No, because in Wingrave's adhering to that order, a ruthless impassivity took puling emotions out of the proverbial equation. That detachedness was what had compelled him to track down his betrothed after she'd gone gallivanting about England with another man. An adherence to duty and title was what kept life ordered and clear.

His frown deepened. He'd gotten away from those tenets which had guided him in his adult years.

Having allowed Helia Mairi Wallace, a captivating stranger, into his household, Wingrave had reverted to the pathetic child he'd once been.

He'd not make that mistake again.

With that renewed resolve, he made a swipe for the pile. In his haste, Wingrave knocked the stack over the side of the desk. Faded ivory, white, and yellowed letters rained down upon the floor.

Cursing, he stood, dropped to his haunches, and proceeded to gather up his mother's belongings.

Once he'd them all tidied and stacked, Wingrave made to rise, and then stopped.

From the corner of his eye, he caught a small, lone scrap—another rectangular label. This one did not contain his or Angela's name, but rather, an unfamiliar one: Mairi.

Haltingly, Wingrave looked at the pile of his mother's correspondences, and he came slowly to his feet.

He sifted through the envelopes. Each bore his mother's name.

Who was Mairi? And why had his mother kept those letters?

Scrunching his brow, Wingrave set the bundle back on the desk, and reached for one.

He unfolded it and skimmed the words written there.

> Oh, Caroline.
>
> I write to you with the most miraculous news. After so much heartbreak, I am about to deliver my precious bairn. I feel him moving and kicking. I have not previously shared my pregnancy in my previous letters as every time I've done so, I then had to write another informing you of another devastation.

Wingrave passed over to the end and the signature at the bottom of a long letter.

Your most loyal and loving friend,
Mairi

His gaze fixed to the joy-filled missive, Wingrave grabbed another, swiftly opened the letter, and read.

My dear friend,
First, you maintained my marriage would be a loyal and loving one. Then, following the eight miscarriages of babes I wanted with all my heart, you promised there'd one day be a babe for me. As always, you proved to be correct once more, when you predicted I carried not a boy and heir but rather, a feisty, strong-willed girl. Oh, Caro, Bruce is overjoyed. He rocks her to sleep each night, and as he does, his eyes glitter with tears and pride. He tells her stories of the great things she'll do and everything he'll teach her.

Wingrave paused in his reading and tried to imagine a world where the Duke of Talbert would have ever been anything but livid and disappointed that, after years of trying and failing to conceive an heir, he'd instead sired a daughter.

There wasn't one. There wasn't such a world. To the duke, daughters were acceptable only following the birth of a required and desired heir and spare, and then, with their only purpose being to expand the power and riches of the Talbert line.

Despite his earlier resolve, it proved nigh impossible to not envy a child so beloved by her parents.

Absently, he skimmed the last sentences.

She is the center of our universe, as radiant as the sun.
We've named her Helia—

Wingrave stumbled. His mind froze. His gaze remained locked on the page.

"Helia *Mairi Wallace*," he said, and shock pulled the name out as a soft exhale.

Miss Helia Mairi Wallace hadn't been lying when she'd claimed a connection—albeit a secret one, unknown to all—to the Blofields.

He reeled under the enormity of that discovery.

All along, she'd been telling the truth, which meant he could absolutely not allow her to set out on her own, and she needed, in fact, to remain here.

A heady relief filled Wingrave. That profound, undeniable emotion had absolutely nothing to do with the idea of her staying, and absolutely *everything* to do with the fact that he'd not been duped.

Stuffing the note inside his coat pocket, he quit his mother's office.

"Helia *Mairi* Wallace," he thundered, irritatingly frustrated that she didn't instantly appear.

He took the corner quickly and collided with Humphries, sending the man's always impeccable slicked brown hair sliding out of place.

The servant tottered on his feet but managed to keep himself upright. "My l—"

"Miss Wallace," he barked.

His butler tilted his head quizzically.

"Magnificent auburn curls, Humphries. A big, mischievous smile. Sparkling green eyes."

The man's eyes went big and glinted with an even greater stupefaction.

Bloody hell. Wingrave didn't have time for this.

"This high." Wingrave held a palm up to the lady's respective height. "She showed up on my doorstep in the midst of a snowstorm. Does any of this sound familiar?"

Humphries found his voice. "Yes, my lord, very familiar."

"Well, that is reassuring," he said sarcastically.

"It is just your description—" The other man stopped midsentence.

The very fine thread of Wingrave's patience snapped. "*Yes*, Humphries?"

A flush filled Humphries's cheeks. "The lady is not here."

Wingrave's spine went erect.

An unnerving disturbance in his chest upset Wingrave's usual stoicism. "What exactly does that mean?" he asked on a grim whisper.

All the color bled from the butler's lean face. "She's gone o-out?"

He narrowed his eyes. "She's gone out. Is that a question, Humphries?"

"N-no. She's not left, my lord. Just gone out."

"Alone, in the cold, when she's still recovering from a bloody illness, Humphries?" he hissed.

Humphries looked one breath away from breaking into big, blustery tears.

Good. The fellow had better be afraid. Very afraid. "Where has the lady gone?"

"The Frost F-fair, my lord."

He furrowed his brow. "The Frost Fair," Wingrave repeated.

Humphries gave a juddering nod.

"What the hell is that?"

"The River Thames, my lord."

This entire day had gotten turned upside down. "A fair is being held *on* the Thames." He resisted the urge to jam his fingertips against his suddenly throbbing temples.

His butler beamed. "The water's frozen, it has. Hasn't done so in decades, my lord."

The young butler's trepidation faded with every word he spoke and was replaced instead with an incongruously childish excitement that belied the unwelcome worry that slithered around Wingrave's chest.

"There's all manner of revelry taking place, my lord: ninepins, skating, sled races."

Wingrave gritted his teeth. The stubborn chit didn't have a jot of common sense. She'd risk her still-fragile health.

"Why, even the prince regent has attended the festivities and—"

"I don't care if God and Satan united on the bloody event and struck an eternal accord," Wingrave snarled.

"My apologies, my lord," the servant whispered.

Wingrave jabbed a finger at the butler. "If she comes to any harm, you and anyone who allowed her to leave this household will be sacked without a single reference." He hissed, "My horse."

Dropping a jerky bow, Humphries backed away. "Yes, m-my lord. First thing."

"Don't tell me, Humphries," he thundered. "Just bloody do it."

"Yes, my—" The servant caught himself, and then tripping over his feet, Humphries raced off to do Wingrave's bidding.

Fired. Every last one of them would find themselves fast unemployed if she relapsed.

And what of you? a voice silently taunted. *You are as much to blame.*

He should have ordered her to remain indoors. As if a headstrong Helia would allow anyone to forbid her from doing anything.

He, however, was not anyone. *I am the unpliable Marquess of Wingrave.*

Wingrave steeled his jaw and strode to the foyer.

The moment he collected her and brought her home, he'd build a goddamned tower and stuff her inside, if need be, to keep the chit from doing any more goddamned harm to herself.

Not even five minutes later, he found himself astride his black stallion, a powerful creature who'd always been as angry as its rider, and on his way to the damned Frost Fair.

Chapter 16

He was a descendant from the younger branch of an illustrious family, and it was designed, that the deficiency of his patrimonial wealth should be supplied either by a splendid alliance in marriage, or by success in the intrigues of public affairs.

—*Ann Radcliffe, The Mysteries of Udolpho*

Numb with fear, Helia desperately fought the panic that threatened to pull her under.

She'd made an enormous and costly misstep.

She'd let her guard down.

Helia attempted to keep up with Cousin Damian, but not because she had any desire to go anywhere with the new earl. Though of average height, he possessed the brawny strength of a blacksmith or pugilist, which robbed Helia of any choice. His punishing hold and the pace he'd set threatened to tear her arm from its socket.

On the annual visits he'd pay Helia and her family, the current earl would greedily assess the furnishings and hangings as if making a catalog of that which would one day be his, and she'd disliked him for that affront. She'd made it a habit to avoid him at any point she could.

It hadn't been until Cousin Damian came to claim his seat at her beloved father's throne that she'd understood the extent of the evil in his soul. The constant browbeating. The taunting promise to toss her on the streets, where she'd be made a whore, if she did not become his countess.

In the time she'd spent in London with Anthony, she'd somehow managed to believe herself safe and insulated from the threat which had sent her fleeing her beloved homeland and all that was familiar to her.

Helia bit her quivering lower lip hard.

Now, back in the mercenary bastard's clutches, she railed at herself for that carelessness.

And yet, for all the dread, Helia's Scot's pride, spirit, and stubbornness wouldn't be broken by this ruthless, heartless Sassenach—nor by any man.

While the earl forced her along the unfrozen perimeter of the Thames, Helia yanked her arm in a futile attempt to free herself.

Based on the lack of reaction from her cousin, Helia's attempts may as well have been the indiscernible fluttering of a gnat.

Desperation crested in her breast and Helia frantically fought for control of her arm. "Will ye lighten your grip?" she gritted out.

The earl didn't let up on the unforgiving pace he'd set. "You know, I don't think I will," he rejoined in cool, crisp tones infused with a terror-inducing false cheer.

Helia swallowed past the fear that formed a lump in her throat.

She'd be damned if she let this monster see her inquietude.

"Ye dinnae think ye will? Or ye dinnae believe ye will, my lord," she said, her breath coming in noisy spurts. "Because the former suggests you may be persuaded."

He stopped so quickly and unexpectedly, Helia went flying forward. His punishing grip, however, wrenched her back.

Helia cried out.

Suddenly, he released her arm with a like velocity that sent her tumbling in the opposite direction.

The earl made no attempt to break her fall.

Helia came down on rock-hard earth, frozen from the winter's cold. Pain radiated from the place where her buttocks made contact with the ground, and that excruciating throbbing shot up her lower back.

Helia's hair, having come loose from the sled ride—which now felt a lifetime ago—hung in a tangle over her face.

Angrily shoving back that makeshift curtain, she glared up at her brutish cousin.

Only when she'd at last looked at him fully did he speak. "The only thing I may be persuaded to do is place you over my knee, toss your skirts up, and redden your stubborn arse," he said dispassionately. His eyes darkened. "In fact, I would enjoy that task immensely."

With his slightly hooked nose, nearly black irises, and features too angular to be pleasing, he'd an unforgiving harshness to him.

Helia's breath came hard and fast; each noisy inhalation and exhalation stirred clouds of white upon the air.

The new earl, on the other hand, wore a bored expression. "After being led on a merry chase from Scotland to London in the heart of winter and in the midst of a snowstorm, I'm growing remarkably short of patience."

Nay, he wasn't a tall man, but with Helia flat on her arse as she was, the earl towered over her like the mightiest silver fir.

To compensate for that advantage, she angled her neck enough to get a crick and scowled. "Och, but I dinnae ask you to come for me."

"There's nothing more to discuss." He consulted his timepiece and then returned that gold chain to his jacket.

"I've had about all I can take of you, Miss Wallace," he said softly, with a lethality she'd never before known a quiet murmuring could possess.

She fought the dread twisting around in her stomach.

Determined to get on equal footing, Helia pushed herself to a stand.

She fixed a sneer on the earl, one even Anthony would have been hard-pressed not to admire.

Anthony! She forced herself to not think of him now. Doing so would only weaken her, and she needed all her wits about her.

"Given your annoyance with me, then, ye should be all too glad to l-let me go." Helia hated that she couldn't contain the faint entreaty there.

The earl didn't rise to the bait or take that offer—not that she'd truly believed he would.

"I wish I could," the earl said. He gave her a harsh look. "*Trust me,* I do wish that were the case. The very last thing I want is an intractable country bumpkin as my wife." He considered Helia with a calculating gleam in his eyes. "No. Regretfully, I've no choice *but* to make you my countess, Miss Wallace."

He took a step toward her and Helia jumped back.

"Given you are familiar with the c-concept of 'ch-choice'"—the stammer to her words had nothing to do with the cold—"then you'll understand when I say, in matters of who I will or will not marry, I'll make my own decisions. And I *choose* not to marry you. In fact, I dinnae want a bluidy thing to do with ye, *Mr. Draxton.*"

The new earl looked faintly amused at that slight. "It appears there is one way we are in accord, Miss Wallace."

He flicked a piece of imagined lint from the collar of his grey-and-blue greatcoat. "Alas, your witless father was rubbish at finances," he hissed, wringing a gasp from her. "And the only money he left with his insolvent estates was, in fact, your dowry, and as such, *you.*"

Her fingers curled into claws. "Ye boggin, doaty dobber, shut yer pus," she hissed. Then the rage, frustration, and sorrow she'd suppressed at the unfairness of her situation set her free.

Helia launched herself at the new earl; she pummeled his chest with her fists. "You cannae hold a candle to my da."

He captured her wrists in a single hand and swiftly put an end to her rebellious efforts. "I'll allow that to be true . . . given he's dead," he said in that bored way.

A crimson fury fell over her eyes. Snapping and hissing, Helia managed to wrench her hands free of his grasp. Knowing she was no match for his strength, she heeded her father's long-ago lesson and brought her knee up to catch Mr. Draxton between his legs.

He cursed and intercepted her efforts.

The earl clamped a viselike touch on her knee, and even beneath the many layers of fabric of her dress and cloak, that punishing cinch brought tears flooding to her eyes.

Helia continued to wrestle with Mr. Draxton.

She may as well have been a child for the effortless way in which he deflected her attempts.

Until, drained of energy and out of breath, the fight went out of her.

Helia sagged.

"Amusing as I find your efforts," he drawled, "I've grown tired of your unruliness."

The earl collected her arm once more.

Helia glared. "You can drag me off to the ends of planet Earth, and your efforts will be in vain. I willnae marry ye."

"We shall see which of us wins this battle of the wills, Miss Wallace." He considered her a long moment. "And I must confess, I've found myself beginning to enjoy your feistiness."

There could be no mistaking the explicitness of the hard gaze he passed over Helia.

The taste of bile filled her mouth, and she choked back that acrid sting.

This time, as he pulled her along, Helia couldn't muster the sufficient strength to fight.

From astride his mount, Erebus, Wingrave spotted Helia in an instant.

Even several furlongs away and with her back to him, the staggeringly bright crown of Helia's auburn curls stood out, a spot of radiance within the vapid, colorless revelers who dotted the horizon.

Wingrave released a huge exhalation of pent-up breath he'd not even realized he'd been holding.

She was . . .

She was . . . speaking with someone.

He frowned.

Nay, more specifically, she stood conversing with a *man*.

Every muscle tightened in Wingrave's frame.

Under him, his mount danced around nervously.

He eased the tension in his legs, and as he set Erebus toward the pair, Wingrave stroked the horse's withers.

The man's finely cut garments marked him a gentleman of some means, but his powerful, compact body more closely resembled those of the longshoremen on these very wharves.

Wingrave kept his gaze intently on the exchange between Helia and the smartly dressed stranger.

She'd insisted she'd nowhere else to go and no one else to whom she could turn, and yet, at this moment, that didn't appear to be the case. The pair spoke with an air of familiarity.

A burning sensation started in Wingrave's stomach, and his fingers tightened reflexively on the reins.

Maybe that was why she'd sought him out this morning? But then he'd taken her in his arms and come at her with accusations and charges, all of which had proven to be wrong.

He didn't know who the hell the man was, but Wingrave hated him on sight. He had a savage need to take the bastard apart at the limbs.

Just then, the man shot out a hand and grabbed Helia by the upper arm. She twisted and wrenched against his hold—to no avail.

A low, instinctual, primitive rumbling reverberated in Wingrave's chest.

Dead. He'd kill him, resurrect him, and then murder him all over again.

Consumed with a vicious bloodlust, Wingrave set Erebus into an all-out gallop. "Go," he growled.

The stallion took flight.

All around them passing festivalgoers shouted and raised their fists in outrage. Uncaring about all of them, uncaring about any but one, he only urged his horse into a breakneck pace.

The closer he drew to Helia and the man who dared to put his hands upon her, Wingrave registered new details: the tracks of tears upon her cheeks.

An unholy rage consumed him—that fury an unrelenting conflagration whose flames swallowed him from the inside out.

He'd made her cry.

That would be the fool's last act.

Sharpening his gaze on the one who'd dared touch her, Wingrave slowed his approach so as to not trample Helia.

The pair, engaged in a struggle, looked up.

Helia's eyes gleamed with a joy and relief that filled him in every corner.

Wingrave, however, tunneled all his focus on the weather-beaten bastard.

The stranger's harsh, angled features conveyed shock.

Helia took advantage of her captor's distracted state and bolted away.

Wingrave jumped off his mount and launched himself at the other man, greeting him with a fist to the face.

The compact man's head went flying back. Blood spurted like a crimson geyser from his already crooked, hooked nose; however, impressively, he retained his feet.

Not surrendering his advantage, Wingrave struck another blow, this time to the bastard's right cheek. Then, in rapid succession, Wingrave brought a right hook to the man's left.

That at last managed to take the whoreson to his knees.

His chest heaving, Wingrave was on the shit-sack in an instant.

He sent his foot flying and caught Helia's offender square in his hard, flat stomach. The force of that collision brought his opponent down on his back. Another time connecting with that solid wall of muscle would have hurt like hell.

Not now. Now, a mindless, bestial wrath raged within at the man who'd dared touch her.

"Anthony!"

Wingrave hurled himself atop the prone figure. He continued to beat the already bloodied face, finding a barbaric satisfaction in doing so. "I'll kill you," he rasped between each blow.

Something soft landed on his shoulder. Snarling, he shrugged it off.

In his mind, he saw only Helia.

He punched the bastard again.

Helia, with her tear-streaked face.

And again.

The bastard's hands upon her.

And again.

"Anthony!"

In the end, Wingrave's given name emerged in the form of a strident cry, managing to cut into his mindless assault.

His chest heaved. Wingrave blinked slowly to clear his vision of the pinpricks of rage dotting his eyes.

Out of breath from the force of his exertions, he staggered away from the lifeless, bloodied form beneath him.

Helia stared blankly at the bruised and beaten man before them. She slowly lifted stricken eyes to Wingrave.

Helia, intrepid as Joan of Arc herself, had never once gazed upon him with that fear. Now those emerald-green irises glittered, such consternation in those always innocent depths, it brought Wingrave crashing to the moment.

"You are all right?" he gruffly demanded, curling his bloodstained gloved fists at his sides.

Dumbly, wordlessly, Helia nodded.

"You're certain, because I'll—"

"F-fine," she quickly cut him off. Her gaze slid back to the unconscious man sprawled at her feet. "I a-am f-fine."

Only, her face wan as it'd never been and her arms curved tightly about her middle, she appeared anything but well.

He stood and took a quick step near her.

Helia scrambled away; she backed away from Wingrave so quickly she nearly tripped on her skirts.

He reached out to help steady her. Then it hit him with all the weight of a thousand stones raining down on him.

She is afraid . . . of me.

Helia grappled with her throat; the long column bobbed wildly. "Is he dead?" she whispered.

As if on cue, a slight, almost inaudible groan filtered through the air.

Anthony glanced at the bloodied mess of a man sprawled beside them. Unfortunately, he'd not finished him.

"He lives," he said coolly.

From the barbarity that'd taken hold and relief at stopping Helia from being forced off, a safer, far healthier annoyance grew in their place.

"We're leaving," he bit out.

Helia wavered. "Sh-should we simply l-leave him here in the cold?"

Raising an eyebrow, Wingrave settled a glassy stare on her. "And you care if we do?"

She hesitated. "I . . . I w-wouldn't see him die on m-my account."

His nostrils flared. An irrational jealousy rooted in his belly.

"If you were so worried about the gent's fate, you shouldn't have gone running around London like a pea-wit," he snapped, effectively silencing her.

That explosion didn't make him feel better. It only left him feeling petty and small.

"We're leaving," he repeated. Wingrave snapped a hand forward. *"Now."*

In an unlikely display of submissiveness, Helia bowed her head and skirted the now stirring gentleman.

Wingrave gritted his teeth. Here he'd thought there couldn't be anything more miserable than feeling those puling emotions of regret and shame. Only to discover something far worse and more debilitating—jealousy and fear.

Staring after her retreating figure, Wingrave gave his head a shake, and fetched Erebus.

Chapter 17

She shrunk from the new scenes of misery and oppression,
that might await her in the castle of Udolpho.

—*Ann Radcliffe, The Mysteries of Udolpho*

Later that night, long after the entire household had taken to their beds, Helia sat on the leather button sofa in the ducal library. Everyone but the occasional squeaking mouse, and the mouser in pursuit, now slept.

Nay. Not all human beings residing here had found rest this day.

Unbidden, her gaze went to the office door. On her meandering through the household, she'd passed a parlor. From under the beautifully carved door, bright light had spilled in an indication that someone remained awake.

Anthony.

From where she sat, Helia drew her knees tight to her chest and rested her chin atop the fabric of her white cotton chemise.

After Anthony had pulverized the earl, he'd escorted Helia from the Frost Fair to the warm comfort of his household, where they'd parted ways. They'd spoken not a word.

She climbed the stairs to her guest rooms, and he stalked off in the opposite direction.

That'd been the last she'd seen of him.

Anthony had nearly killed her cousin.

Or maybe he did, a voice whispered.

Helia shivered.

Given the new earl's cold, unfeeling ruthlessness, he deserved a dark fate, but . . . Anthony had almost ended the other man, and worse, he'd done so because of her.

As a man who so prided himself on his self-control, he'd resent that she'd gone out and he'd had to not only collect her but also fight a man on her behalf.

The fact he'd stayed away from Helia and only sent Mrs. Trowbridge to ask after her was proof of the marquess's irateness.

Helia stared absently at the flames that gracefully swayed and danced in the hearth. *Why would he want to see you?* He believed she'd lied about her reasons for having come to Horace House.

No doubt all out of patience with her, Wingrave would, in the eventual meeting, turn her out for having gone off.

Being honest with herself, she acknowledged that cowardice had sent her into hiding.

Despise her all he might, Helia owed it to Humphries, John Thomas, and all the staff who'd shown her kindness to speak on their behalf and ensure their continued employment.

That didn't make her dread this exchange any less.

Helia climbed to her feet, and her cotton skirts fluttered about her ankles. On stockinged feet, she padded across the room, making her way to its front.

She drew the panel open and dipped her head out into the hall, empty but for the shadows dancing on the satin wallpaper.

Helia made herself take the unwanted walk to the door she'd cowardly rushed past earlier that night.

Maybe the marquess was no longer there.

Why, it'd been *hours.*

Perhaps he'd since sought his chambers and retired for the night.

That would grant her a brief reprieve before she had to face him.

Too soon, Helia reached that pretty pink-and-white-painted panel. She hovered there. Angling her head, she leaned in and strained her ears for any hint of sound from within.

The thick hum of silence proved her only companion this night.

Immense relief filled her.

Tomorrow. She'd approach Anthony and speak about his staff tomorrow.

Helia had turned to go when the faint rustle of papers reached her.

She stopped in her tracks and closed her eyes.

Bluidy hell. She wasn't going to get off that easily, after all.

Before her courage deserted her, Helia lifted her knuckles and knocked.

She waited for the room's occupant to call out in his endearingly impatient tones.

And moments later, she remained waiting.

Helia tried again, this time louder.

She ceased her rapping and stared at the door.

He didn't want to see her. Only a blistering fury could account for his intractable silence.

Battling herself, Helia worried at her lower lip, and then resolutely, she let herself inside.

Every thought left her head: Her reason for being here. The events of the day. All of it.

Anthony sat behind a mahogany desk, the smooth surface covered in neat stacks of papers. Engrossed as he was in whatever note he read, he'd failed to note Helia's arrival.

Her gaze lingered upon him. Anthony, with his height and overwhelmingly powerful build, couldn't be more out of place in this space. He couldn't be more out of place on the delicate wood-cane desk chair he occupied.

Sans jacket and cravat, the marquess, from what she could see of him from the waist up, wore but a loose lawn shirt that gaped at the neck and revealed a whorl of black curls.

Her mouth went dry with something she wished were fear, but now—after his having brought her body to exquisite surrender—she recognized all too well as desire. That wicked yearning flooded her belly and stirred that suddenly sensitive place between her legs.

Go. Leave. Flee.

Fear didn't urge her to take flight, but the inexorable pull he had over her did.

Helia drew the door shut softly behind her. Still, Anthony remained intently focused on that faded yellow page.

"Hullo," she called tentatively.

It was only as she ventured deeper into the room and had reached several paces away from his desk that she realized—he'd not heard her.

All at once, Anthony looked up.

Surprise filled his usually stony eyes, which gave quick rise to annoyance.

"What do you want, Helia?" His hard lips formed an angry white slash.

She froze midstep, but then made herself continue her approach.

"I am sorry to interrupt," she said softly, when she'd reached him.

He spoke sharply. "Not sorry enough to not interrupt."

"No," she acknowledged.

She told herself to not be offended by his irascibility. He'd shown himself to be a man who despised being caught unawares. He always behaved more churlishly in those instances, as if he were angry at her and himself for having failed to hear . . .

Helia stilled. Her mind whirled with a sea of thoughts and remembrances.

A tense exchange with Anthony.

"Don't you knock, Miss Wallace?"

"I did and quite loudly. *You didn't—"*

His black eyebrows snapped together. "What is it?"

She whipped her focus his way.

"Is this what you came for?" he whispered, coming to his feet with a menacing languor.

Thump.

Helia's gaze darted to the black cat bounding out from behind the desk and thoroughly ruining any attempt from Anthony at scaring her.

Shock brought her brows up.

Anthony glared, silently daring her to mention the fact he'd had the cat on his lap.

"You were keeping company with him," she whispered.

A flush dusted the edge of his cheekbones. "He interrupted my damned solitude, the same as a certain someone." He looked pointedly at her.

She couldn't suppress the soft smile that formed. "It is all right you love him," she said thickly. "I shan't tell a soul."

"I don't love anyone," he snapped.

"Aye, I believe you've said as much."

He narrowed his eyes. "But *you* don't believe it." There was another warning there.

She'd never been one to scare easily. "I believe it's possible for one to tell oneself with words they don't love anyone or anything, but that doesn't keep the emotion from living in here." Helia touched a fist to her chest.

"Why are you here?" he asked in a tone that indicated he'd absolutely no intention of continuing this particular dialogue.

"I came to speak on behalf of your servants. They are not to bla—"

"This is why you've come?" he taunted. "You storm my office—"

"In fairness, I didn't storm it as much as knock, but you didn't seem to hear me."

"To save my delinquent staff?"

"They were in an impossible place. They were taking directives from me and received no specific guidance from you."

"Taking directives from you, my dear?" He flashed a lazy, jeering grin. "That in and of itself is a sackable offense."

Helia angled her head. Anthony sought to get a rise out of her. She'd come to know him well enough now to see that he buried his vulnerability in the form of harsh tones and steely grins. Inside, however, he, like anyone else, hurt. The marquess just concealed his far better than most.

"You won't fire them, then," she finally said.

"Is that a ques—"

"No," Helia interrupted. "You won't. I know it."

He chuckled. "My, how confident you are, my dear." With a panther-like grace, he slowly unfurled each of his six foot three inches, stretching. "On what grounds," he purred, "have I proven to be a benevolent lord of the household?" He glided languidly from behind the desk.

He stopped just a foot away.

She knew what he intended. Still, her heart hammered and Helia had to dig the tips of her toes into the floor to keep herself planted where she stood.

Shaken by his nearness and her body's awareness of him, Helia did not back down.

She lifted her eyes to his. "You allowed me shelter, Anthony, when I was nothing but a stranger who gave you only my word—"

"You're still a stranger," he jeered.

"And still, you let a stranger share your home."

"It is not a home," he spat.

Aye, she'd agree with him on that score. This household possessed none of the familial closeness and warmth that made a house a home.

She'd not, however, let him distract her from what they actually discussed—him and the goodness in him.

Helia raised her gaze to his. "You cared for me when I was ill," she reminded him. "And then when you found nothing which linked our mothers, even then, you *still* did not turn me out, Anthony."

Something flashed in his eyes this time. Not his usual annoyed or harsh glint but something *vague* and indecipherable.

"Enough," he said, his warning whisper proving fiercer than any rage-filled shout. "I'm not some pathetically merciful lord."

How very sad his views of life and love, in fact, were. "There's nothing pathetic in showing mercy, Anthony," she said gently. "And I do not want you to fire anyone because of me."

His mirth faded. He locked a hard stare on her. "Caring about others and not yourself? It is a foolish thing to do."

"I—"

"Let me guess," he interrupted dryly. "You disagree?"

"In fact, I do."

He again folded his arms at his chest. "Absolutely shocking."

Her lovely lips only dipped down farther at the corners. "You're being sarcastic."

Anthony brought his hands together in a derisory little clap. "You are becoming somewhat more worldly, Miss Wallace."

He stopped. A muscle rippled along his jaw. "I will not fire anyone."

Helia's heart swelled, along with the smile on her lips.

"I don't want to hear anything else on—" He scowled. "Why are you smiling like that?"

Her grin grew wider. "How am I smiling?" She knew precisely what he spoke about. His reluctant goodness had an inspiriting effect, and she could not suppress a grin, even if her staying here were dependent upon hiding her joy.

Anthony scowled. "Do not get it in your head that I in some way care about those in my employ."

Helia adopted a somber expression. "Of course not."

His brows dipped menacingly, and he snarled like an angry lion. "I don't even care about the people who gave me life."

Her smile instantly fell. How lonely, how sad his life was. She yearned to take him and show him the good that existed in the world.

"The sole reason I've not fired them this time is because I've grown tired of having this discussion repeatedly with you, Helia. In the future, might I suggest if you're actually worried about costing my servants their employment, you'd not put them in a position of doing something that will see them *un*employed."

For all his forceful protestations and repeated denials, there could be no doubting from the leniency he'd shown that he was not only the benevolent lord he insisted he was not, but that good dwelled within his guarded heart.

She bowed her head with an appropriate deference. "I understand." *Him.* She understood him so very well.

He grunted. "Good. I am pleased that is settled."

Going on tiptoe, Helia whispered into his left ear, "I am falling in love with you and ah'm scared to death."

Anthony quickly turned his head. But for a frown, his face otherwise remained expressionless.

Oh, my god. And at last, it made sense. *This* was what the housekeeper had alluded to. "You cannot hear," she breathed.

Rage tightened Anthony's features, and his swift transformation into an angry beast sent Helia stumbling away from him.

"What did you say?" he raged. As soon as the question exploded from his lips, Anthony blanched, and as if he'd realized what he'd asked, he, too, retreated a step.

Helia bit down hard on the inside of her cheek. It was the first he'd ever faltered before her, and she hated the sight of his suffering.

A man as proud and strong as Anthony would see any loss of hearing as a complete failing, a sign of weakness and vulnerability.

How much did his partial deafness account for the guarded man he was now?

Helia found her feet and her voice. "It is all right, Anthony," she said softly. "You are no less because of . . . of . . ."

His glare cut through her, and her words trailed off.

"Say it," he seethed.

"Say it," he repeated, in a deathly quiet tone, more dreadful than any of the thundering he'd done. He'd not, however, hurt her. She knew that all the way to her now anguished soul because she knew *this* man. He'd cared for her with his own hands.

"You are no less of a man because you cannot fully hear, Anthony," she finally said.

Anthony's body tensed.

He'd not thought she would speak those words.

And then, it was as though she'd imagined all hint of vulnerability in Anthony.

He donned one of his coolly sardonic grins. "Do you truly believe I see myself as a *lesser* man, my dear?"

Anthony used that "my dear" like Helia was a recalcitrant child. She recognized it as an attempt to protect himself.

"No," she said calmly. "I have no doubt you are a man who knows his worth, strength, and power. You are a king among men."

Anthony drew back.

Her avowal had taken the wind out of his ire, and it'd also restored the hard, square set to his broad shoulders and the usual swagger he wrapped himself in.

"That is right, Helia," he purred. "I know exactly my worth. Others, however, see any imperfection as something to be pitied."

"Others, such as your father?"

He laughed, an actual mirth-filled expression at odds with his next revelation. "The duke would have to be capable of something *other* than disdain for anyone he deems inferior."

Disdain for his son? What a bloody monster. With every small detail Anthony had shared in Helia's time here, he'd proven all the tales of the duke's awfulness were true.

Anthony sharpened his gaze on her. "Now tell me, have there been servants with loose lips who've shared tales about how I lost my hearing?"

She shook her head. "No, they are loyal to you," she assured him.

She'd come to learn Anthony was the reason servants remained on staff despite having a cruel employer. They knew the duke would not live forever and respected the duke-in-waiting enough to suffer in their services.

Anthony eyed her a long moment—no doubt he searched for the veracity of Helia's admission.

"My brother," he said suddenly, unexpectedly.

Afraid if she so much as breathed, Anthony would stop sharing parts of himself with her, Helia made herself remain completely motionless.

"One winter's day, I urged him to join me for a skate at the lake. The ice broke and he disappeared into that opening. I went in after him. He fell sick and died. I fell sick and lost half my hearing."

How succinct a telling for such a significant and tragic part of Anthony's life. And how much the death of his beloved brother in fact accounted for the Anthony had become.

Everything hurt. Every single part of Helia, from her chest to her soul to her toes, ached.

"You needn't look at me like that, Helia," he said, with more unwarranted amusement.

"How do you believe I'm looking at you?" she asked quietly.

"As though I'm some poor street urchin in need of saving. Evander's death nearly destroyed me."

Evander. His older brother now had a name. Helia stored it in her heart.

Anthony slipped an arm about her waist and drew her close. "But I am stronger for it." He placed his lips near Helia's temple. "I may have lost hearing out of one ear, but from that day forward, I became invincible. Untouchable."

And she absolutely believed he'd told himself that so many times as to believe it.

He flicked his tongue along the shell of her ear. Shivers of desire radiated from that tiny place he caressed.

Which was also likely why he now used her desire as a diversion from an uncomfortable topic.

She'd not be distracted. Helia laid her palms along his chest. "I—" Everything she'd intended to say fled her head. Her breath audibly caught.

Apparently she *would* be distracted.

God, he'd the chiseled hardness and beauty of a bronzed bust of David. Reflexively, she smoothed her hands over his warm, unyielding chest muscles.

The hard, mocking glint in those sapphire irises said he'd sensed her body's awareness.

"I certainly don't have any interest in discussing old memories. Perhaps you didn't just come to plead for me to show my staff clemency, love?" he asked on a suggestive purr.

Anthony glanced pointedly at her hands, which still absently stroked him. "Maybe you came for another taste of what you had this morning? Hmm?"

She flinched, his vulgar words each landing like a well-placed barb. He sought to put up that wall between them. These words, they came because he sought to protect himself.

"Or," he taunted, and rubbed a palm crudely over the hardness tenting his trousers and lawn shirt, "maybe you've come to return the favor and finish me off this time?"

Helia's entire body burned with a blush.

Anthony gave a caustic laugh and let his arm drop.

Stop! He's trying to elicit this reaction. This was the mechanism he relied upon to push away anyone who got too close. Helia swallowed several times.

She edged her chin up. "I know you speak crudely when you are trying to run me off."

I know you speak crudely when you are trying to run me off . . .

It'd worked this afternoon. Funny how quickly she'd figured out Wingrave's efforts. It unnerved the hell out of him. *He*, who'd always been impassive, should be nonplussed by this fey creature.

Since he'd found her at the Frost Fair, an altogether *different* focus—about not their mothers' relationship but the company Helia had kept that day—had commanded his attention.

Determined to unsettle her and steady himself, he folded his arms at his chest. "Very well. I've allowed you your piece, Helia. Now it is *my* turn."

Her brow wrinkled with a consternation that couldn't be feigned. "What do you—"

"Surely you aren't stupid enough to believe we will not discuss your meeting earlier, Miss Wallace," he interrupted frostily.

"I don't . . ." She shook her head.

"What?" He sneered. "Have any idea what I could possibly speaking about? Not the burly fellow I thrashed within an inch of his life today?"

At speaking those words aloud, Wingrave's heart pounded hard against his ribs. *I lost control. What is happening to me? What is this tiny, innocent imp of a woman doing to me?* She was a fire in his blood and burning down the man he'd shaped himself into.

Enraged, with her as much as himself, he took a furious step closer. "Do you have nothing to say?" he hissed.

Her lips parted and formed a perfect little open-mouthed moue. "Oh," she said weakly. "That."

His cock gave another randy leap as he imagined slipping the head of his shaft between those lips and rage tunneled through him.

He drew in a breath through his nostrils and reined in his rapidly soaring emotions.

Except as he stood there, the clock ticked the passing seconds, and each grating beat sent his frustration spiraling and spiraling.

"That is what you'll say, Miss Wallace?" he finally bit out, when it became apparent she didn't intend to say another word apart from the useless response she'd just given him.

Helia hesitated and then gave a little nod.

And through the maddening rage and frustration, Wingrave found the first spot of amusement in longer than he remembered.

He laughed. "This is rich."

"What?" she asked haltingly through his fit of hilarity.

"I, who would be content to never speak a word with you or anyone, now find myself compelled to hold a discussion, and you, who are chattier than a magpie, have of a sudden gone silent."

He stopped laughing and sharpened a stern gaze upon her. "Very well, I'll be first to do so. Why don't we begin with an identity of your companion at the fair, Miss Wallace."

Helia twisted her fingers in the fabric of her nightwrapper. "'Companion' suggests a friend," she said quietly. "He is *no* friend." She pressed her lips firmly together.

When it became apparent Helia would contribute not one thing more, he again crossed his arms and leaned a hip against a nearby sturdy, embroidered armchair.

"Who was he, Helia?" Wingrave asked, with gentleness he'd never believed himself capable of feigning.

It took a herculean effort, but he gritted his teeth to keep from demanding she spit out the bastard's identity.

His forbearance paid off.

Helia nibbled at her lower lip a moment and then finally capitulated. "Cousin Damian."

Cousin Damian? He furrowed his brow. "Who the hell is—" Wingrave stopped. The past interrupted the present.

H-he is n-not a guardian. He is my cousin, and h-he inherited after my da passed.

Wingrave rubbed the aching muscles of his nape. Christ. It'd all been true. Every last piece of it: the distant cousin, blackhearted enough to fit the page of even the most fatuous gothic novel.

"Cousin Damian," he echoed, this time with a humorless laugh. "He doesn't look—" Wingrave stopped short.

Helia lifted a smart auburn eyebrow. "He doesn't look like you expected he would?"

Curse the minx for being the only person in the whole of the god-damned kingdom who somehow knew his unspoken thoughts.

She didn't let up. "What did you expect, a paunch and oily hair and pockmarked skin?"

Amusement dripped from her question.

Wingrave resisted the urge to squirm. For that *was* the manner of man he'd envisioned.

Her eyes twinkled, and that captivating glimmer knocked the thoughts from his head.

Helia leaned up and in. "He isn't a *gothic novel* villain." Her expression darkened. "He's a *real-life* one."

A real-life one . . .

More of their previous discussion on *Cousin* Damian wrenched Wingrave back to the present.

"Never tell me? He locked you in your rooms and denied you meals until you consented to be his bride."

"He didn't d-deny me m-meals on a-account—o-on account, he—"

"He didn't deny you meals on account . . . ," he said between clenched teeth.

Confusion filled Helia's gaze. She shook her head.

"*You said* he didn't deny you meals on account of . . . and didn't finish the thought. What were the reasons he did not deny you meals?" he bit out.

Understanding filled her eyes. "Oh. You remember that."

She went quiet again.

"Helia, what were the reasons he did not deny you meals?" He snapped out each syllable of that question.

"He didn't, on account that he didn't want a wraith for a bride and couldn't have me dying on him as he needed my dowry."

An unholy rage descended over his vision.

A guttural, animallike growl escaped Wingrave. "Did he ever put his hands on you before today?" Because he'd end him. He'd hunt him down and rip Cousin Damian's beating heart from his chest and make him watch while he consumed it.

Helia must have seen the promise of death in his eyes.

She gave her head a quick shake. "No!" she said with alacrity. "He didn't. He only locked me in my rooms and . . ." She stopped short of giving Wingrave what he sought.

"Surely you don't seek to protect the bounder?"

"I seek to protect *you*, Anthony."

Protect him.

He drew back at the unexpectedness of a statement that should be ridiculous—*her* protecting him.

Wingrave attempted to scoff . . . and yet, no one had protected him. His mother had always been a coward—not that he didn't understand why. Being wed to a cruel bastard like the current duke would do that to a woman. His *father* had himself caned Wingrave both for the slightest offenses and to make his unexpected heir stronger.

He tightened his mouth.

It was also how he'd come to discover he didn't need anyone other than himself. Armed with that reminder, he dusted a speck of lint from his shirtsleeve. "My dear, I'm from one of the oldest, longest lines in the realm and future Duke of Talbert. I assure you, I do not require protection from anyone."

Helia's eyes sparkled. "How very fortunate for you that you may move through life without ever suffering any consequences," she said dryly.

He gnashed his teeth in frustration.

How could she be so casual? How could she crack quips when they discussed the bastard who'd dared touch her today?

"I would regret you hurting someone on my behalf."

An image slithered forward of Helia as she'd been locked in her rooms, at the mercy of that dastard. "Killing someone," he corrected for accuracy's sake. "I'll feast on his fists for dinner."

Helia paled.

Wingrave made another attempt to go, but Helia remained as tenacious as a stubborn weed.

"I won't have you act in violence on my account." She grimaced. "That is, any *more* violence. You are a good man—"

"And killing him would make me a better one."

Helia's lips twitched. "You don't believe that, Anthony," she said tenderly. "That's just one more of those things you tell yourself."

He stared at her for a long while. Who *was* this woman? "God, how could anyone be as naive as you?" he asked, in abject perplexity.

"I'm not naive. I just don't believe violence is the answer," she murmured, smoothing her palms over the front of his shirt.

The air grew charged, like the earth just before a lightning strike.

As one, they looked down, registering her tender touch upon Wingrave.

His pectoral muscles bunched under her innocent caress. His cock went instantly, painfully hard. From a virgin's untried touch? What madness possessed him?

A detestable and incessant frustration beat within him—at himself. He possessed enough self-control to not be moved by a lily-pure innocent.

Wingrave glanced pointedly at her palms, which still rested on him. "What is it about you, Helia Wallace?" he murmured to himself.

He slid a palm over her hip, and fisting the fabric tightly, he drew her close. Helia went unresistingly.

"I don't know what you mean," she whispered, her words tremulous, her voice breathless.

She clenched and unclenched her legs like one trying to assuage an ache that had built there.

He reveled in her desire.

"I was right, earlier," he crooned. "You do want to come again. Very well. You do not have to toss me off." *Yet.* "I'm more than happy to pleasure you, love."

Wingrave guided Helia back until her buttocks rested on the edge of the desk and then dropped to his knees.

Never taking his gaze from her wide-eyed one, Wingrave grinned, and inch by slow, deliberate inch, he pushed her nightskirts higher. Ever higher.

"Wh-what are you d-doing?" she whispered throatily when he'd reached her knees.

"What am I doing?" Wingrave caught her left calf in his hand, and as he leaned down, he raised the smooth, graceful limb close to his mouth and paused. "Why, I am kissing you, sweet."

Her eyes grew to the size of globes.

With that, he touched his lips to the place her knee connected with her sinfully lush thigh.

A low, hungry moan filtered from her lips. She caught the lower one between her teeth and bit.

Wingrave chuckled. "Oh, that is just the beginning, sweet."

Helia trembled. "Wh-what are you doing?" she whispered again.

He'd long derided rakes and their pitiful fascination with deflowering debutantes. But with the hot, musky scent of Helia's desire, he understood why they risked their bachelorhood for a taste of that forbidden fruit.

"You want me to tell you and ruin the surprise?" he teased.

She nodded.

Another low laugh rumbled in his chest. "Of course you do."

Withholding that which she sought, he slowly kissed a path up the expanse of her thigh. He licked and nipped a trail higher and stopped.

With his head framed between her legs, and his mouth a breath away from her fiery thatch, he at last gave her the naughty words that, in her untried innocence, he didn't even think she knew she sought.

"I'm going to take you in my mouth, sweet Helia. I'm going to bury my tongue in your tight, wet slit."

At his words, she reflexively lifted herself toward him, and his mouth at last had a taste of what he hungered for.

"I'm going make you come so hard and so good you're going to curse and scream like a naughty girl."

His shaft grew painfully hard at the mental image he painted for the both of them.

Another low, slow, desperate moan escaped Helia, and she began to undulate wildly, grinding her muff against his mouth and taking what Wingrave still withheld.

A sweat broke out on his skin. He wanted to give her the climax he'd just promised. When he'd wrung every last bit of come from her honeypot, he'd shove a knee between her legs and sink himself ballocks deep inside her.

Tormented by a want he'd never known with any woman, Wingrave groaned long, low, and loud.

"Anthony," she begged, arching her hips, "I have never felt the way you make me feel."

He thrilled with a powerful sense of male satisfaction that he'd been the one to awaken her to the wonders of lovemaking. It wasn't enough.

Wingrave placed a tender kiss on the inside of her right thigh. "How do I make you feel?"

Helia angled her body up enough so their eyes met.

"Like that feeling on the warmest, clearest summer day," she said softly. "Where you lie upon the highest peak of the greenest hill and stare up at the clouds as they float past." Her eyes slid closed, as if even now she witnessed the scene unfolding. "Only, this with you . . . it is like . . . I'm one of those clouds drifting past."

He'd never done that. Even in those distant days before he'd lost his hearing and life had been more uncomplicated.

Cynical from birth, he wanted to taunt her with that childlike image she painted. Except, he found himself besieged by an even greater yearning to know that tableau with her.

With her?

His heart thumped weirdly in his chest. Why should he want to take part in such a simplistic passing, with Helia Wallace, at that . . . with *anyone?*

Helia opened her eyes. She moved her innocent gaze over Wingrave's face in a tender search.

She stretched a palm out, and with an aching tenderness cupped Wingrave's cheek.

He swallowed with difficulty.

For while he'd reveled in the skilled, sure touch of the most experienced courtesans, Helia's roused something different, but no less powerful.

No, her whispery-soft touch proved *even* more profound for the nescience of it.

Done with these unnerving thoughts and feelings she'd roused, he ended the earlier sexual games he'd played with her, and gave Helia what she—and he—truly craved. Mindless sex.

Growling, he buried his tongue inside her sodden channel.

Helia hissed; her entire body tensed.

And then, as he teased her nub and lapped her, she rocked herself closer, pushing herself against him.

She had a mild, musky scent more potent than the opium mixed with spirits he'd favored in his university days.

Good. This was safe. This was something he knew. Something he felt comfortable with. Not the puling sentiments she'd roused.

Without breaking focus on her cunt, he stretched his hands up and filled his palms with her pert, tempting breasts. Through the thin fabric of her nightshift, her nipples peaked. Wingrave gave them a deliberately sharp yank.

Helia moaned and tangled her fingers in his hair.

"Like that, do you, kitten?" he whispered between each stroke of his tongue.

She pressed him closer to her core and rammed her hips up.

"Uh-uh," he chided and drew back. "You know I like those naughty confessions from you, love." Wingrave gave her another deliberately taunting lick.

"Yes," she cried out. "I love it, Anthony."

When he still didn't give Helia what she craved, she gripped his head hard and pushed Wingrave where she wanted him.

Her wily power and determination sent another rush of blood to Wingrave's already throbbing cock; his balls tightened.

He gritted his teeth against his body's lustful yearnings and continued to withhold that which her body yearned for.

Wingrave released a long sigh against Helia's soaking thatch. "I am afraid that will not do, Helia."

She whimpered. In a clear attempt to steal what she sought from Wingrave, she rocked back and forth.

He chuckled and buried his nose in her curls.

Helia cried out.

Wingrave breathed deep of her salty juice. "Your sweet puss weeps for me, love."

With a heroic effort, he stopped.

Helia's rapturous shout gave way to an agonized wail. "Anthony," she keened.

"*Tell me,*" he demanded in harsher tones. "Do you like when I'm rough with your nipples, Helia?" Wingrave followed that question with another sharp tweak.

"*Yesss,*" she sobbed. "I *love* when you are rough with my nipples."

"Good girl," he praised.

Rewarding her capitulation, Wingrave plunged his tongue inside her.

Helia collapsed on the desk and lay sprawled with her legs parting even more widely.

Around them, notes and papers fell to the floor like an ivory vellum rainstorm.

Wingrave intensified his ministrations. Alternately, he sucked her nub and swirled his tongue in a slow circle inside her. Fast and then slow.

Incoherent, gasping utterances spilled from her lush mouth. "Mm-hmm," she moaned.

"Christ, Helia. You are so fucking wet."

At his words, her juices flowed and coated his tongue. He licked up her salty wetness.

Growling and hungry for this innocent woman as he'd never been for the most skilled courtesan, Wingrave lapped wildly of her nectar like Helia was the first and last meal he'd ever know.

Gritting his teeth, Wingrave reached a hand down and gave his randy cock a tug.

That yank did nothing to assuage the discomfort of his raging lust. Instead, his blood fired ten degrees more.

Helia's thrusting took on a greater urgency, her movements jerky. But still, she remained tense, her hips undulating wildly in search of the surrender she desperately sought.

"You taste so good, Helia," Wingrave breathed, and stroked his tongue over her clitoris.

She whimpered.

Helia slowly, unevenly pushed herself up onto her elbows. She looked at Wingrave with confused, lust-filled eyes.

"Anthony," she whispered pleadingly.

"Aww, you're in pain," he crooned. "I'll help you, love." Not breaking eye contact, he rubbed his painful erection. "I am, too," he said huskily.

Helia's eyes widened.

Stroking himself through his trousers, Wingrave dived back into worshipping her cunny. "I'll suck you until you scream with pleasure and a blissful surrender," he said, in a harsh, ragged promise.

Helia ground her teeth and pumped her hips angrily against him.

"You're close, love," he purred. "Come for me, sweet kitten."

Then, Wingrave, still tormenting her with his tongue, inserted a finger inside her slick, tight channel.

Helia's lithe, beguiling body tensed.

His head still buried in her cunny, Wingrave stole a glance up.

Helia's eyes remained big, wide, unblinking circles.

He pressed his tongue hard.

That was all she needed.

Helia came. She screamed, cursed, and sobbed through her surrender—as he'd known she would, the naughty little thing.

The taste of her sweet nectar flooding his mouth left him half-mad, crazed with an insatiable lust. As he continued to wring every last drop of her, Wingrave's cock trembled.

Wingrave gritted his teeth and fought the urge to come in his trousers like some pathetic green lad with his first whore.

Apparently, for all his previous doubting, the Lord proved real, after all, for Helia let loose one last small, delightful gasp and collapsed, depleted from Wingrave's endeavors.

He gave her one final lick. She quivered.

"Good girl," he praised, rewarding her with a gentle kiss upon her silkily soft inner thigh. God, how he wanted to fuck her.

She'd let him. He knew he could have her.

So take her.

A weak, shy, but grateful smile wreathed her lips, and that rakish voice in his head grew distant.

She'd be ruined if he did this.

She is already ruined. Take what you've been wanting since she stepped inside your goddamned household.

An inner war he'd never before faced waged within him.

The difference was, the lady might be ruined in society's eyes, but she remained a virgin—in only the sense of the word anyway.

The thick fringe of her reddish-brown lashes swept low and concealed Helia's stunningly bright green eyes.

Her heaving chest settled into a smooth, slow, even, up-and-down rhythm.

Like a cat who'd landed the cream, Helia burrowed into the letters that made a small, ineffective blanket under her, and slept.

Wingrave remained on his knees between her legs and stared up at her.

Of all the times to develop a fucking conscience.

He drew her skirts gently back into place—both to keep her limbs warm from the chill of the room and to save himself from the suffering of staring at her glorious cunny.

It didn't help.

Wingrave clenched his eyes tight and wrestled for control of this all-powerful hungering.

I'm not a goddamned shad-bag who can't control his baser urges.

Of course, with this insatiable lust, one would never know it.

His shaft pulsed and throbbed with a desperate hungering for a release of his own. Having coaxed Helia's untried body to her first orgasms, however, proved too much for even his worldly experience.

Neither wanting to wake her from her rest or ask her to tug him off, Wingrave reached for his rock-hard length.

Never once taking his gaze from Helia's delicate, freckled features, he freed himself.

Then, closing his eyes, he saw her as she'd been just moments ago, both shy and yet also possessed of a glorious lack of inhibition.

Wingrave gripped the edge of the desk in one hand and took his cock in the other and began to pump his shaft.

Gritting his teeth, he moved from base to tip.

All the while he saw Helia in her exquisite gloriousness as she'd eagerly lifted her hips in search of surrender. Using his thumb, Wingrave applied a light pressure to the underside of his cock.

His breathing grew harsh and harder.

He squeezed as he stroked himself, giving his base extra attention.

Only, the steamy words he'd drawn from her lips were not the ones he recalled as he pleasured himself. Instead, her soft, lilting voice while she'd tried to put her feelings to words whispered around his mind.

Like that feeling on the warmest, clearest summer day . . . where you lie upon the highest peak of the greenest hill and stare up at the clouds as they float past. Only, this with you . . . it is like . . . I'm one of those clouds drifting past . . .

At the back of his ballocks, pressure built.

Wingrave fumbled his spare hand about for his jacket.

He snatched the kerchief just in time.

Wingrave stiffened and then came in an exquisitely fierce orgasm. He groaned and continued to pump his shaft, until he'd emptied himself of every last drop of come.

Spent, he collapsed forward. His head collided with Helia's legs. She stirred but remained sleeping.

It wasn't enough. It wouldn't be enough.

His breath settled into an even pattern and he cringed. Good God, he'd just brought himself off while she lay sleeping on his mother's desk. Apparently, Wingrave was more depraved than he'd ever credited himself with being. He, of all men, possessed a moral sense.

With a disgusted grimace, Wingrave dropped the soiled kerchief still clutched in his fingers.

He stood, then carefully lifted Helia in his arms. She immediately curled against him like the cat he'd sooner chop his tongue off than admit he enjoyed petting.

Wingrave carried Helia to a nearby pale-green-and-pink silk brocade sofa.

He lay her down . . . and only so that she did not roll off the makeshift bed, Wingrave lay beside her . . . and soon, he joined Helia in sleep.

Chapter 18

Virtue and taste are nearly the same, for virtue is little more than active taste, and the most delicate affections of each combine in real love.

—Ann Radcliffe, The Mysteries of Udolpho

A low-pitched rumble slipped into Helia's deep, dreamless slumber.

She tried to open her heavy lashes, but far too content to burrow into a warm, welcoming heat, she gave up the fight.

The edge of consciousness she hovered on drew her back, deeper and deeper into that blissfully welcoming, calm nothingness.

Then there came another reverberation. This time, more resonant, it lightly shook Helia's frame and released her from her torpor.

She managed to open her eyes, only to have them meet a curtain of inky blackness.

Still hazy from the fog of sleep, Helia blinked several times to adjust her gaze to the dark.

What in blazes? Where am I?

All the while, she attempted to make sense of her whereabouts.

Her eyes more adjusted to the dimness, Helia looked about . . . and froze.

Then it all came rushing back. The shameful, wicked, wanton, and God help her, wonderful climax Anthony had coaxed from her body.

The feel of his tongue inside her. The lewd words he'd rasped against her womanhood—she'd loved every single one. She'd thrilled at the things he'd done to her and said to her and—

A low, sonorous rumbling—that same sound which had penetrated her sleep—cut into her unchaste thoughts and she glanced down.

Her heart stopped.

Anthony.

Her hair lay in a tangle of curls about his soundly slumbering form.

His body, rock-solid beneath her, conferred a delicious heat that erased any chill from a long-extinguished fire.

She was ruined.

She'd known that the moment she stepped through the doors to this house, and that's why she didn't feel panicked and horrified.

But this was a different sort of ruined.

Anthony, the Marquess of Wingrave and future Duke of Talbert, Helia's lover, had ruined her for all men.

"Lover," she whispered, tasting the sound and feel of it.

All her life, there had been expectations of her and for her. Her parents had envisioned a respectable Scottish husband for Helia. Mr. Draxton sought to make Helia his wife. There'd always been dictates about her and chains around her. She'd just not realized it until now, when she was fully and completely ruined, in every way.

Only, her life hadn't turned out the way she'd thought it would. And now she found herself Lord Wingrave's lover, and without a single regret.

Helia angled her head up and studied him.

Why would she regret having lain in his arms? She'd been ruined in name, which was ruined in every way. At least, she'd have known this wonderment she found with Anthony and in his arms.

From his slackened lips, slow, even breaths escaped him. Sleep lent a gentleness to the marquess's otherwise harshly beautiful features. In rest, an aura of peace and softness hung over him. As if only in his body's absolute quietude could Anthony truly let his walls down.

Helia laid her cheek upon his lightly furred chest. Underneath her ear, she heard the solid, steady, reassuring thump of his heartbeat.

Sighing, Helia closed her eyes and absorbed his warmth and strength. She gently stroked a hand back and forth over his shoulder.

How peculiar. Even in rest, Anthony managed to confer a consolation that all would be well. Even though she knew he'd despise it were he to know, in Anthony, Helia felt . . . safe and protected.

Despite his often-crass words and cynical sneers, at every turn, time and time again, he'd cared for her.

He—

A low, resonant rumble started in his chest, and then Anthony emitted an unmistakable but immensely endearing snore.

As though angry he'd nearly awakened himself, Anthony frowned and stirred faintly in his sleep.

She held her breath until his own, once more, settled into a smooth, even pattern.

Helia's lips turned at the corners in a smile. Why, he managed to be cross with even himself.

Anthony's big, broad form shifted under Helia. That slightly restless repositioning sent a loose black strand falling over his brow and lent him an even softer, more approachable air.

Helia melted inside.

She closed her eyes.

I am not falling in love with him. I . . . love him.

Helia waited for the dread that discovery should bring. Terror, however, did not come.

Rather, she found herself filled with an absolute sense of calm. Nay, not calm. Rightness. From the moment he'd met her in that foyer, barefoot and filled with fury, there'd existed something between them.

At least on her part.

She chewed at her lower lip.

Except time and time again he'd shown he felt something for her. That was, something *other* than annoyance and disdain. Those were the only emotions he allowed himself to reveal with his eyes and words.

With his *actions*, however, he showed the manner of man he truly was: one who'd venture out on a cold winter day and, like a knight of old, champion a lady in peril.

And the way he'd touched her and kissed her . . .

An increasingly familiar ache built between her legs. She yearned to shift and squirm in a bid to relieve some of that pressure, but she bit her lip and fought the urge so as to not wake him.

Surely a man could not do the things to her that Anthony had and not feel some affection and regard for her.

When he'd rubbed his erection through his trousers, he'd shown in a most vulgar way he desired her. She wasn't so naive in the details surrounding copulation. Helia understood men spilled their seed when they achieved the desired state in lovemaking.

Yet he'd restrained himself and given only Helia pleasure.

Helia propped her chin atop his chest and gazed up at him. "Who are you, Anthony?" she whispered. She moved her gaze over his resting features. "Angry marquess or wounded man who is afraid to let anyone in?"

She, however, knew the answer.

She yearned to help break down his barriers so he could be free to be the man he truly was.

Her heart faltered.

For she wouldn't be here. As he'd pointed out, he'd not found any link between their mothers, and ultimately, when he decided she was well enough, he would show Helia the door.

Would he be able to do that?

And yet, what was the alternative? That he'd allow her to remain indefinitely as a guest of his family?

All the warmth and contented satiation lifted. Restlessness ran through her.

Unable to sleep, even with his body snugly pressed against hers, Helia carefully climbed off Anthony.

A loud, shuddery breath escaped him and Helia remained motionless above him, until he'd shifted back and forth on the sofa.

Anthony flipped onto his right side so he faced the back of the sofa and then resumed snoring.

Helia glanced around the office. Her gaze landed on a blanket draped over a green embroidered Gainsborough armchair tucked in the far-left corner of the room.

On stockinged feet, she hurried over, fetched the throw, and then stopped.

Unblinking, lest the image change, Helia stared at the soft blanket she held in her hands. Close as she was to the soft, woolen fabric, she now took in the details which had been previously obscured by the room's darkness: the weathered pink and even paler sea-green checkered pattern. That proud tartan of Clan Fraser.

Helia gasped and her fingers flexed reflexively.

The blanket fell to her feet.

Heart hammering, she hurriedly rescued the blessedly familiar throw and clutched it close to her fast-beating heart.

Surely, surely, this could be no mere coincidence? Why should the duchess, who by Anthony's own admission kept no secrets from her powerful husband, own the checkered fabric which belonged to people whom the duke despised?

Not only that, what were the chances the duchess would, and that it should also happen to be Helia's family tartan?

Another bleating snort split through the quiet.

Helia jumped.

While her thoughts whirred, Helia returned to Anthony's side.

She traced her gaze over his sprawled frame. He'd curled up into himself as though in sleep he sought to make more space for his large, powerful physique.

Mayhap that pink and sea-green was nothing more than a coincidence. Those beautifully delicate hues proved an ideal match for the ebulliently decorated room.

"And maybe you're just so very desperate to be connected to the Blofields so you won't have to be separated from Anthony," she whispered to herself.

His deep, sonorous breathing proved the only response to her musings.

Coming out of her thoughts, Helia gingerly brought the throw over his resting form. She remained motionless for several moments more so as to not wake him.

Once assured he slept still, Helia turned her focus to the mess he'd made of the duchess's office.

Don't you mean the mess you both made of her office? a deprecating voice reminded her.

An image of Helia perched on the edge of the delicate mahogany desk played like a stage performance in her mind. Her fingers tangled in Anthony's hair as she shoved his face into that most intimate place.

She pressed her palms to burning cheeks.

Those efforts didn't do anything to dull the heat.

For a second time, she'd behaved like a wanton. She'd not only surrendered to his advances, she'd shamelessly *embraced* Anthony's every kiss, every caress, all of it. All of *him.*

Helia, determined to bury those sordid memories, dropped to her haunches and gathered up those papers at the foot of the Duchess of Talbert's desk.

She stacked them neatly, and tapped the pile lightly upon the floor to make that stack even, then moved her attention to those on the right side of the desk.

"You taste so good, Helia," Anthony breathed, and stroked his tongue over her clitoris.

She whimpered.

"Aww, you're in pain," he crooned. "I'll help you, love."

Helia exploded to her feet. "Enough," she whispered furiously. *Do not think of what took place on this desk and in this office.*

Helia finished collecting every neglected page and returned them to the desk. She had begun to set the messy surface to rights, when her gaze alighted upon a crisply folded newspaper. The sheets were entirely too perfectly inked and faded white to be aged by time.

Curiously, Helia availed herself of the copy of *The London Times*.

She stole a peek over in Anthony's direction. Once she confirmed he remained sleeping, Helia carefully unfurled the newspaper.

She quickly skimmed the contents and then stopped at the top center.

Scandal of the Century

What lady should not wish to be the next Duchess of T?

Helia paused and her pulse picked up.

> Certainly, wedding the distinguished and powerful Marquess of W is a dream to all . . . except, that is, the one lady he'd been slated to marry—the Season's most breathtaking beauty, a Diamond of the First Waters, betrothed to the marquess before she'd even formally debuted.

> The future duke found himself left standing at the altar as his betrothed walked off with another man, the Viscount C, a lesser gentleman—in every way. Only an uncouth cad would dare interrupt a wedding ceremony in progress and declare his love with the groom at the bride's side.

> This author expects Lord W may have any woman he
> wants . . . that is, if his heart might recover from this
> greatest of degradations.

Helia's heart thudded in a sickening beat against the walls of her chest.

"Oh, Anthony," she whispered, her heart breaking for him . . . and herself. "No wonder you've become such a curmudgeon," she murmured to herself, rereading those sad words inked in black.

Was it not enough he'd suffered the abuse of his father and the neglect of his mother? He should find his heart broken, too?

"And what reason is that?"

Helia gasped. She jerked her head up so fast her neck muscles wrenched.

At some point, Anthony had not only awakened, he'd stood. He now *rested*, with a hip dropped upon the arm of the sofa he'd slept on only moments ago.

Anthony's near-obsidian black lashes swept low until they'd swallowed up his sapphire eyes. He studied Helia with a cool smile on his hard lips.

A knot formed in her belly.

"Interesting reading," he remarked, in a pleasant voice that belied the steel within it.

Blinking furiously, Helia dropped her gaze to the stiff, oversize sheet clutched damningly in her fingers.

When she looked up, Wingrave remained there, contemplating her with an incisiveness in his icy eyes that swiftly killed the illusion of a lazy boredom.

Unnerved as she'd never been, not even during Mr. Draxton's browbeating, Helia dipped her tongue out and traced the seam of her lips.

The marquess sharpened his eyes on her. Nay, not her, rather that slight movement of her tongue.

Anthony's eyes glowed with an incandescent heat that could have melted the immense snow the storm had left upon the London streets below.

She immediately flattened her lips.

He chuckled, straightened, and started over with long, languid steps.

He's trying to unnerve me.

He's trying to scare me.

To cow me.

To send me running.

Alas, if her fleeing proved his ultimate goal, he'd best do better than don menacing, seductive looks. The peril behind her was far greater than the danger before her.

He stopped a pace away. "Tell me, sweet, who is the curmudgeon you spoke of?"

Through the haze he'd cast by his presence alone, she recalled belatedly, he'd discovered Helia reading—and more and worse, he'd been awake long enough to hear her *talking* about him.

Alas, she'd long ago discovered honesty proved the most effective means to disarm a person.

Helia cleared her throat. *"Y-you,"* she managed.

Anthony blinked those coal-black lashes slowly.

She found her feet. "I was talking about you, Anthony," she repeated. "*You* are the curmudgeon."

He sent an icy brow arcing up. "Ah, and I take it you've gathered the cause of my curmudgeonness."

"'Curmudgeonness' isnae a word."

"Neither should be 'curmudgeon,' but here we are," he said sardonically.

She gave him a gentle look. "I ken what you are trying to do, Anthony."

Crossing his arms, he leaned down and whispered, "Just what is it you *ken* I am doing?"

She ignored the mocking emphasis he placed on that particular word he'd appropriated.

Helia tipped her chin up. "Ye are trying to divert my attention away from . . . from . . ."

"*Yesss.*" Anthony flicked his index finger across the tip of her nose. "Why don't you be so helpful as to enlighten me about this astounding discovery you've made."

The jeering glimmer in his beautiful blue eyes dared her to speak. She didn't fear him. She didn't believe she ever really had.

"You had your heart broken," she said softly, and even as she uttered that avowal, her heart cracked.

Surprise replaced the marquess's customary cynicism. In fact, in the time she'd been here in the duke's household, it marked the first crack in his otherwise unflappable demeanor.

"You must have loved her greatly," she managed past a tight throat.

He flashed another one of those empty, mocking grins. "My dear, I'd have to possess a heart to have it broken."

"That's what a man with a broken heart *would* say."

"Nay, that's what a man with no heart *does* say." He considered her a long while, before speaking. "It must make you feel better."

She tipped her chin at a defiant angle. "What?"

With slow, sweeping, pantherine steps, Anthony walked a languid circle about her.

Helia didn't back down. Rather, she turned her head as he went, following his every move.

He stopped just beyond the edge of her right shoulder so she had to crane her neck back or turn and face him.

Anthony made the decision for her.

He placed a hard, possessive hand on her right shoulder, and his left, upon her hip. "If you believe I'm capable of love, Helia," he breathed against the shell of her ear, his words a husky threat mixed with a promise, "then you've no idea what I'm capable of."

Despite her resolve and faith in the marquess, a shiver traipsed over her spine.

His brows dipped, and she couldn't sort out whether his blue eyes reflected back her own desire, or a like yearning on his part.

"I've already told you, Anthony, I'm not afraid of you." And . . . she meant it. He did, however, unnerve her as no one had before.

His icy smirk said he knew it.

Only, he didn't know. Not really. Not truly. Helia's fear . . . it had nothing to do with Anthony, but instead, with everything he made her feel. And if she were being honest with herself—what he made her long for. Things no good, virtuous, innocent lady should long for.

Anthony flicked his tongue over the shell of her ear, and she trembled as that whispery sough of his breath both tickled and tormented.

She wavered on her feet, and her back found purchase against the hard, muscled wall of his chest.

Then he filled his palms with her breasts and rubbed the pads of his thumbs over the peaks pebbled not with cold but from a shameful desire.

"S-stop," she croaked.

Anthony instantly ceased his stroking and extended his arms, so they framed Helia on either side.

"Is that what you really want, Helia?" He dangled forth that husky temptation. "For me to stop touching you?"

Her lashes fluttered wildly, and she gave thanks he couldn't see her body's reaction to him.

Shamefully, wantonly, she wanted him to do all those things he'd already done to her and with her over and over.

"Well?" he prodded seductively. "Shall I cease my caresses or give you more of what I gave you earlier?"

His thick, rigid erection prodded her buttocks.

Helia's center throbbed, and she shifted and squirmed in search of relief from that ache.

Still, without bringing his hands in contact with any part of her body, Anthony touched his lips along the curve of her neck. The tenderness of that kiss belied all the coldness that'd met Helia since he'd awakened.

That gentleness threatened to undo her.

Helia reflexively tipped her head to allow Anthony better access.

"Hmm?" he whispered. "What is it to be, love?"

She closed her eyes. What was it to be? Or what did she *want* it to be? Helia well knew, in this instant, Anthony only used her body's hungering for him as a means with which to distract her from a topic he didn't wish to discuss.

Slowly, Anthony raised his arms and brought his hands closer, ever closer, to her breasts.

She bit the inside of her cheek hard enough to draw blood, and then with a silent curse, she managed to find her voice.

"Aye, Anthony," she said, not knowing where she discovered the might to resist his magnetizing pull. "Ah want ye to stop."

He stilled; his body tensed.

He'd not expected her rejection.

But then, why should a man so skilled and capable in the art of lovemaking expect anything other than a woman's capitulation?

Anthony placed his mouth near that sensitive spot on her neck once more. "Liar," he whispered.

She swallowed spasmodically. Aye, he knew her in so very many ways. Helia was afraid she'd never recover when they were brought apart.

Anthony let his arms fall to his sides.

As though he'd not set her body afire, he casually stepped away and stood so they faced one another.

By the granite look he leveled on Helia, she may as well have merely imagined all beneficence in his earlier embrace.

"Let me take a moment and clear your innocent head of any imaginings you cooked up," he said bluntly. "The duke and duchess hand-selected Lady Alexandra Bradbury to be my bride on account of her impeccable bloodlines."

Unlike Helia, whose Scottish blood made her someone the duke would never approve of. It shouldn't smart. Helia was a proud Scot, and yet somehow, knowing she'd not be considered enough for Anthony left her hurting all over.

"No," he continued, pulling her back from her own pitiful ruminations. "Their efforts would one day spare me from the onerous task of finding a bride of my own."

He snorted. "I couldn't care less *who* the duke selected as long as the lady was passable enough to bed. Not that I'm so very particular that bedding my wife should prove onerous," he added as more of an afterthought.

Helia flinched. For his absolute indifference served as one more harsh, unwanted, but necessary reminder that all the things he'd done to Helia had not meant anything to him. Any woman would have done.

The muscles in Helia's belly contracted.

She stood before Anthony, talking with him, but it felt like she was on the outside, watching a performance between two actors she didn't recognize unfold before her.

Each horrid utterance to fall from Anthony's lips turned each beautiful act between them into something sordid and *dirty*.

Helia grappled with her throat. "S-surely you cared that you were compatible and friends?" Her voice emerged as a whisper.

"Friends?" He tossed his head back and howled with a biting amusement. When he'd composed himself, Anthony gave Helia a pitying look. "A friendship with one's spouse?" he repeated. "How *plebeian*."

With every brutal word Anthony uttered so very casually, Helia's horror grew and grew.

She could only stare at him.

He was even more damaged than she could have ever imagined. If she had any sense, she'd take this recent discovery and keep a far distance from him.

What was wrong with Helia that the part of her heart he'd somehow claimed begged her to help him learn to love and feel . . . anything other than this cold nothingness?

"She came to the marriage without a dowry," he shared about his former betrothed, like it was dull gossip he recounted to some gent at the clubs.

Unlike Helia, whose father had ensured there would be funds for her, even if his estates had been unprofitable since Napoleon began wreaking havoc all over the Continent.

"But she was beautiful," he said, equally cool and aloof.

But she was beautiful . . .

Despite Anthony's detached assessment of the woman, he'd been so very close to marrying her it still managed to hit Helia like a kick to her solar plexus.

Anthony proceeded to rip Helia apart from the inside out.

"The lady was a Diamond." Just as the papers had described. "Fair. Pale blonde hair."

Also unlike Helia. Who, with her very auburn curls and even more abundant freckles, missed only a tartan to mark her as a Scot.

She curled her hands into tight fists.

"The lady ran off with another, a McQuoid."

A McQuoid. A fellow Scot. Now his early derisiveness about Helia's origins made sense.

Anguish threatened to crush her heart.

"Even knowing she'd likely spread her legs for him," he continued, knocking Helia from her miserable musings and adding more kindling to her jealousy, "I was still willing to overlook her loss of a maidenhead. In fact, I assured her she could continue bedding him after we wed."

Tears burned her eyes. "How very big of you, my lord," she said, her voice thick.

Helia's bitterness seemed to penetrate Anthony's apathetic accounting. He sharpened his gaze upon her.

"Do not look at me like that," he ordered, his voice harsh.

A tear squeezed out.

His nostrils flared and he jabbed a finger at Helia. "Like I didn't tell you, like you didn't know exactly what type of man I am."

Another drop slipped down her cheek, and another.

He glared. "Like that! Stop!"

"A-all right," she whispered, her voice wobbling.

Fury blazed from his eyes. He took an angry step toward her, and she automatically backed away.

Helia's hip collided with the corner of Her Grace's desk. The wood bit sharply into her side and she welcomed that pain, as around her, the notes she'd assembled took a second tumble to the floor.

And then, every last horrible thing that happened this day hit some manner of peak, and at last Helia cracked under the weight.

Anthony blanched. "Stop." This time there was a note of desperation in that command.

"A-all r-right," she repeated, and unable to meet his horrified eyes, she dropped her gaze to the pretty floral Aubusson carpet underneath her, and then froze.

Through the cloud of that shimmery water at her eyes, she registered the duchess's name on a folded note.

It wasn't, however, that which froze Helia where she sat, but rather, the familiar scrawl.

Her focus locked on the old letter. Helia quickly grabbed the sheet, unfolded it, and shock slammed into her.

She worked her gaze over the page again and again, but nothing changed: not the meticulous, graceful lettering. Nor the name inscribed at the very bottom of the loving note.

Emotion welled in her breast. In each word written, Helia heard her mother's lyrical voice as she regaled her friend, the duchess, with tales of Helia's first hunt alongside her father.

She read and reread those treasured lines and then slowly lifted her gaze.

From under black lashes, Anthony stared back with hard, cruel eyes.

Helia stumbled over her thoughts, before finding the courage to challenge him. "It appears, of the two of us, *you* are, in fact, the liar, my lord."

Chapter 19

To him alone her heart turned, and for him alone fell her bitter tears.

—*Ann Radcliffe, The Mysteries of Udolpho*

She'd stopped her weeping. That was good. Wingrave abhorred those drops as signs of weakness. Oh, there'd been plenty of false ones from mistresses who'd sought grander gifts when he'd tired of their affections. But those, he took for what they were—a manipulative attempt to wheedle more gifts and more money and more of his time in their beds.

This display from Helia, however, proved unnervingly real—she didn't cry because she desired something from him, but rather, because of him.

Why should that stir this peculiar discomfort in his chest?

Suddenly, her shock and sadness lifted, to be replaced with an indomitable spark.

The lady was a quivering, apprehensive, weepy chit one minute, and the next a fierce, ferocious spitfire who boldly called Wingrave out.

That contradictory display of shy kitten and tempestuous lioness fired his blood.

"You've gone silent, my lord." Helia raised a delicate red eyebrow. "Nothing to say?"

"If I said the things I'm thinking to you, kitten," he said silkily, "you'd find yourself on your back, begging me as I pumped between your legs, this time until we both came."

Her cheeks fired. "You are saying that to distract me. I won't be distracted, Anthony." She paused. "Not this time." That latter part she uttered as though a reminder for herself.

Actually, he gave her only truths. Wingrave found himself consumed with a ferocious hungering to possess her, this mindless lust the likes of which he had never known with any woman. He'd be damned, however, if he admitted that craven yearning.

Like some Spartan-warrior princess, Helia tipped her chin up at an obdurate angle. "All this time, I've sworn my mother was a dear friend to yours, and all along, you insisted that couldnae be because I'm a Scot and yer ma would nah keep company with the likes of a Scot."

"For accuracy's sake," he drawled, "I indicated my father would never condone such a fellowship, and that remains true." Wingrave favored her with a mocking grin.

Helia stared at him with big, wide, hurt eyes. "*Everything* is a game to you," she whispered.

"Nothing is a game to me, sweet. I don't have time for them."

She remained planted there; she looked at Wingrave with a disbelieving glimmer in her gaze.

Then, giving her head a disgusted little shake, she sifted through the notes and quickly scanned them.

Methodically, Helia set aside some in favor of others.

Through her investigation, Wingrave stood there, forgotten.

It was a foreign position in which to find himself. This brazen hoyden was the only one who'd ever shown him anything less than the due regard his position, rank, and power merited.

And Anthony got a thrill out of her willful disobedience.

"Need I remind you those are not your private correspondences, Miss Wallace," he coolly warned.

"Aye." She didn't so much as deign to glance up from her survey.

Another wave of lust flashed through him.

"One can argue that given these notes were written by my mother, I'm at least half their rightful owner."

With that cheeky pronouncement, she tucked them in the pocket of her night wrapper.

"You cannot have rightful ownership of letters that were sent by another to another, my dear," he said, more amused than annoyed at her audacious display.

Helia stopped in the middle of the floor and glared. "Try to take them from me." She dared him with both her words and gaze.

More. He wanted to take even more from this sassy Scot.

Wingrave gave her a lecherous appraisal. He glanced pointedly at that piece of furniture where she'd lain sprawled and open to him. "I find myself positively titillated by that prospect."

She eyed him with a chary expression.

Wise girl.

Then, it was as though the fight left her. "You lied to me," she said, her gaze wounded.

Anthony balled his hands sharply. How bizarre he should prefer her insolence to this serene sadness.

"I didn't get around to mentioning it because you took yourself off like some twit, and nearly got yourself raped by and married to your dastardly cousin," he said between gritted teeth.

They remained at an impasse; each stared at the other.

Helia looked away first, breaking the deadlock. She gave her head a shake. With her shoulders drawn back, Helia took a wide berth around Wingrave.

His brow dipped, and he stared in absolute consternation as she continued sailing toward the doorway.

And then it hit him.

"Just what the hell do you think you're doing?" he barked.

People didn't walk away from him.

"Leaving," she said, without breaking an impressive stride.

Apparently, this chit did, however, walk away from him.

Wingrave gnashed his teeth.

The hell she would.

He took a step toward her.

Even with the sizable lead Helia had on him, Wingrave overtook her in three long strides.

He slapped a palm over the panel, anchoring the door shut.

Unfazed, Helia's scowl only deepened. "Move yer hand, my lord."

When fired up, her brogue thickened, and he found himself not repelled but further lured by whatever siren's spell she'd cast. He dipped his gaze to the rapid rise and fall of her chest; the pink, erect tips of her breasts pressed invitingly against the thin fabric of her modest night garments.

"That is, unless ye find yerself in the habit of trapping women who want nothing to do with ye," Helia taunted.

"I confess, kitten," he said, desire thickening his voice, "I've never found myself in this position."

"Never tell me, because *all* women want ye?" she dryly asked.

"Yes."

Helia rolled her eyes. "Well, I am nah that woman." Her expression hardened. "Now move."

"I'll do so happily."

Like a good girl, she waited patiently.

"When?" she snapped, like the naughty girl she truly was.

"After you tell me just where it is you're going with those letters you've pocketed." Boldly, Wingrave slipped his fingers inside that pocket and caressed not those pilfered notes, but rather her soft, flat belly.

Her lithe muscles lost the tension in them. The graceful column of her neck moved.

He stroked his hand lower, so that he brushed the dark curls shielded by that cotton.

Her thighs slipped apart, and Helia bit her lower lip.

Suddenly, Wingrave stopped, and her body sagged.

Still, he made no attempt to withdraw his hand.

He bored his angry gaze into Helia's dazed, desirous one. "Tell me," he demanded sharply.

She blinked furiously, then snapped upright, as if jolting herself out of the haze he'd placed over her.

"I'm l-leaving."

She thought to just leave? The audacity. The gall. She'd just up and go, without so much as a parting farewell?

Wingrave narrowed his eyes on her and removed his hand from her person, denying her body the pleasure she sought.

Good, let her. He didn't need a bloody goodbye. He'd be better off. His hands would finally be clean of her, and she'd be someone else's problem—his *mother's*.

You're a bloody liar. You've not only become accustomed to having her near, you hunger for her. With her innocence, fiery spirit, and strength, she'd imprinted upon him.

Nor, for that matter, was Helia truly the duchess's problem. Her Grace may have maintained a secret friendship with a Scottish woman through the years, but the Duke of Talbert would never countenance having a spirited, red-haired, heavily freckled Scot amongst them.

No, the duchess had challenged the duke but once—at Wingrave's wedding ceremony to Lady Alexandra. The day Dallin McQuoid had stepped forward and objected to the union on account of his *feelings* for Lady Alexandra, Wingrave's mother had lent her support to the love match. That bold showing had seen the duchess banished by the duke for the rest of the London Season—and a vow on His Grace's part to send her to a madhouse were she to stage any further displays of rebellion.

Helia took advantage of Wingrave's tumultuous ponderings. She hastily drew the panel open.

She managed to get only a foot in the hall before Wingrave shot an arm around her waist and drew her back inside and against him.

"The hell you'll leave," Wingrave rasped harshly against her ear. She belonged to him and only him.

"What do you want, Anthony?" she pleaded, and that crack in her composure made him feel a way he didn't want to look too closely at, and certainly didn't want to *feel*.

"The duchess will not help you," he scoffed.

"Why are ye being so cruel?"

"I'm cruel by nature, my dear, but in this instant, I'm giving you only the blunt truth, Helia." He jerked his head back, toward the letters her mother had written his.

"Do you truly believe, given the fact she said nothing at all about your mother to anyone, that she'll freely own a connection to the departed woman's *daughter*?"

A fierce and welcome fury surged through her sadness. "Do you truly believe I can go to your mother now?" she cried. "As you predicted from the start, my reputation is ruined . . . and I have no place to turn." Her misery-tinged outburst echoed around the room, and this first real display of hopelessness in the always naively optimistic miss jolted him to the core.

Helia stepped out of his arms, and with her head held high, she left.

As she glided, all in white, like a specter wandering the halls of Horace House, Wingrave stared after her proudly retreating figure, transfixed.

Lust fired in his veins. Like that great untamed king of the jungle, Wingrave filled his lungs with the heavy scent of sex that lingered in the room.

Even on her own and without any options or anywhere to turn, over and over she'd proven intrepid. She possessed an imperial fearlessness and courage that set her apart from every other woman he'd ever known and would ever know.

Never had he wanted to possess any woman. But then, only Helia had revealed an indomitable spirit that marked her as his ideal mate. It was why, from the very start, he'd not turned her away from his foyer.

It was why he'd let her remain and cared for her when she'd faltered and fallen ill. Like a savage in the jungle, he'd possessed an inherent, animalistic knowing that Helia Wallace belonged to him, and he was the one to safeguard her.

His gaze slid over to the desk where he'd buried his mouth in Helia's muff and wrung another climax from her sweet lips.

His breathing grew shallower; his pulse throbbed in his veins. He wanted to fuck her whenever he wished, which would also be whenever she wished, because he'd keep her so sated, she'd never tire of the feel of him between her legs.

Yes, he needed to have her. He'd never be full in control of himself unless he had a claim to her. Not just her body.

He wanted her in every way, and he would have her. He'd have her body and soul, so she belonged to him and only him.

For too long he'd failed to see the truth laid bare before him. She was the only woman strong enough and courageous enough to be his partner and wife.

He'd rectify that prodigious error.

Growling, Wingrave quit his mother's office, and set off in hot pursuit of the one he sought.

Like a beast with the scent of his mate compelling him, Wingrave beat a quick path along the route Helia would have taken to her chambers.

The moment he reached her rooms, he didn't even stop; he tossed her door open.

Helia, in nothing more than a new chemise, and poised with a knee on the bed, gasped. She remained frozen with her nightskirts rucked about her knees.

Hungrily, he drank in the sight of her shapely limbs and imagined himself shoving them apart and lying between them and pumping himself inside her until he filled her with his seed.

Her innocence had snared him from the start—a virginal offering of the gods Wingrave had, for far too long, rejected. Not anymore. Never again.

The fabric clenched in her bloodless fingers slipped. Helia hurriedly readjusted her grip.

"Anthony?" She stared at him with big, luminescent eyes. "What are ye—"

With the heel of his foot, he kicked the door closed behind him and stalked toward her.

An emotion somewhere between fear and desire flitted across her gaze, and he reveled in male primality.

"Mine," he proclaimed in guttural tones.

Those crimson eyebrows, as fiery as Helia's spirit, nearly touched the lady's hairline.

"You are mine," he repeated, this time infusing steel within that avowal so there could be no doubting she belonged to him and only him.

Her chest hitched.

"You love those words, Helia," he growled, and gently caught her by the nape. "Because you *know* you belong to me."

"I belong to no one, Anthony." She caught her lower lip and leaned into his touch; her body's easy surrender to him made a liar of Helia, but her fight further fueled his lust.

"No," Wingrave whispered.

He swept his gaze over her flushed, freckled cheeks. Even those light-brown, tan, and red specks set her apart from every other banal, dull-featured lady who'd ever walked amongst Polite Society.

"You don't belong to anyone." Wingrave tightened the grip he had upon her. "*Me*, Helia," he repeated. "You belong to *me*."

———— ⚜ ————

You belong to me.

Anthony's possessive declaration, which stripped Helia of ownership of self and put it squarely in the hard, unforgiving hands of society's darkest lord and wickedest rake, should repel her.

Instead, she felt resurrected from the ashes of her recently broken life, and reborn anew for the male dominion he'd declared over her.

For so very long, she'd yearned to be his, and knowing he shared a like hunger for her stripped her of pride, and God forgive her, Helia was all too content to surrender and submit in the ways he demanded.

In this moment, with his body arced over her partially bent frame, everything from his words to the way his big, powerful body towered over her granted Anthony supremacy.

Still, however, there existed enough shreds of self-control and pride within Helia that she managed to resist him.

She scrambled up onto her knees so that she could meet Anthony's gaze.

The feather mattress dipped under her shifting weight and proved her foe as it abetted the marquess's attempt of mastery over Helia.

She, however, would not bend.

Helia laid her palms upon Anthony's hard, broad chest. The heat of him pierced all the way through his lawn shirt and burned her palms with the delicious warmth of his sinewy body.

Reflexively she curled her fingertips into him; her nails dug into that material and left crescents upon it.

Anthony's muscles jumped under her touch, and she reveled in the knowledge that she, a small woman, impotent in so many ways, should wield this power over him.

"I want ye, Anthony," she said softly.

A charged, savage shadow flickered across his gaze.

"But I'll be no man's mistress, Anth—"

Her declaration ended on a gasp as Anthony shot a hand out.

He caught her wrist in a gentle but completely unbreakable grip.

"I'd cut out the eyes of any man who ever dared to look at you," he whispered. His scorching eyes drilled all the way through Helia. "I'd chop off the hands of anyone so stupid as to touch the woman who belongs to me."

Helia shivered with a shamefully wicked thrill at that lethal, protective promise. Since her parents' passing, she'd been on her own, reliant upon herself to stay alive and keep herself safe.

How very alluring it was being in the care of a man who'd declare himself her steadfast sentinel.

He placed a fierce, unapologetic kiss upon the inside of her wrist. "Marry me."

Even though Anthony's wasn't a request but rather a lordly demand, she went warm all over.

"You'll want for nothing. As my queen, your crown will drip with diamonds, and the shine of gold will blind the mere mortals who dare look at you. Everyone will live to serve you."

Some shameful, wicked part hidden deep inside her reveled at the fantastical world he painted with his evocative imagery. "These are th-things, Anthony," she said softly, reminding him as much as herself.

"I will fill your every day and night with mindless pleasure," he murmured.

She did not doubt it.

Suddenly, he tightened his grip and fiery rage filled his eyes. "No man will ever dare touch what is mine, and you will never want anyone other than me, because I will assuage your every yearning so just thinking of the things I do to you will make you come."

Helia's heart missed a beat as she recalled how he'd encouraged his former betrothed to keep a lover after they wed.

That this virile man should expect *Helia's* fidelity sent another rush of heat between her legs and brought her eyes shut.

Anthony wasn't done with her.

"I will protect you with my very life. I will kill for you." With each vow, his eyes blazed brighter and brighter from the gleam of every promise made. "And if needed, I would give my life so you may live."

She fell further and deeper under his spell.

Anthony wrapped a hand about her waist, and as he pulled her against him, Helia went unresistingly.

"Then, in the afterlife," he whispered against her temple, "I will be your watchman, whose only purpose in death is to stalk and destroy every person who so much as walked in your shadow."

She drew in an unsteady breath.

In the bastion of his arms, Helia truly knew what it was to be protected and safe. He was a savage, muscle-bound warrior of old. With Anthony near, no harm would ever befall her.

Anthony made to take her mouth in another possessive kiss.

Helia pressed her fingertips to his lips, stopping Anthony as much as herself from surrendering to him.

His low, feral, angry growl vibrated against her fingers.

"Why do ye wish to marry me, Anthony? I would have you tell me." She delivered that as much a demand as any of the many he'd put to her.

As if enflamed by Helia's boldness, he moved his eyes over her face with a savage intensity.

"I have never known any woman like you, Helia. I have never met *anyone* like you. You possess a strength, fire, and spirit that somehow make me stronger. Align yourself with me," he urged, shadowy, like they were a medieval couple of old, forging an alliance in the now.

Anthony withdrew his gold watch fob.

Helia stared on confusedly as, in quick order, he freed his gold timepiece and let it fall forgotten to the mattress. Anthony removed his signet ring and wordlessly held it up to Helia.

He slipped the gilded intaglio piece upon the fob. "Bind yourself to me in name, soul, and body, Helia."

Then, without ever taking his eyes from hers, Anthony placed that golden, everlasting chain about her neck.

The cold metal of the makeshift necklace settled in the crevice of her breasts.

Trembling, Helia touched her fingertips to a shackle that, when conferred by Anthony, brought her, as its wearer, a liberation from fear and the strictures binding her as a young, unmarried woman.

It did not escape her that he'd not said "heart," and that organ clenched in her own chest in response.

With everything Anthony proffered this night, Helia should seek nothing more from him, but she proved greedy and ungrateful for wanting most the only gift he continued to withhold.

Suddenly, with the skill only a rake could surely manage, he cupped Helia's buttocks, shoved her skirts up, and palmed her already damp curls.

His masterful skill drew a sharp exhale from between her teeth. "I want you, Helia," he said sharply. "But I want you every night and in every way." Anthony slipped a finger inside her sinfully wet channel. "And I know you want me, too."

More. She wanted him *more.*

Helia bit her lower lip hard enough that she tasted the metallic tinge of blood in her mouth.

Savagely, Anthony kissed her; he sucked those sanguine drops like they were a life-sustaining nourishment from which he drew his strength.

Helia whimpered and met each bold, possessive slant of his lips.

She yearned for this man in every way. She longed to crest more of those rapturous peaks in his arms. She *wanted* to belong to him and wanted him to belong to her.

As if he'd heard and sought to fulfill those yearnings, he lured her with the sensuous promise of more.

"I will see you well loved every night so that when we, London's most powerful couple, appear together, gracing mere mortals with our presence, your legs will tremble from how often I've fucked you, and everyone will know at one glance I've laid claim to you, and that you belong to me."

She bucked against the one finger buried inside that he now teased her with. He rewarded her efforts by adding another long digit.

In search of another surrender, Helia panted and rocked her hips.

216

Anthony's dark irises gleamed with male triumph, and he continued to give her what she so desperately craved.

But she also wanted more . . . *with* him.

Helia drew back.

His gaze, angry and black, speared her with an exacting glint.

"Ah dinnae want a marriage of convenience, Anthony," she explained through hard-to-draw breaths. "Ah want—"

"The only thing convenient about our union will be all the ways in which our relationship was ordained by the gods," he interrupted. "Now, Helia," he purred, tugging off his shirt. He tossed the lawn garment over the edge of the bed. "I'm going to make love to you. With my body, I'll mark you as mine and claim you as my queen. With you at my side, together, we will not only take on the *ton*, we will also conquer and rule the whole world. I'll claim your body this night, and seal the pledge we've made, and tomorrow? Tomorrow, you will belong to me in every way. Just as I will belong to you."

He pushed his trousers down, revealing his rampant erection.

Anthony kicked aside the pants so he stood resplendently naked before Helia.

Och, God. Her mouth went dry. He was a magnificent specimen of manhood.

"Ye find me passable enough to bed, Anthony?" She somehow found the ability to tease him with those words he'd once spoken to her.

Anthony frowned. "Passable enough . . . ?"

Helia, empowered by the same power Eve had held over Adam, gave him a brazen smile.

Anthony looked her over approvingly. "You minx," he said in husky praise, as he looped an arm around her waist. "I see that wry glimmer in your mischievous eyes. Do you know what I'm going to do to you, Helia?" he whispered, his words like sin itself.

She was capable of only the tiniest shakes of her head. She lifted her gaze to his. "I'd rather ye show me."

Anthony stilled. "God, you are magnificent, Helia." The glint in his eyes darkened. "Then, let us get on with it."

She shivered at the ravenous way in which he devoured her with his gaze.

Anthony pulled Helia into his arms and crushed his mouth over hers. Unlike the earlier kisses, aggressive in their own right, these were even more frenetic. He nipped and bit her lips: the lower, the upper, their corners.

She whimpered, and he took that parting of her lips as a surrender. Perhaps it was.

"I'm going to take your small hand and wrap it around my cock," he said harshly against her mouth. His vow didn't bring fear; rather, with it came an agonizing throbbing.

He moved to the edge of the bed, so his feet were planted on the floor, and Helia scooted nearer him.

"I'm going to teach you how to tug me off, little love."

As promised, Anthony took her fingers and guided them over his long, proud erection. He proceeded to show Helia exactly what he'd meant with his dirty promise.

Heat crept across her cheeks, and Helia buried her head against his shoulder.

"Ah-ah, little love," he scolded. "There is no embarrassment between us, and certainly not in this. Not in my arms. Not in my bed. Now, *touch* me," he demanded.

He'd already guided Helia's hand up and down smoothly, slowly, teaching her, until she caught on to the rhythm he so loved. "Just like that," he gritted out, his features strained.

By the tensing of his features and the pleasure-pain radiating from his eyes, he favored her efforts greatly. Helia thrilled at the knowledge she could move him as he moved her with his touch.

"Christ, that feels so bloody good," he rasped.

His wicked words and the feel of his hot, steely rod in her fingers sent wetness flooding to that hungry place between her legs.

From almost her first night within this dark, sinister household, she'd craved things she'd not known about or understood at the time. Since then, he'd opened her eyes to the wonder to be had in his arms, and she yearned for all of it—all the mysteries of her body and his that remained, as of now, still unexplored.

Helia grazed her fingertips lightly over the plum, round tip. She resumed her exploration. Veins pulsed and bulged on the thick rod. A crystalline bead pebbled and then leaked from the tiniest slit.

Fascinated, Helia smoothed the pad of her thumb over that lucent fluid, smearing it around the head of his penis.

Anthony emitted a deep, guttural, pain-filled growl.

Helia instantly stopped and looked up.

"Do. Not. Stop." He bit out each harsh syllable of that order.

Helia did his bidding. She continued to stroke him up and down, over and over, until his eyes slid closed and obscene curses fell from his lips.

Recalling the potent effect his mouth had upon her, Helia lowered her head to Anthony's lap and tasted of that clear fluid; the salty taste of him filled her mouth.

A low, animalistic groan shook Anthony's whole body. "How did you learn that, sweet?" he hissed.

Helia hesitated and, with a frown, glanced up. "Ye dinnae like i-it," she stammered. "I-I th-thought ye might enjoy it like when ye k-kissed me—"

His eyes bored into Helia's. "I do not like it," he rasped. "I love it." He cupped her possessively at the nape.

Brought to life by both his primal grip and approval, Helia licked his length. She trailed a path of kisses along the rock-hard shaft.

He teased his fingers along her jaw, urging her to open. "Please, sweet, take me in your mouth," he implored.

Exhilarated at having been the one to reduce Anthony, this proud, powerful man, to begging, Helia moved up and down on his length. Each time she took him a bit deeper.

"Less teeth, little one. Yes, yes, that's it," he said through gritted teeth, as with his words and low groans he guided her exactly toward what he sought. "God, I want to come in your mouth so bad."

Anthony shoved a hand under her chemise and slid two fingers inside her.

She moaned and her channel tightened around his long, strong digits. While she sucked him, he rewarded her efforts by stroking Helia in time to the same rhythm she'd set with her mouth.

Soon, their grunts and moans filled the room.

Then, with his usual mastery, Anthony pulled Helia off him, flipped her onto her back, and towered over her as if she were some kind of pagan sacrifice beneath him.

"I'm going to give you what you want, Helia," he said, harsh in his declaration. "I'm going bury myself ballocks deep inside you, so deep, you can't tell where I end and you begin."

She whimpered.

But he wasn't done. Mercilessly, Anthony continued filling her ears with a carnal imagery that drove her wild.

"I'm going to pump myself inside your quim, over and over, until you're mindless and begging to come."

Anthony, further torturing her, wrapped his hand around his thick length and stroked himself as he'd taught Helia.

Helia moaned and rocked back and forth to bring herself some relief of the agonizing ache he'd wrought.

With his spare hand, Anthony reached down and pressed his palm against the soaking entrance of her body.

He smeared Helia's juices all over her curls and rubbed the glistening fluids over his shaft, until, Helia, incoherent with need, thrashed her head wildly back and forth upon the mattress.

"Please, Anthony," she cried, furiously lifting her hips.

Anthony came down over her, inserted a knee between her trembling thighs, and parted her.

Then, with a torturous languidness, he slid the tip of his rod inside Helia.

At last!

Suddenly he stopped, and Helia keened in misery as he denied her what she craved. "Please."

His black gaze seared her all the way through. "I'll be the only one you beg for your pleasure. Is that clear?"

She managed a shaky nod.

"Say the words," he rasped harshly. Anthony gave her another inch of his length, before he again stopped. "Tell me, and I'll give you more of this."

"Only you, Anthony!" Helia screamed. "You will be the only one I ever surrender my body to. I am yours."

His eyes glinted with that hard, possessive gleam . . . and something more. "And I am yours, Helia, my marchioness, my queen."

With that, Anthony claimed her lips and buried himself to the hilt, deep inside.

She cried out and her entire body spasmed in bliss, relief, and some parts discomfort.

For even as her soaking channel had eased his entry some, his enormous shaft stretched and filled her virginal channel.

Anthony brushed a sweaty curl back behind Helia's ear and placed a kiss upon her damp brow. "Have I hurt you, little dove?" he asked hoarsely.

"It feels . . . you feel so good, Anthony." Her center throbbed from the force of her need. "Please, don't stop loving me." Helia, in a bid to spur him on, thrust her hips up.

"Never," he rasped, and her words and gyrations seemed to unleash him.

In a powerful rhythm, his body moved over Helia's. He stroked his length inside her, until that now familiar pressure built between her legs.

She yearned for that peak. Helia hurt with the force of her need for release. Still, Anthony withheld that gift, keeping it an elusive goal that she arched and begged for.

Biting her lower lip, Helia wrapped her arms about him and dug her nails sharply into the contoured muscles of his back. She leaned up into Anthony so as to somehow get herself closer, to no avail.

The harsh angles of his face were drawn tight, and he gritted his teeth like he, too, fought the same battle within that Helia waged with herself.

"You feel so good," he rasped. "So bloody good." He drove himself harder, deeper inside her, and then, at last, Helia reached that glorious zenith.

She screamed her surrender to the ceiling. She screamed Anthony's name.

Anthony stiffened over her, and then with a low, guttural groan, he spent himself inside her; as promised, he filled her with his seed, and she continued coming.

Helia gasped, her entire being jolted by the resplendence of at last being joined with him.

"I love you, Anthony," she cried, and then collapsed onto the mattress.

The echo of her avowal danced around the walls and off the ceiling . . . only to linger, and then fade into nothingness—unreturned.

Chapter 20

O! useful may it be to have shewn, that, though the vicious can sometimes pour affliction upon the good, their power is transient and their punishment certain; and that innocence, though oppressed by injustice, shall, supported by patience, finally triumph over misfortune!

—*Ann Radcliffe, The Mysteries of Udolpho*

The following morning, Helia and Anthony, without any fanfare, and with only servants as witnesses, were married.

The ancient-looking vicar, with nascent tones, who'd been unable to deny the future Duke of Talbert's demands, performed a perfunctory ceremony that joined Helia and Anthony until death did part them.

She and Anthony had promptly adjourned to the dining room for their wedding breakfast, whereupon her husband had ordered the servants to leave. The door hadn't even fully closed behind the last footman when Anthony placed Helia on the edge of the dining table.

He'd lifted her skirts and feasted upon her. Anthony, like a flesh-and-blood Lothario, had wrung climax after climax from Helia, until her center had pulsed and gone nearly numb from the intensity of his loving.

Then he'd left.

And she'd not seen him since.

Helia, curled up on the throne-like chair she'd commandeered in the duke's office, rested her chin atop her right fist, and stared out at the single yew tree in the distance.

Absently, Helia played with the chain Anthony had placed around her neck, with the ring that marked her as his.

Even now, thinking of all the things he'd done to her this morn left her shamefully wet between her legs.

Helia didn't doubt he desired her. Countless times he'd made her body sing and taught her something new in the art of lovemaking. He hungered for her the very way she ached for him.

Of course, knowing Anthony's reputation and his lusty appetite, she'd anticipated they'd spend hours making love—which they had.

Aside from that, she didn't know what else she'd expected of their marriage—

Helia pulled a face. "Liar. You know precisely what you expected." *And still expect.*

When Anthony had barged into her chambers last evening, he'd filled her ears with the most beautiful of promises. With all that and the security, safety, and stability he vowed, how could she want for more?

Furthermore, although he'd not said he loved her, Helia knew with every *other* word he'd uttered that he cared for her, respected her, valued her, and wanted her to be his partner in life.

But she wanted more. She was the greediest of creatures, having so very much from Anthony, but only truly wanting the one thing he withheld—his heart.

Groaning, Helia dropped her head along the back of her seat.

From their first meeting he'd been clear—he didn't deal in that intolerable thing called love.

Where Helia had been born, raised, and nurtured by that emotion, Anthony's almighty parents had withheld it. The one person he'd freely loved had been taken from him.

"Is it any wonder you became the man you did?" she whispered.

He saw that grand emotion as the greatest weakness and had fully insulated himself from all people.

Incorrectly and heartrendingly, Anthony had come to the erroneous conclusion that his loving others brought with it pain, loss, and weakness.

Helia took in a shuddery breath.

Wind knocked at the windowpanes in Mother Nature's forlorn assent.

This time, Helia felt him before she heard him.

Anthony slid his arms over the back of the chair. "Look at you, taking over the duke's offices," he whispered against her ear. "My wife. My marchioness." With each claim, he took a bite of her sensitive lobe. "My future duchess, my queen."

With a maddening slowness, he ran his skilled hands over her body.

He still wore his fine leather riding gloves, an indication—and reminder—that he'd only just returned.

Anthony filled his palms with her breasts.

Her breath caught sharply in a telltale sign of her desire.

He chuckled, a deep, throaty rumble that indicated he knew all too well the effect he was having on her.

How easily he roused her to an all-consuming lust. And yet . . . she wanted more than that.

If she let Anthony have her now, without any hesitation on her part and with no discussion of his abrupt departure today, she'd never truly be his equal.

With a strenuous effort, Helia pushed his palms away.

He grunted. A man of his talents would never be familiar with any form of rejection of his attentions. The reminder of how many women there'd been before her left her more than a little piqued.

"I prefer it here, Anthony," she said evenly. "The view of the gardens is superior. *That* is my reason for being here."

"Do you know where you'd prefer it more, dearest Helia?" he asked, tempting her as he slipped another hand over her breast. "In my arms. In my bed. On this desk. Hell, anywhere and everywhere."

This time, with a far greater struggle, she gently but firmly took his wrists, so her fingers made a makeshift shackle around them.

Not that she deluded herself into believing he couldn't or wouldn't break that weak binding were he to so wish it. Her fingers didn't even manage to go all the way around Anthony's wrist.

But in this instant, he allowed her power over him and this exchange, and she loved him all the more for allowing their relationship to be one where they were equals.

"Are you cross with me, love?"

Love . . . Her heart skittered a beat. This time, that endearment emerged with a softness he'd never before infused within it.

"Ye've been gone," she said huskily.

Anthony stared at her for a long moment. *"And?"*

And she dreaded the discussion about what had sent him running but wanted to have it. "Ye left on our wedding day," she said, a gentle rebuke.

He continued to study her, and then a flash of understanding sparked in his eyes.

Suddenly, Anthony scooped her up.

Helia emitted a squeak as he flipped their positioning so he sat enthroned upon the ducal chair and she, with her skirts rucked high about her waist, sat astride his hips.

"Oh, kitten," he murmured, a soft smile on his hard lips. "Never tell me you believe I've gone to find pleasure with another woman."

Actually, she hadn't. She'd been far more concerned he'd gone into hiding because he'd married her and now felt stuck.

"No." She paused and wrinkled her brow. "*Is* that something I should be worried about?" She found herself possessed of an all-potent, venomous jealousy for every woman who'd come before her, and for every one who'd seek a place in his bed even with him now married.

He made a tsking sound. "Oh, Helia, you still have not gathered that forevermore you are the only woman I will ever have in my life and bed."

Anthony brushed a palm over her cheek, and she leaned into that intoxicating caress. "You are a fire in my blood. I will *never* tire of you, wife. I will continue to discover new ways to worship your body and make love to you and will only run out of them when I either die or the earth folds into darkness."

He gave her a sharp look. "Do you understand me, Helia?"

She trembled, liquefied by the devotion of this once great rake. *For me.* He swore his fealty and fidelity to her.

Helia nodded.

Anthony tweaked her nose playfully. "I still did not answer your question, though, did I?"

"No." Some of the tension went out of her; inner coward that she was, they'd not have the discussion about her declaration—at least not now.

"Do you want me to?" he teased.

"Only if you *wish* to tell me."

"Very well. If you aren't curious . . ." He started to rise, but Helia wrapped her arms about his neck and held firmly on to him.

"I may be mildly curious, husband," she murmured.

"Only mildly curious?" Again, Anthony made to stand.

Laughing, Helia clung more tightly to him. "Very well. I am *outrageously* curious. Are you satisfied?" she managed to get out through her mirth.

He covered her mouth with his, in a punishing kiss that robbed Helia of breath, and she kissed him back with a like fury and passion.

All her earlier questions and worries of where he'd been faded. Not a single cogent thought could exist in her head when he made love to her.

A commotion out in the hall suddenly reached them, and then rapidly approaching footsteps. "Where the hell *is* he?"

That austere, commanding tone could belong to only one man—the Duke of Talbert.

Bloody hell.

The office door exploded open, and Wingrave's parents stood frozen at the threshold.

The duchess was regal as ever, her features largely untouched by age, but for a few slight creases at the corners of her eyes.

His ashen father, with a height similar to Wingrave's and far greater bulk from too many spirits and candied fruits, had presence alone that would have roused a man to fear. That, however, coupled with a ducal title that went back to 1326 made the Duke of Talbert a chilling menace.

For anyone and everyone—everyone other than Wingrave.

The duchess gasped and promptly covered her eyes.

Her husband, on the other hand, took in the tableau of a pale Helia and Wingrave's hold upon her. As he did, his eyes grew wider and wider until rage made them large circles.

Any other time Wingrave would have thrilled at having his father find him in the goddamned ducal office and claiming this space as his own.

Not this time, not with Helia's legs dangling on either side of his lap, and him a handful of front falls from plunging himself up and in her.

Wingrave carefully helped Helia to her feet and made sure her skirts were drawn into place to provide deserved modesty, and then stood beside her.

"You have terrible timing, Duke," he drawled. "You should have remained in the country. Your color is shite."

The duke, previously never speechless, found his voice. "I would still be there if I hadn't received word about what you've been up to!" he thundered.

This meeting had been inevitable. It'd been clear that eventually word of Helia's presence here would slip out, carried by some servant's loose lips, or as witnessed by someone during the lady's many ventures outdoors.

"Is something wrong with *both* of your goddamned ears?" the duke hissed.

There'd been a time that insult would have hit the very mark his sire intended. Now, Wingrave flashed a cold, mocking smile.

Bright-red, angry splotches formed on the duke's cheeks. "You dare to insult me?"

"I wouldn't give it a second thought." Wingrave arced an eyebrow. "In this particular instance, however, I'm merely speaking the truth."

His father's eyes bulged, and it was a wonder they didn't pop out of the old bastard's head.

Wingrave's bold and brave wife cleared her throat, and as the duke swung his gaze her way, Helia made herself the target of his wrath.

She dropped into a flawless curtsy. "Yer Grace. It is verra lovely to meet—"

"What have you done, Wingrave?" the duke thundered over the rest of her greeting.

Helia drifted nearer to Wingrave.

Wingrave gritted his teeth. He wanted her in his rooms and away from this ugly—about to get uglier—exchange.

With that goal in mind, Wingrave collected Helia's palm in his and headed for the door. "Step aside, old man."

"The hell I will," the duke barked. With an impressive speed for a man his age and size, Wingrave's father stormed inside. The duchess only just made it into the office before her husband slammed the door and planted his bulky frame between Wingrave and Helia's escape.

Wingrave's mother hurried to the corner of the room.

"Anthony. Are ye all right?" Helia whispered, hesitant and made timid by his goddamned father.

But she did not run.

"I am more than fine, love," he murmured. "Just a blustery old man."

"*Love? Anthony?*" the duke roared. And it was a testament to his rage that the duke ignored the slight on his character. "Why the hell is this *Scot* calling you 'Anthony'?"

From the corner of his eye, Anthony caught his mother hurrying to hide behind the long velvet curtains. "Goddamn it, answer me this instant, Wingrave."

To protect her from the old bastard's wrath, Wingrave positioned himself between Helia and the duke. He locked stares with the man who'd sired him but had never really been a father. Not in the ways Helia had described her own.

"This proud, beautiful Scot?" Wingrave asked in suitably solemn tones. "She is my wife."

His Grace's cheeks grew mottled; his eyes flared so big all the whites were exposed.

In anticipation of the impending storm, Wingrave reached a hand behind him and found Helia's fingers; they were steady and warm, as they would be, his magnificent, undauntable goddess.

The duke boiled with rage. "You stupid, stupid man," he whispered. "You did this to best me."

"Actually, I didn't." Wingrave flicked a cool, bored gaze over his sire. "I'd have to care one way or another about you or your opinion and I don't." He steeled his jaw.

Before Wingrave knew what Helia intended, she stepped out from behind him and took her place at his side.

Wingrave glanced briefly down at his wife; Helia looked up and gave his fingers a squeeze in support.

"I married her because she is a bold, courageous, strong, honorable woman who I am proud to have as my wife and the next duchess."

"She is a goddamned Scot," the duke hissed.

"Indeed." He inclined his head. "Also, that is likely what makes her all those things I so admire her for. She's not some vapid, puny English miss who'll cower in the shadows."

Wingrave looked toward the corner, where his mother even now listened. She'd stood up to the duke once—and only once—before.

"Perhaps this would be a good time for you to point out my wife is also your goddaughter, Mother?" he called, offering her the opportunity to speak up, and also understanding if she couldn't.

His mother stepped slowly from the shadows. There she was, that woman from the church . . .

"Goddaughter?" the duke thundered, his bulbous nose flaring.

Wingrave's mother disappeared into the shadows with a far greater speed than she'd stepped out of them.

He understood.

Through the years, Wingrave had been all too happy to secretly provide her with the funds the duke had denied her—for the pleasure he found of thwarting his sire, of course. But were the duke to decide to commit the duchess, there was nothing Wingrave could do. To the world and the law, the duchess was a possession that could not be taken away.

"You stupid, stupid man!" The duke wagged a wrinkled finger at Wingrave. "You, with your broken ear and defiance—it should be your brother who lived."

Before Wingrave could issue a droll reply, Helia spoke up. "How dare you?" She glared at the duke. "You evil, evil soul. Your son? He is one *thousand* times the man you are and is the one truly good thing you've done in your life."

Veins along the duke's big, broad brow bulged. *"You,"* he raged. *"You've* done this."

Blinded by fury that anyone would dare speak to Helia so, Wingrave took a furious step toward the duke when Helia spoke.

"If by that you mean I fell in love with your son, then, yes, you are correct," she said, with such stoicism in the face of the duke's wrath, Wingrave growled with fierce approval and hunger for his queen.

Ruddy color suffused the duke's cheeks. *"Love?"* he scoffed. His Grace turned all his fury back on Wingrave. "Is *that* how this one tricked you? With some innocent act and words of that false, puling emotion of *love?"*

Helia took another beautifully bold step toward the duke. "Given the horrid way you've treated your son and clearly bully your wife, I can say with absolute confidence love isn't real . . . at least for someone such as you."

I seek to protect you, Anthony.

That avowal she'd recently made Wingrave, the one he'd rebuffed, he now let in, a feeling still unfamiliar but . . . right, and welcomed.

"You are incapable of and undeserving of that sentiment," Helia continued. "But for your son, your wife, and every other person with an actual soul and heart in their beings, love is very much real."

The quiet calm in Helia's voice proved more powerful than any of the duke's bellowing, and Wingrave fell only further under her siren's spell.

She'd managed the impossible—to silence his sire.

The duke's cheeks grew mottled and more florid. "You talk about love. The only thing you *truly* love is that you're now set to be a duchess," he hissed. Spittle formed at the corner of his mouth.

Helia didn't back down in the face of his fury. "No, Your Grace. One does not love power. One craves and needs power. Love, on the other hand, is unselfish. It requires nothing and gives everything."

Suddenly, the duke narrowed his eyes. "I know what you did. You waited until I'd gone and then came here." He spoke that *discovery* to himself. Rage blazed all the brighter in his ruthless eyes. "You seduced my goddamn rake of a son."

He looked to Wingrave. "Couldn't you have just made her your goddamned mistress? You could have tupped her anytime and married an estimable, well-bred Englishwoman who brought something of value to—"

The duke's vitriolic diatribe ended on a squeak.

Wingrave had wrapped a hand about the old bastard's thick neck. "Do not ever, I repeat, *ever*"—he tightened his grip for emphasis—"utter so much as a word about my wife that isn't the highest praise and adulation, or I will happily end you, and make her the duchess she was and is now destined to be."

He'd not been able to protect his brother. The duke had threatened to send Wingrave's mother to a madhouse were Wingrave to intervene on the duchess's behalf.

But it ended here. It ended now.

"Anthony," Helia murmured, resting her hands on the muscles that bulged even through the heavy fabric of his greatcoat. "Mercy," she whispered.

Wingrave lingered his hold a second more. "It is only because of my queen's benevolence that I don't happily end you." He abruptly released the duke.

His father's expression turned black. "I'll petition the king, Wingrave. I'll have it annulled."

He smirked. "I assure you, this union is very much consummated, *Duke*."

The duke slammed a fist into a porcelain urn that rested on a nearby side table. The tall, cobalt-blue vase exploded into a sea of tiny shards upon the marble flooring.

Blood dripped from the old bastard's wrist.

Helia stared on with horror in her revealing eyes.

"And I'll have you know," Wingrave continued, the calm to his father's storm, "your threats of sending your wife away end this day. Should you attempt to have her placed in an institution, I will freely speak about how your own insanity led you to place a woman most respected, revered, and appreciated by the *ton* into a cell."

Spittle formed at the corners of the duke's limp mouth.

Done with the duke, now and forever, Wingrave looked to the shadows, where his mother remained.

He motioned for her to join them.

The duchess inched out.

"How dare you threaten me?" the duke shouted, and the echo of his vitriol sent her into hiding once more. "How dare you seek to control that which is mine?"

"I do so very easily, *Father*," he said mockingly. "Because your days on earth are numbered and power is mine. You know it, and you hate it."

With that, Wingrave looked to Helia. "Come," he murmured, guiding her toward the door. He'd not have her see any more of this.

There'd been a time when Wingrave would have relished nothing more than a good row with the nasty bastard. Now, however, with Helia in his life, he'd no interest in battling his father and instead had a desire to spend every goddamned moment of his life loving her and simply existing in her presence.

"Where are you going, Wingrave?" his father bellowed. "We are not done. This is not done. Return this instant."

Behind them, the duke cursed and shouted.

There came a great, resounding crash.

Helia paused and glanced back.

Like some wild, rabid beast, Wingrave's father grabbed everything in his sight and upended it.

He grabbed a gilded clock in one hand and a vase in the other and hurled them at the wide double doors.

The crash of shattering glass came over and over as he chucked every fragile piece that adorned the room until he stood amidst the shards of his crumbling empire.

Panting and crazed as any madman bound for Bedlam, the duke flitted wild eyes about.

Wingrave's sire, with every delicate piece now broken before him, squatted and, with a savage roar, hefted a gilded and marble console table over his head—

"Oh, my God," Helia whispered.

"There's no god in this," Wingrave said, guiding her face away from the melee. "This is the Devil's work."

He tried to tug her free, but in the face of mayhem, Helia lingered still.

"Helia," Wingrave said loudly over the duke's din.

"We are not leaving her with him, Anthony."

Wingrave looked toward his mother's hiding spot and stretched a hand toward her.

Amidst the duke's destruction, the duchess rushed to join them. Without hesitation she placed her fingers in Helia's welcoming ones.

Wingrave gave his wife and mother cover.

As he shut the door behind them, the cacophony of furniture flipping and the duke's unintelligible shouts and curses continued behind them.

"He is not always like that," the duchess whispered, when they'd reached the end of the corridor.

"He is." Wingrave wouldn't lie about what a monster the duke was.

The duchess's steps slowed, and Helia allowed the older woman to stop.

His mother cast a distracted glance over her shoulder.

"What is it, Your Grace?" Helia asked softly.

"I must go to him."

He and Helia spoke as one.

"No," he said, his voice sharp where Helia's was gentle.

"Your Grace, you do not," his wife murmured. "He just needs some time to release his anger, and then I expect he'll be in a better frame of mind."

The duke wouldn't.

And the duchess knew it. That was why Wingrave's mother had a worried glimmer in her eyes and wrung her hands together the way she did.

Suddenly, the duchess ceased those frenetic movements, and as she drew back her shoulders, she had more the look of that brave woman who'd stood up in the middle of a church in challenge of her husband. "I am the one who calms him, Anthony. You know that."

He knew she was the one verbally battered by the old codger, and that whenever Anthony had intervened, the old bastard had made it worse for her.

"Don't go to him," he said quietly, all the while knowing what she intended and that there'd be no stopping her.

The duchess gave him a watery smile. "You've always been a good boy, Anthony." With tears in her eyes, she glanced at Helia. "I am so very glad my son has found you."

Helia made to speak when a thunderous bellow cut into the tender moment, ending it all too quickly.

"Go," the duchess urged, and when neither Helia nor Wingrave made a step to leave, she hurried off the way they'd come, back to the fray.

Several corridors later, the unmistakable sound of the duke's rampage continued, only slightly muted this time.

Helia's eyes bled with grief; sadness lined her every exquisite feature. "Oh, Anthony—"

He grunted. "I am sorry you were subjected to that. We will not remain here. I have holdings of my own and will all too happily take you away from—"

Helia pressed two fingers against his lips. "I am not hurting for *m-me*," she said, her voice catching. "I am hurting for your mother and sister. But more, I am hurting for *you* and the life you've known. I will have you know, with me as your wife, I promise you will only be loved and live in a household filled with that emotion you've been denied and are so deserving of."

His throat . . . it moved in the oddest of ways. Something in his eyes pricked, making it hard to blink.

He'd feared loving anyone made him weaker, and put anyone he cared about in peril. Only to discover, love somehow made him stronger. Nay, *this* woman's love. He'd fought it—and her—at every turn.

"I am done fighting," he murmured, more to himself, and he found . . . peace in that, a sense of absolute rightness made all the more profound by a final, noticeable thump and then quiet from downstairs.

Helia's eyes softened. Joy glowed from their dark-green depths.

He pressed his forehead hard against hers so that their gazes met. She'd been long deserving of the words she'd spoken to him so many times now. Ones he'd been too much of a coward to give her. Not anymore.

"Helia," he said gravely, "I—"

A horrible, drawn-out, animalistic wail cut off the rest of his avowal. Wingrave stiffened.

"No. No. No. No. No." That single-word litany rang out, over and over, in his mother's shrill cries.

There came a clamoring and the rush of footfalls. As one, he and Helia looked, just as a breathless Mrs. Trowbridge rounded the corner. "M-my lord," she rasped, her cheeks wan, her eyes stricken. "His Grace, the duke . . . is dead," she whispered.

———— ❦ ————

Eight hours later

Wingrave stood in wait outside the duke's grand suites; his back braced against the wall and his arms folded at his chest, he stared unmovedly at the adjacent door.

All the while, his mother, the duchess, sat on an upholstered armchair which had been stationed outside her husband's rooms and wept quietly into her kerchief—just as she'd done since she and Wingrave had taken up position here.

Devoid of disdain and filled more with pity, Wingrave glanced at his mother's bent head.

How . . . odd. How strange. It was illogical in every way. His mother . . . actually cared about the duke. Maybe even loved him.

A time before, Wingrave would have felt disdain for her having any sense of devotion to the man who'd been her—and their entire family's—oppressor.

As it so happened, now he found himself pitying her.

At last, the door opened.

They looked over as Dr. Hall, the same family physician who'd failed to heal Wingrave's brother, exited with the same leather bag he'd carried from a different set of rooms many years earlier.

The duchess jumped up.

Dr. Hall looked solely at Wingrave. "My lord, may we speak?"

The message and meaning were clear; the doctor didn't intend to include the duchess in the discussion about her husband.

Wingrave inclined his head.

He and Dr. Hall walked several paces, putting some distance between themselves and the duchess.

The minute they stopped, Dr. Hall set his bag down, removed his spectacles, folded them, and tucked them in the front of his pocket.

"I fear it is grim," the doctor began.

"He's not dead, then?"

"He is not." Hall's features grew strained. "However, I am sad to report, the duke will not make the recovery you hope for."

All the while they spoke, the duchess strained her neck in an attempt to hear the exchange.

Hell would freeze before Wingrave's own wife ever allowed herself to be denied information from anyone. No doubt she'd have shut herself away in the rooms and guided the incompetent physician's every action, before ultimately taking them over herself.

"Given His Grace's collapse," Dr. Hall was saying, "and his lack of reflexes, inability to speak, and . . . vacant expression, I can safely—but sadly—conclude he suffered some internal hemorrhagic rupture. I am so very sad to say."

The old bastard had driven himself to an apoplexy. He hadn't died, but knowing his sire as he did, Wingrave could safely conclude death would be a preferable state to bedbound and without any brain function.

Odd, he found himself capable of some pity for the mercenary duke, after all.

"Thank you," Wingrave said.

"If there are any services I may provide—"

"None. You are done here. Your tenure as the Blofield family physician ends this day."

Dr. Hall's jaw slackened. "M-my l-lord?" he stammered.

"That will be all."

Dismissing the physician outright, Wingrave returned to the duke's door.

His ashen mother worried her hands together. "A-Anthony?" she whispered.

Anthony. He was finally Anthony again. Perhaps she'd already gleaned the news and sought to reclaim some ownership of herself and her decisions.

Wingrave placed a hand on her shoulder, leaned down, and whispered the duke's fate.

She sucked in a shaky breath and emitted a small, indistinctive sound from her throat.

He gave her shoulder a gentle squeeze, and then with her standing in wait, he let himself inside the dark, shadowy room.

His father, attired in a long gown, and with a sheet and coverlet draped over him, lay as still as death upon the big mattress.

Wingrave stopped at his bedside and looked down.

Like a hot sun had melted his face, the duke's features drooped on both sides. Drool pooled at the corners of his mouth.

Wingrave, not taking his gaze off his father's frail form, dragged a nearby chair over and seated himself.

Steepling his fingers, he stared over the tops of them. "You were a terrible duke, you know," he stated, matter-of-factly, into the quiet. "I didn't realize I was becoming you, and wouldn't have realized, had it not been for the glorious woman I made my wife."

The duke's lids lifted; his gaze was surprisingly sharp, despite his condition, so much so that Wingrave wondered if the bastard had struck a deal with the Devil, all to defy the fate Hall had laid out for him and to retain the power he so coveted.

"Ah, the beast awakens," Wingrave remarked.

The duke's slack lips wobbled, revealing a tongue as dead as the old man's heart, and no words emerged . . . only more saliva.

"How awful this must be for you," Wingrave murmured. "Not anyone else. You were a miserable cur. But I've not come to tell you all the ways in which you were a malevolent duke, father, and husband. With you unable to speak, where would be the fun in that?"

The duke continued to stare vacantly back.

"I will keep this quick." Wingrave dropped his hands atop his lap and leaned forward. "You've scared your daughter, wife, servants, and, for that matter, *anyone*, for the last time. They will not miss you. They will not mourn you. They will not even visit. You will exist as nothing more than a ghost who goes unseen amongst us."

His father's gaze remained vacant, but for a distant glimmer indicating that somewhere in there, the duke not only heard but understood exactly what Wingrave said.

Wingrave flattened his lips into a hard line. "Your time as duke is done. Your reign ends and belongs to me. It all belongs to me, and with Helia, my wife, we will rule with strength and a benevolent good for those who are deserving and a relentless might for any who dare cross us."

A choking, rasping sound started in his father's chest and got stuck in his throat as a low, wet gurgling.

Without a backward glance, Wingrave left his past and marched on to his future.

Chapter 21

"Why all this terror?" said he, in a tremulous voice. "Hear me, Emily: I come not to alarm you; no, by Heaven! I love you too well—too well for my own peace."

—*Ann Radcliffe, The Mysteries of Udolpho*

Her knees drawn close to her chest, Helia sat on the floor in the corner of the same guest chambers she'd occupied upon her arrival, days, weeks—a lifetime—ago.

Even with the sun glaring brightly through the filmy curtains, the room remained chilled from the absence of a fire in the barren hearth.

That cold filled every corner of her numb being.

Anthony had worried that those who were close to him ultimately suffered. Helia had struggled to help him realize differently.

She didn't delude herself into believing Anthony carried any affection for his father. How could he, after all?

What her husband would take from this was that his actions had brought about another death.

He'd blamed himself for having encouraged Evander to go skating with him and saw himself as responsible as opposed to understanding it'd been a tragic accident.

Only, in the end, everything Anthony had taken as fact and feared—even as he would never dare admit to that emotion—had come true.

He'd been so very close to letting down all his walls and trusting and smiling . . . and then pain and heartache and loss had revisited this household, all because of Helia.

Or that was how Anthony was likely to see it. And why shouldn't he? The entire reason for the duke's explosion had been because Anthony had married her.

She squeezed her eyes shut and hugged herself even more tightly. Once again, her efforts proved futile. The memories of the duke's violent row with Anthony, the thunderous shouts, the breaking glass, the toppling furniture; it all came rushing back.

What now?

Cowardly as it was, she didn't want to know. She wanted to remain hidden away in this room, shut away from Anthony, and what was to come.

The hinges of the door squeaked as the panel opened.

Let it be a diligent maid. Let it be a footman. Or . . . or any servant. Just do not let it be . . .

Anthony.

Alas, the universe wouldn't even grant her a slightly longer reprieve.

From where he stood in the entryway, her husband, wearing a dark frown, did a sweep of the room.

Helia hunched her shoulders and made herself as small as possible.

She should have known better.

Her slight movement instantly beckoned Anthony's notice.

His gaze sharpened on the corner she'd made hers for the better part of the morning and afternoon; Anthony frowned.

"Helia?" he said, pushing the door closed behind him with a quiet click.

He was across the room and at her side in three long strides.

Her gut clenched. She hated his frown as much as she cherished, craved, and loved his elusive smile. "An—*my lord*," she quickly corrected, in tremulous tones.

His scowl deepened. "'My lord'?"

Oh, God. The worst had happened. "Your G-Grace?" she whispered. She made to climb to her feet and pay proper due in the form of a curtsy to her husband.

"What are you doing down here?" he demanded, and joined her on the floor before she could even stand.

Because duchesses behaved a certain way and that most definitely did not include hiding in corners.

She couldn't manage anything but a question of her own. "Your father?"

His jaw tightened. "Lives, but not in any sense he'd want to."

Helia stared confusedly at him.

"He suffered a catastrophic apoplexy," he said flatly. "It has robbed him of the ability to speak, walk, or use his hands."

Her gut roiled. First he'd lost his brother, and now his father had suffered perhaps an even worse fate. *I'm going to be sick.*

"I am so, so sorry, Anth—my lord." She got past the thick ball of emotion in her throat.

He stared at her like she'd sprouted a second and third head. "Why in hell are you calling me 'my lord'?"

Grief did strange things to people. Having lost her parents, Helia knew that all too well.

"I . . ." It was too much being this close to him. Needing to stretch, needing to move, needing distance from him, Helia stood and presented him her back.

"Yes?" he snapped.

"I thought you might prefer it?" That slight uptilt managed to turn her response into a question.

"*Prefer* it?" he asked bluntly. "And why would I?"

That brought her up short. A sliver of hope slipped inside her breast. She faced him once more.

"I know you feel as if you are responsible when those close to you suffer." She held her palms up. "Just as I know I'm the one responsible for your father's fit and resulting impairment."

With every word that flew from her lips, Anthony's gaze darkened.

Missing a beat, Helia stumbled back a step. "And if you wish for me to go away . . ." Her voice broke.

Oh, God, how she'd miss him. Her heart would cease to beat and then wither and die in her breast.

He glared for her to continue.

"If you wish for me to leave, I understand. I've already asked for my belongings to be packed."

Anthony said nothing for a long while, and Helia sat in the misery of his silence.

Then a low, murderous rumble shook his frame.

"You've packed your bags," he said between tightly gritted teeth.

Biting her lower lip, Helia nodded.

Suddenly, he shot a hand out, caught her by the waist, and hauled her against him.

She gasped . . . and then made the mistake of meeting his gaze. Those nearly black irises gleamed with a raw ferocity.

He lowered his head, so that she had to tip her neck back.

"You better have packed for two, love, because if you think for one moment I intend to let you leave me, I will track you down to the ends of the earth, and claw my way to heaven and snatch you back from the hands of God himself."

Tears blurred his beautiful, beloved visage. Her mouth trembled furiously.

He wasn't done with her.

"You are mine," he rasped. Anthony gave her a slight shake, and the chain bearing his signet ring rattled about her neck as if to add further weight to his affirmation. "And I am yours. Do you hear that?"

Helia gave a small nod.

"Do you *hear* that?" he repeated, this time more forcefully and with another greater shake.

A sob escaped her, and Helia caught it too late behind her fingers. "A-aye."

Anthony searched her face like one in seek of the veracity of her confirmation, and with a harsh growl, he again snatched her close.

Helia wept; her tears dampened the front of his shirt. She cried so that her entire body shook, and still she could not stop, not even with the quiet, soothing words Anthony whispered into her ear.

"I th-thought you would blame me," she said between tears.

"Why would I blame you, love?" He placed a tender kiss at her temple, softening that chastisement.

"I challenged him. I pushed him—"

"Helia, my father's actions and behavior this day, and every day, belong only to him."

She opened her mouth to further protest, but he kissed her to silence.

Her lashes fluttered wildly.

"Now," he murmured, "you are going somewhere."

Helia's lashes flew open.

He tweaked her nose. "With me, Helia. I am your warrior, your king, and also your shadow. Where you go, I go, too."

With a mysterious set to his features, Anthony removed a long strip of black satin fabric from inside the front of his jacket. He made to twine the soft cloth about her head.

Helia drew back. "What are ye d-doing?" Her voice trembled in both wicked anticipation and fear.

"Trust me."

And she did. She trusted him to keep her safe and protected and to treat her like the queen he insisted she was.

A short time later, a blindfolded Helia sat nestled alongside Anthony on the carriage bench. A warmed blanket upon her lap and heating bricks added an impossible heat on this winter's night.

"May I take this off?" she murmured, already reaching for the black satin fabric he'd gently fastened about her head.

"I'd rather you didn't." The velvet squabs dipped, and Helia found her legs shoved farther apart. "It heightens the pleasure."

She knew what he attempted to do.

With a tantalizing languor, Anthony pushed her skirts up, higher and higher, and despite his denial, she removed the blindfold and gazed upon him.

Helia slipped her fingers through his hair, already knowing his intentions, and wanting them, but she made herself stop, preventing him from giving her what she hungered for.

He glanced up with a question in his eyes.

"I know," she said softly.

His frown deepened.

"I know you are showing me that which you are unable to say." She gently stroked his loose, ink-black curls.

Anthony placed a kiss on the inside of her thigh. "What is that, love?"

His question contained none of the rancor that'd been so much a part of their exchanges before.

"It is going to be fine." Helia touched her palm to his cheek, and held his gaze. "We are going to be fine."

Emotion blazed from within his eyes; an understanding passed between them.

They knew one another's thoughts. They knew one another's souls.

"It is going to be all right," he vowed.

Anthony placed tantalizing kisses along first her right inner thigh, and then her left. As he did, the sough of his breath upon her hot flesh made the ache between her legs unbearable.

And then, he buried his tongue inside her slit.

Helia moaned and lifted her hips.

Unhurried in his attentions, Anthony made love to her with his mouth.

All the while, the carriage rocked under them, that slight back-and-forth bouncing heightening the effects of his efforts.

At last, Anthony brought Helia to a gentle, but no less transcendental, climax.

Gasping, replete, Helia collapsed into the velvet squabs and allowed her heart to find its normal tempo.

A powerful wave of emotion threatened to bring her under. She would never not want him. He was the very air in her lungs. The reason her heart beat.

Tenderly, Anthony dropped a kiss atop her damp curls and then drew her skirts down into place.

The bench dipped as Anthony joined her. "It was good, love?"

"Good?" A sated smile played at her lips. "You strutting rooster, you ken it was splendorous."

He grinned, flashing two rows of perfectly even, pearl-white teeth. A loose black curl fell over his eyes, giving him a boyish look, and her heart melted.

Dark, enigmatic marquess. Masterful, attentive lover. Naughty, bonny boy. Guarded, hurting man. She loved every dazzlingly different facet of him.

"We're here," he murmured.

It took a moment to register that at some point the carriage had come to a stop.

Here? "Where is 'here'?" She reached for the gold velvet curtains.

Anthony caught her hand and effectively intercepted her efforts. "Uh-uh." He touched his lips to the delicate place where her hand met her wrist.

Helia's breath hitched. *How is it possible for such a small kiss to have this dizzying effect?*

Anthony shot a fist up.

The carriage dipped. There came a slight hurry-scurry, and then the footman, John Thomas, drew the door open.

Helia went to steal a peek outside, but as Anthony made to exit, his broad frame completely blocked the entrance and robbed her of that attempt.

When his feet touched the ground, John Thomas reached a hand up. She made to place her gloved fingertips within his palm.

Anthony growled; that menacing sound caused the servant to stumble several steps away from Helia.

In the nighttime still and winter's quiet, there came John Thomas's telltale audible nervous swallowing. The man fell back into the shadows.

That imagined threat gone, Anthony, in one fluid movement, caught Helia by the waist and helped her down himself.

"You know, you've scared poor Mr. John Thomas," she chided the moment her feet touched the snow-covered ground.

"Good," he said tersely. "No man touches what is mine."

Butterflies danced around her belly.

That possessive threat was softened as he carefully drew her fur-lined hood into place.

Helia caught his hands and linked her fingers through his; she forced him to look at her. "Do you truly believe I could ever want anyone but you, husband?"

"No," he said bluntly, with a deserved masculine conceit. "But I do not trust any man won't lust after you and be compelled to do something as foolish as daring to touch you." His eyes darkened. "Then I'd be forced to kill him."

She shivered with a shameful ebullience.

He raked a savage gaze over her. "Come, love," he said in gravelled tones. "Let me show you what I've been up to."

Anthony placed her fingers in the crook of his elbow. She allowed herself to be led by him.

As they walked, Helia took in their surroundings.

Then Anthony brought them to a stop. Her stomach clenched, and Helia stared, unblinking, at the shore like she passed a horrific carriage accident.

She closed her eyes, but the onslaught of memories and emotions overwhelmed her senses.

The only thing I may be persuaded to do is place you over my knee, toss your skirts up, and redden your stubborn arse . . . In fact, I would enjoy that task immensely.

We shall see which of us wins this battle of the wills, Miss Wallace . . . And I must confess, I've found myself beginning to enjoy your feistiness.

"Look at me, Helia."

Anthony's gratingly harsh command penetrated the hell of that day. She forced her eyes open.

"Why have you brought me here?" she asked thickly.

He caught her by the shoulders and drew her close. His indomitable gaze speared Helia's unsteady one.

"The man who dared to touch you stole ownership of that day and your happiness." Fire burned from within the deep-blue depths of his fathomless eyes. "No one"—he gave her a slight gentle shake—"shall take anything from you. Tonight, with me at your side, you reclaim what he took. You will purge him from your thoughts, Helia, so only the memory of your time with me lives in their place."

The ferocity of that decree stole all the breath from her body.

"You are ready," he proclaimed on Helia's behalf.

And she was. With Anthony at her side, she found herself steadied by his words and formidable presence.

"I am ready," she confirmed.

He grunted his approval.

Together they went. The closer they got, Helia evaluated the frozen Thames through lenses devoid of fear.

This winter wonderland was a place she'd been before. But at the same time, this frozen part of London was discrepant in every way. Where before the provisional fairground had rung out with the loud, joyful resonance of festivalgoers, now a tranquil peace remained in its stead.

And yet, the sweet, pleasant smell of roasted chestnuts and freshly baked bread filled the air; those scents mingled with the inordinately loud call of peddlers offering their goods.

The rough, playful whine of fiddles combined with wassailers singing a quick tempo rendition of "Auld Lang Syne" lent a cheer that managed to further drive back any dark remembrances.

At last they reached the edge of the ice.

Dazed, Helia stopped and looked about. "Where are all the people?"

"Aside from those who work the event, you and I are the only ones here, Helia."

Helia whipped her head up to look at Anthony; she searched for signs he jested—only there were none. His features remained as coolly implacable as ever.

"The only way to ensure we are in control of any and all memories made this day is to erase everyone from the equation," he explained.

He'd closed down the whole Frost Fair so only she and he could be here.

Tears clogged her throat and blurred her vision. "You did this for me?" she whispered.

"It is all for you. Anything your heart desires, anything you want, crave, or need, will be yours."

As if to demonstrate that very promise, he inclined his head.

A young lad hastened over at a pace that sent his wool cap tottering on his head.

He held up a small red-and-green cloth, tied with a pink ribbon. "Roasted chestnuts for ye, Your Ladyship." The child flashed a crooked smile.

Helia fell to a knee. "Why, thank you very much, good sir. Tell me," she said as she loosened the ribbon. "Are you the fine maker of these sweets?"

He pulled at his tattered lapels. "Indeed I am, Yer Ladyship."

Helia helped herself to one. She chewed the earthy, rich-tasting goody and closed her eyes. "It is more magnificent than I could have imagined."

The four-foot-three-inch fellow grew several inches more under that high praise.

"Your parents must be very proud of your accomplishments . . . ?"

The lad shifted back and forth in his boots. "Ye want anything else, Yer Ladyship?"

Helia nodded. "Do you know, I do. My husband . . ." She glanced up at the taciturn figure above them.

The child lifted his gaze and instantly blanched.

"Lord Wingrave and I have been searching for someone to make toasted chestnuts as good as yours. Isn't that right, husband?" Helia gave her husband a stern look.

"No," he muttered.

She narrowed her eyes.

"Maybe?" he rejoined, this time.

Helia shook her head and mouthed, "Try again."

"Yes," he gritted out.

Helia beamed and recalled the terrified lad's focus. "You have such talent for this. What is your name?"

"Knox."

"Mr. Knox," she continued.

"Just Knox, my lady."

"Very well, Knox. I can only imagine the wonders you'll do in a kitchen. That is, if you are searching for employment?"

The boy choked. "Y-Yer Ladyship?" he squeaked.

Helia sighed. "It is as I feared—you are already employed in someone's kitchens, no doubt a baker—"

"No! Don't got no work. That is, no regular work." He puffed his chest out. "It'd be an 'onor to work in yer kitchens, Yer Ladyship." He dared a peek at Anthony. "And yers, Yer Lordship."

Helia clapped her hands around the chestnuts. "Splendid!" She proceeded to give him directions to the waiting carriage, along with a message to deliver the driver.

Knox frantically bowed. "Ye willna regret this, Yer Ladyship. Oi promise."

She scoffed. "Of course I won't. I know a thing or two about delectable sweets. Isn't that right, husband?" She directed that up to a stonily silent Anthony, giving him another chance.

He grunted; his hard features remained impassive.

The grinning boy glanced up at the marquess, and again his smile instantly faded.

Like he feared the offer would be rescinded at any moment, the boy took flight.

Helia came to her feet and dropped her bag of chestnuts into her cloak pocket. "Do you make a habit of scaring children, Anthony?" she drawled.

He gave another grunt. "I didn't do anything."

She smoothed the lapels of his black, satin-trimmed greatcoat. "No," she murmured, tenderly stroking him. "Not with anything you said or did, but what you did not confer. Children, they need assurances of warmth and kindness."

He stared at her like she'd gone mad. "What good will *that* do them? Better they understand the world is a cold, dark place."

Anthony sounded so truly confused, her lips twitched. "Better they are armed with affection and love so that they are prepared to face the cold, dark world you describe."

He drew back.

She'd gotten through to him, some.

"I want our children to know they are loved and so very much wanted, Anthony," she said softly. "I want them to realize we will protect them and help them and hold them when life is cruel. I want our children to be loved the way you would have wanted Evander loved."

The stupefied expression on his face deepened.

"It is all right—I will help you along the way," she promised.

Helia withdrew a sugared treat from her pocket and popped it in his slightly agape mouth.

Like a child who'd gotten caught with his hand in the cookie jar, Anthony stole a furtive glance about.

At that poignant reminder of all the things he denied himself, a vise tightened about her heart.

"Come," she said, taking over to lead the way, and this time, *he* went cooperatively.

That pliability proved short lived. "As we are discussing one another's habits, love, tell me: Do you go about hiring every London street waif you meet?"

She scoffed. "I hardly hired *every* street waif. Just the one lad." *For now.*

"For now," he said bluntly.

Helia stared up at him.

"You didn't need to say it, love. I saw the intent in your glittering eyes."

She forced them to another stop. "And what is so wrong if we do offer employment to children and people in need?" she asked. "By your own words, do we not have a veritable kingdom, Anthony? You, who possess the riches to pay vendors and send away festivalgoers, can hire every poor soul in London and still have a fortune to last you and our children for centuries to come. So why should we not—eek."

Anthony wrapped an arm about her waist and drew her close. Before she could even catch her breath, he covered Helia's mouth in a long, hot-blooded kiss.

She melted into him and his embrace and met every glide of his lips and tongue.

Too quick, Anthony broke that kiss.

He placed his lips against her temple. "My glorious, benevolent queen," he whispered harshly. "There is no one like you."

"A benevolent queen requires a benevolent king, Anthony," she gently reminded him.

She braced for his rejection.

"I'll show benevolence only to those you deem worthy," he vowed.

Warmth suffused her breast. For a man so proud and insulated, Anthony's was a significant concession. He fought to maintain the fortress about him, but each day, in every way, he slowly but surely let those walls down—for her and only her.

Her scrutiny went on too long.

Anthony frowned. "What is it?"

"I love you. That is all." There was no dread over his anticipated reaction to her quiet pronouncement.

The sharp planes of his cheeks grew flushed. "Helia," he said gruffly.

"Someday you will become comfortable hearing those words and accepting them, Anthony," she said softly. "I don't know when you heard those words last—"

"Helia," he clipped out.

"But I'm going to continue telling you, Anthony, and one day, you'll be at peace and comfortable with my lov—"

"Helia!"

She stared wide-eyed at him.

He drew back and gripped her arms. "Listen to me, love, there are no buts in this. You are my queen, and your holdings include my heart."

Anthony placed her fingertips against the place where that organ beat in his chest.

Her breath caught. She frantically searched his beloved face.

What is he saying?

His eyes sparkled with an unchecked light and warmth she'd never before seen him so freely reveal.

"What am I saying?" he murmured, reading her thoughts as he was so apt to do. He made a tsking sound. "Shame on me for not being clearer and for having left you in doubt for far too long."

Anthony dropped to a knee. "Until the stars go dark and the moon falls and the tides cease their movement"—his eyes blazed with the strength of his vow—"I love you, Helia, my duchess, my queen. Stand beside me in life and in every—"

"Aye!" Sobbing and laughing, Helia launched herself into her husband's arms. "Ah love ye, Anthony, my duke, my king, my lover, my friend. Anthony, my duke, my king, *I'll love ye 'til the day I die.*"

And with that pledge of their partnership, Anthony kissed Helia hard, marking eternal his promise to her.